MARVEL

A NOVEL OF THE MARVEL UNIVERSE

DOCTOR STRANGE

DIMENSION WAR

NOVELS OF THE MARVEL UNIVERSE BY TITAN BOOKS

Ant-Man: Natural Enemy by Jason Starr

Avengers: Everybody Wants to Rule the World by Dan Abnett

Avengers: Infinity by James A. Moore

Black Panther: Panther's Rage by Sheree Renée Thomas

Black Panther: Tales of Wakanda by Jesse J. Holland

Black Panther: Who is the Black Panther? by Jesse J. Holland

Captain America: Dark Designs by Stefan Petrucha

Captain Marvel: Liberation Run by Tess Sharpe

Captain Marvel: Shadow Code by Gilly Segal

Civil War by Stuart Moore

Deadpool: Paws by Stefan Petrucha

Doctor Strange: Dimension War by James Lovegrove

Guardians of the Galaxy: Annihilation – Conquest by Brendan Deneen

Loki: Journey into Mystery by Katherine Locke

Morbius: The Living Vampire – Blood Ties by Brendan Deneen

Secret Invasion by Paul Cornell

Spider-Man: Forever Young by Stefan Petrucha

Spider-Man: Kraven's Last Hunt by Neil Kleid

Spider-Man: The Darkest Hours Omnibus by Jim Butcher, Keith R.A. DeCandido, and Christopher L. Bennett

Spider-Man: The Venom Factor Omnibus by Diane Duane

Thanos: Death Sentence by Stuart Moore

Venom: Lethal Protector by James R. Tuck

Wolverine: Weapon X Omnibus by Marc Cerasini, David Alan Mack, and Hugh Matthews

X-Men: Days of Future Past by Alex Irvine

X-Men: The Dark Phoenix Saga by Stuart Moore

X-Men: The Mutant Empire Omnibus by Christopher Golden

X-Men & The Avengers: The Gamma Quest Omnibus by Greg Cox

ALSO FROM TITAN AND TITAN BOOKS

Marvel Contest of Champions: The Art of the Battlerealm by Paul Davies

Marvel's Guardians of the Galaxy: No Guts, No Glory by M.K. England

Marvel's Midnight Suns: Infernal Rising by S.D. Perry

Marvel's Spider-Man: The Art of the Game by Paul Davies

Obsessed with Marvel by Peter Sanderson and Marc Sumerak

Spider-Man: Into the Spider-Verse – The Art of the Movie by Ramin Zahed

Spider-Man: Hostile Takeover by David Liss

Spider-Man: Miles Morales – Wings of Fury by Brittney Morris

The Art of Iron Man (10th Anniversary Edition) by John Rhett Thomas

The Marvel Vault by Matthew K. Manning, Peter Sanderson, and Roy Thomas

Ant-Man and the Wasp: The Official Movie Special

Avengers: Endgame – The Official Movie Special

Avengers: Infinity War – The Official Movie Special

Black Panther: The Official Movie Companion

Black Panther: The Official Movie Special

Captain Marvel: The Official Movie Special

Marvel Studios: The First 10 Years

Marvel's Avengers – Script to Page

Marvel's Black Panther – Script to Page

Marvel's Black Widow: The Official Movie Special

Marvel's Spider-Man – Script to Page

Spider-Man: Far From Home: The Official Movie Special

Spider-Man: Into the Spider-Verse: Movie Special

Thor: Ragnarok: The Official Movie Special

MARVEL

A NOVEL OF THE MARVEL UNIVERSE

DOCTOR STRANGE
DIMENSION WAR

ADAPTED FROM THE CLASSIC STORIES
BY STAN LEE AND STEVE DITKO

JAMES LOVEGROVE

TITAN BOOKS

DOCTOR STRANGE: DIMENSION WAR
Print edition ISBN: 9781803362588
E-book edition ISBN: 9781803362595

Published by Titan Books
A division of Titan Publishing Group Ltd
144 Southwark Street, London SE1 0UP
www.titanbooks.com

This Titan edition: August 2025
10 9 8 7 6 5 4 3 2 1

This is a work of fiction. All of the characters, organizations, and events portrayed in this novel are either products of the author's imagination or are used fictitiously. Any resemblance to actual persons, living or dead (except for satirical purposes), is entirely coincidental.

FOR MARVEL PUBLISHING
Jeff Youngquist, VP Production and Special Projects
Sarah Singer, Editor, Special Projects
Jeremy West, Manager, Licensed Publishing
Sven Larsen, VP, Licensed Publishing
David Gabriel, VP, Print & Digital Publishing
C.B. Cebulski, Editor in Chief

© 2025 MARVEL

Cover art by InHyuk Lee

No part of this publication may be reproduced, stored in a retrieval system, or transmitted, in any form or by any means without the prior written permission of the publisher, nor be otherwise circulated in any form of binding or cover other than that in which it is published and without a similar condition being imposed on the subsequent purchaser.

A CIP catalogue record for this title is available from the British Library.

EU RP (for authorities only)
eucomply OÜ, Pärnu mnt. 139b-14, 11317 Tallinn, Estonia
hello@eucompliancepartner.com, +3375690241

Printed and bound by CPI Group (UK) Ltd, Croydon CR0 4YY.

This book is dedicated to
Stan and Steve
who made the magic happen

PROLOGUE

A LONE figure staggered through the mazy streets of Greenwich Village. It was late at night, and a pounding downpour had driven most Manhattanites indoors. But not this man, who moved along the slick, rain-spattered sidewalks hunched over, trembling, seemingly in the grip of profound torment.

He was searching for a particular townhouse, and at last he found it, on the corner of Bleecker Street and Fenno Place. The residence was made distinct from its neighbors by the large, circular skylight set into its angled roof. With nine panes arranged like an asymmetrical tic-tac-toe board, the skylight resembled some arcane ideogram.

The man climbed the steps and hammered on the front door, which swung inward immediately, as though a visitor had been expected. He stumbled across the threshold, and the door closed behind him. He looked round to see that no person had opened or shut the door. It had operated apparently of its own volition. Some automated mechanism, he assumed.

The hallway was spacious and filled with exotic furnishings: ornate mirrors, cavorting statues, intricately fashioned urns. A broad staircase curved upward. Dozens of candles flickered in tall candelabras, and the heady smell of incense wafted through the air.

The man thought he was alone, but then, as if from nowhere, another man appeared in front of him.

This other was tall and dignified-looking, clad in a loose, bell-sleeved dark blue shirt and skintight leggings, with a sash cinched about his waist and a high-collared cape hanging from his shoulders. Suspended around his neck was a golden amulet, square in shape and featuring a closed eye at its center. The ensemble was completed by a peculiar pair of gloves which reached to his elbows and had a spotted pattern somewhat like leopard-print. His raven-black hair was white at the temples and a neat little mustache adorned his upper lip.

He looked, in short, like exactly what he was rumored to be. A student of the occult. An expert in sorcery. A magician.

"Mr. Trent," he said. His voice exuded calm, quiet competence.

"You—you know me?" said his guest.

"The face of New York real estate mogul Ronald Trent is not unfamiliar to those who read the newspapers and watch the news."

"Yes. Yes, of course." Trent was, in his way, famous. Some might call him notorious.

"And you are in trouble," said the magician.

"I am," Trent said. For someone like him, the hardest of hard-nosed businessmen, this was a difficult thing to admit. "How can you tell?"

"All who come to me as importunates are."

"Importun—?"

Before Trent could finish echoing the word, the magician made a beckoning gesture. "This way. Follow me."

"IT'S THE dreams," said Ronald Trent, sitting in the magician's book-crammed study. "The *dream*, strictly speaking. Same one, night after night."

"And what happens in this dream?" the magician asked.

With some effort, Trent collected himself. Being out in the rainstorm had left him bedraggled, his hair awry, his clothing sodden, but this only added to a pre-existing haggardness. There were dark rings around his eyes, and his complexion was tinged with gray, suggesting he had not slept well lately, or indeed at all.

"Every night," he said, stumbling slightly over the words, "I dream of a man in a hooded robe, bound in chains."

"And what does he do, the hooded man?"

"Nothing. Just stares. Stares and stares at me. I can't even see his face—it's hidden in the shadows of the hood—but I know he's staring. It's like… like he's judging me."

"What might he be judging you for?" the magician said.

Trent hesitated briefly. "Nothing. Nothing comes to mind."

"I presume you've sought conventional treatment for your… problem."

"I've been to doctors. To psychiatrists. The best money can buy. Even to a priest. Pills, therapy, praying, none of it helps. This has been going on for weeks. Weeks!" Trent clutched his gaunt cheeks with both hands, shaking his head from side to side. "I'm going crazy! I can't focus at work. I'm barely eating. I dread going to bed. Every time I close my eyes and doze off, I'm there in that place. That same blackened, empty landscape, where everything's all bent and sharp like thorns, and in the middle of it, staring at me, the hooded man."

The magician nodded pensively. "I believe I know what is plaguing you, Mr. Trent, and I believe I can resolve the matter."

Trent looked at him with almost pathetic hopefulness. "You can? Really? I was told I should try you. Rumor has it that you specialize in this sort of stuff. If it's true, if you *can* make the dream stop, you won't regret it. I'll pay you handsomely. I'll tell all my pals about you. I'll make you a celebrity."

"I seek neither wealth nor fame," said the magician. "My only goal is to help my fellow human beings. Go home now, Mr. Trent. I'll call on you tomorrow night."

Ronald Trent left the house on Bleecker Street feeling something he hadn't felt for a long while. The magician's confidence had kindled a flame of optimism in him. His nightmare might finally be over.

TRUE TO his word, the magician arrived at Trent's the next evening. The real estate mogul lived in the penthouse of a tower he himself had constructed, a couple of blocks away from the city landmark that was the Baxter Building, home of the Fantastic Four. His apartment was an opulent palace with sweeping views of the Manhattan skyline.

Seemingly not surprised nor particularly impressed by the extravagance of the place, the magician encouraged Trent to go to sleep as normal, while he would wait in an adjoining room.

"But how?" said Trent. "How's that going to work? What are you going to do?"

"It's very simple," the magician said. "I shall enter your dream, Mr. Trent."

"You'll what?"

"You disbelieve me?"

"No. I mean, yes. I mean, I don't know what I believe."

"You came to a practitioner of the mystic arts for aid, Mr. Trent. Have faith that I know what I'm doing."

Trent could have protested further but chose not to. The man had a point. Trent was desperate. The magician was his last resort. Enter his dream? Sure. If he said so. Why not?

Trent took himself to bed, popping a couple of sleeping pills which he washed down with a slug of bourbon for good measure.

Soon enough, sleep drew its curtain over him.

Then he was there again: back in that dark, twisted place of winding pathways and leafless trees and broken ground, like a world that had been devastated by some apocalypse, where whatever lived and grew, lived and grew stuntedly and soullessly.

And there, too, as expected, was the robed, hooded man, with his burden of heavy iron chains. He stood observing Trent fixedly, and Trent, as he always did, turned aside to avoid that mute, accusing stare, only to find that the hooded man still stood before him. This was the true hell of the dream. Wherever Trent looked, the hooded man was invariably in front of him. If he ran away in any direction, the hooded man loomed ahead. Trent couldn't even close his eyes. The dream prevented that.

Something was different this time, however. Trent was no longer alone with the hooded man.

The magician was beside him.

With calm resolve, the magician approached the hooded man. Trent had never had the nerve do this. He had only ever yelled at the phantasmic figure to leave him alone or pleaded with him for mercy, in either instance receiving nothing but stony silence in return. It certainly had not occurred to him to speak with the hooded man conversationally, as the magician was doing now.

"You," he said. "Whoever you are—whatever you are—why do you torture Ronald Trent in this manner? What has he done to deserve it?"

"He knows," the hooded man replied in slow, sepulchral tones, like a monk intoning a liturgy. "He knows exactly why I visit him in his dreams night after night. He knows his shame. He knows the crimes he has committed. If you do not believe me, ask Chester Crang."

Chester Crang.

The name fell on Trent's ears like a hammer blow.

Of course. That was it. Crang. Crang and all the rest.

The hooded man might have said more, but then came a sound of hooves. They thundered from a distance, growing ever louder as a terrible apparition loomed over the horizon. It sped closer, revealing itself to be a coal-black horse with a horn sprouting from its forehead, like some demonic unicorn. Astride this creature sat a slender wisp of a man. The latter was clad in a forest-green fishnet bodystocking, with an up-pointing collar around his neck and a tattered cape trailing behind. Red eyes leered dementedly from a face as white as chalk, below a shock of jet-black hair.

The magician turned to confront the new arrival. His jaw set into an expression of steely resolve.

"Nightmare!" he growled. "I had a feeling you might show yourself."

"With you intruding into my realm, mage," replied the rider, reining in his mount, "how could I not? Have you come to spoil my fun?"

"I should hope so."

"Pity. I think, however, that you have overestimated your worth, and you will now pay the penalty."

Trent's dream had taken a truly unexpected turn. The magician's presence had upset the status quo, drawing in a new element—this horrendous horse and its even more horrendous rider.

The two of them, the magician and the personage he had addressed as Nightmare, squared off against each other, clearly readying to fight.

And that was when Ronald Trent woke up.

HE WOKE up sweating, tangled in the bedclothes, heart racing, as was the case every time he had the dream.

Things had changed, though.

The hooded man had mentioned Chester Crang to the magician.

If the magician investigated the name… If he learned what Trent had done to Crang, and to numerous others like Crang…

That must not happen.

Trent clawed his way out of bed and reached for the semiautomatic pistol he kept in his nightstand drawer.

The magician was seated on the floor in the room next door, in the lotus position. His eyes were shut tight, his breathing almost imperceptibly slow and light. Trent crept towards him barefoot on the thick-piled carpet. He could scarcely believe what he was doing.

But he had not risen this far in life, had not accumulated so much money and prestige, only to have some Village weirdo ruin it. Kill him, dispose of the body somehow. No one would know.

He racked a round into the chamber of the semiauto and leveled the gun at the magician's head.

Just as he was about to pull the trigger, Trent saw the eye on the magician's amulet open.

Next thing he knew, he was being bathed in light.

The light emanated from the eye, a beam of brilliance that encased Trent, stopping him in his tracks. It was not simply light. It was more than that, much more. It was honesty. It was integrity. It was truth in all its forms.

The light penetrated through Trent's skin somehow. It pierced him to his heart, to his soul. It filled every corner and crevice of him with its illumination, finding the shadows within him, the dark places where he stowed his sins.

Trent couldn't bear to look at it, but neither could he escape it. The amulet's light exposed him to his core, and all the guilt he had ever felt rose to the surface. Everything he had fought to keep down, pretended he was immune to, came seeping out.

He dropped the pistol. He sank to his knees. Pressing hands to face, Ronald Trent started sobbing piteously, like a scolded infant.

When the bout of weeping had run its course, Trent looked up to find the magician, awake now, standing over him. He held the pistol in one hand and its magazine in the other, with the slide on the gun locked back to show that the weapon was unloaded and made safe.

"Wh—what just happened?" stammered a timorous Trent.

"The Eye of Agamotto protected me while I was in my trance state," the magician said. "It shone its light on you, delving into the goodness that still resides in you. Yes, even a man like you, Mr. Trent, has some goodness within him, however small and shriveled it may be. And now you know what you must do."

"Yes," said Trent. "Yes. Chester Crang. A business associate.

I ruined him. Cheated him in several deals. Bankrupted him. Last I heard, he was living out of a rat-infested shoebox apartment in the Bronx, drowning his sorrows in drink. And there've been others. Rivals I've ruined by undercutting them, refusing to pay their invoices, trampling over them on my way to success. So many! One even committed suicide, so I'm told, because of me."

"You have much to atone for," said the magician. "That was what your dream was trying to tell you. The hooded man was a manifestation of your guilt. Perhaps now is the time to start putting things right."

Trent frowned. "I—I don't know. Is it possible? After all I've done?"

"Redemption is always possible. No life is so far gone along the road of damnation that it can't be turned around. Believe me, I know."

The man appeared to speak with authority, and Trent drew encouragement from this. "Yes," he said, his voice filled with righteous determination. "Yes! I can make up for what I've done. I can repay my debts. It's never too late."

The magician gave a thin smile. "It never is, Mr. Trent. See to it that you do what you should, and from then on you will sleep as soundly as a baby."

"I will," Trent declared. "I swear it."

○━━━━━○

BACK IN his townhouse on Bleecker Street, which he had dubbed his Sanctum Sanctorum, Dr. Stephen Strange contemplated a job well done. Ronald Trent would keep his vow, he was certain. Like Ebeneezer Scrooge, he had been changed by a dream vision and nothing would ever again be the same for him.

Strange recalled his encounter with the entity known as Nightmare during his intervention in Trent's dream. He had suspected that Trent's underlying guilt was so strong that it had attracted the attention of the Dream Dimension's most dastardly denizen, who derived his power from the misery of sleeping mortals. Trent had unwittingly been drawn into Nightmare's realm every night in his slumbers, and Nightmare had been feasting off his anguish, like a vampire sucking blood.

Projecting his astral self into the Dream Dimension, Strange had planned on bargaining with Nightmare to leave Trent alone. In the event, the two of them had had a face-off, during which Trent had returned to the waking world. Strange, alerted by the Eye of Agamotto that his physical form was in danger, had fled from the battle before it had even begun, leaving with Nightmare's mocking laughter ringing in his ears.

"Going so soon, Strange?" Nightmare had crowed. "But we've hardly started. Coward! Perhaps you are not all you're vaunted to be. Perhaps the Ancient One chose his disciple unwisely. I have no doubt we two shall meet again, and then we'll test your mettle, Strange. Yes, then we'll see whether you are deserving of the responsibility bestowed upon you."

Nightmare, like most of his kind, was a braggart and a blowhard. Doctor Strange remained confident enough in his magical abilities that he could outmatch almost any eldritch foe, and those he couldn't outmatch he could outsmart.

Yet he had not been a fully-fledged sorcerer for long. However well his master, the Ancient One, had trained him and prepared him, perhaps he did not truly know all the dangers he might face in times to come.

He had chosen a difficult, treacherous path in life, and while there would surely be further successful days like today, he foresaw that there would be perilous ones too. Ones where his life, his very soul, might be forfeit.

Strange sent up a prayer to the great Vishanti, the trinity of gods who guided the hands of virtuous mystics. He beseeched them that whatever trials he faced in the future, he would be equal to the challenge.

Not just for his sake, but for the sake of everyone on Earth.

ONE

IN HIS castle in Transylvania, Baron Karl Amadeus Mordo brooded.

Baron Mordo spent a lot of time brooding. He had much to think about, and much to be resentful about.

Mostly his broodings centered on the Ancient One, his former mentor, under whom he had studied the mystic arts for a number of years. Those years had been spent in the Ancient One's Tibetan mountain retreat, far from civilization, with none of the comforts and luxuries Mordo was accustomed to. Living according to a spartan regime, sleeping on a straw-pallet bed, eating like a peasant. And all for what?

His hope had been that one day, thanks to the Ancient One's tuition, he would command every magical secret there was to know. As scion of a family of magic-wielding aristocrats, Mordo felt that ultimate sorcerous power was his birthright. But whereas his parents Nikolai and Sara had sought only to shore up their personal status by magical means, Mordo had harbored greater ambitions. He'd wished to become nothing less than Sorcerer Supreme.

That dream had been dashed when the Ancient One rejected him for another pupil, Stephen Strange. The upstart American had usurped his place in the Ancient One's favor; soon enough, Mordo had been banished from his master's presence and had made his way home to Europe sullen and defeated, like a dog with its tail between its legs.

That was months ago. Now, finally, Baron Mordo decided enough was enough. With his magical education incomplete, there remained spells and rituals he had yet to learn, ones that would elevate him from adept to mage. The Ancient One had withheld them from him, so Mordo had to take them by force.

A fire blazed in the huge hearth in Mordo's private chamber, which occupied a whole floor in one of the castle's turrets. He watched the flames crackle and writhe, and a broad smile settled upon his face. Mordo was a squarish, heavyset man, with bushy eyebrows and a pronounced widow's peak whose M-shape was mirrored by the W-shape of the thick goatee beard on his chin. Tufts of hair stuck out above his ears, refusing to stay flat no matter how he tried to tame them. He was not handsome but he carried himself with a certain swaggering authority which some might mistake for charisma. The smile he was smiling right now, though, was anything but charming.

He took himself over to a large throne-like chair whose back was carved to resemble a vulture with its wings outspread. Seated, he closed his eyes and willed himself into a relaxed, receptive state. In a matter of moments, his astral form sprang forth from his body. He flew away from the castle, from his hometown Varf Mandra, from Transylvania, from Europe. Travelling at speeds the average mind could scarcely comprehend, his astral form hurtled halfway across the world until it reached Tibet.

Navigating his way unerringly across the jagged topography of the Himalayas, Mordo swooped towards a remote, monastery-like dwelling that nestled against a mountainside: the Ancient One's retreat. Simple whitewashed buildings with bright red pagoda-style roofs surrounded a courtyard where koi carp drifted to and fro in a pool dotted with lily pads. Dusk was gathering over the towering, snowcapped peaks, and windows in the retreat began to glow as yak butter lamps were lit indoors.

Mordo well recalled the routine of daily life under the Ancient One's tutelage. It was a kind of prison, he thought. You rose early, carried out menial tasks, exercised, meditated; only then, after these duties were discharged, were you allowed to commence your studies and practice your spells. The day ended with a second round of domestic activities. Everything had to be done at the appropriate hour and with due reverence and attentiveness. No action—even something as straightforward as, say, lamp lighting—could be performed unless it was performed mindfully.

He descended towards the Ancient One's private quarters, his astral form penetrating the outer wall as though it did not exist. He had wreathed himself in a cloaking spell to disguise his presence but found this measure had been unnecessary. The Ancient One was poring over an antique scroll, so absorbed in contemplation that he was entirely oblivious to Mordo's incursion.

Mordo turned towards the kitchens, where he knew someone would, at this moment, be preparing the Ancient One's evening meal. Sure enough, there was Wong. Zealous Wong, the most loyal of all the Ancient One's domestic staff. He stood at a table, chopping vegetables for soup.

It was child's play for Mordo to enter Wong's mind and seize control of him.

He directed Wong to a shelf laden with traditional local medicines derived from herbs and minerals. One of these was a potent analgesic which, taken in moderation, eased most aches and pains. An overdose, however, could prove lethal.

Mordo compelled Wong to pour a liberal quantity of the medicine into the soup pot, and add plenty of turmeric and cumin to hide the taste. Then, when the soup was ready, the ensorcelled Wong carried a bowl of it through to the Ancient One. Mordo felt Wong resisting him every step of the way, but the servant's willpower was nowhere near as great as Mordo's. He set the bowl before the Ancient One, who acknowledged receipt of it with a vague, distracted nod. Mordo bade Wong to return to the kitchen and sit down on a bench and go to sleep, which he duly did.

Meanwhile, the Ancient One broke off from examining the scroll to spoon soup into his mouth. Mordo's astral form hovered nearby, watching eagerly.

It wasn't long before the wizened old teacher was clutching his chest and groaning. He tried to stand but collapsed onto the cushions of a divan.

That was when Mordo cast off the cloaking spell.

An astral form was invisible to normal human eyes, but the eyes of the Ancient One, even though he was in considerable physical distress, had no trouble seeing Mordo.

"You," he croaked. "Mordo. You are responsible for this. You have had my food tampered with." He attempted to summon up a spell to repel his unwanted visitor, but his hands were no longer responsive and could not form the necessary configurations. Likewise, his whirling brain could not formulate the words that helped channel other-dimensional magical forces. "You would dare do such a thing as this?"

Mordo let out a gloating chuckle. "I would dare *anything*, my erstwhile master."

"What do you want?" the Ancient One gasped.

"Not much," Mordo said. "Merely access to the conjurations you failed to share with me when I was your pupil. You guarded them closely during my time here, and in the end deemed me unworthy of knowing them. That must change. Tell me all I need to know, and I will have Wong fetch you an antidote. If not… Well, a younger, healthier man might recover of his own accord, but you are elderly and frail. Your life is draining away before my very eyes. At this rate, I doubt you will last longer than an hour. The choice is yours, Ancient One. Speak, while there is still time—or die!"

THOUSANDS OF miles away, in his Sanctum Sanctorum, Doctor Strange woke up with a sense of terrible foreboding.

He had learned to trust such instincts. As dawn light filtered around the drapes in his bedroom, Strange got up and dressed quickly. The sense of foreboding only grew as he hurried to his Chamber of Shadows, where he kept his most powerful magical books, artifacts, and esoterica. At some subconscious, preternatural level he was being alerted to jeopardy. The jeopardy involved not himself but another person. He was almost certain he knew whom, but there was a surefire method of checking.

Centermost in the room stood a waist-high plinth topped with a domed lid. Sliding the lid open, Strange revealed a basketball-sized glass sphere that glowed inside with ribbons of coruscating, iridescent light.

The Orb of Agamotto. One of the greatest scrying tools known to humankind. Like Strange's amulet, it was imbued with a tiny fraction of the divine essence of Agamotto himself. The mighty, All-Seeing Agamotto, one of the triumvirate of deities, along with Oshtur and Hoggoth, who comprised the Vishanti.

Strange held his hands over the Orb and attuned himself to its mystical vibrations. This was not unlike searching for a station on an old-fashioned analog radio, turning a dial until a signal came through the static, loud and clear. Magician and artifact became aligned, so that what Strange desired to see, the Orb would show.

An image shimmered into life within the sphere. It was the Ancient One, ailing and helpless, with a wraithlike figure hovering menacingly over him.

Strange had no trouble recognizing the latter.

"Mordo," he murmured, his lip curling.

There was no time to waste. He steadied himself mentally and sent forth his astral form. Body and soul separated, a melancholy sensation, a heartfelt wrench, like lovers parting.

Incorporeal, no longer subject to the laws of physics or biology, Strange flew.

○━━━━━━━━○

MINUTES LATER, his astral form arrived in Tibet and was spiraling down towards the Ancient One's retreat. It was months since he had departed the place, heading back out into the wider world to begin his new life as a magician and use the skills he had acquired to benefit others. Coming here, even as a nonphysical spirit, felt like coming home.

No sooner did he enter the Ancient One's private quarters than Mordo turned towards him. The two of them, in their astral forms, stood poised antagonistically, while the Ancient One himself sprawled on the divan, panting and perspiring, desperately pale.

"I should have known you might come running," Mordo sneered. "Stephen Strange. Teacher's pet. Or do I mean faithful lapdog? Anyway, you're too late. The Ancient One is doomed. Breathing his last. It seems he would rather perish than surrender his greatest magical secrets to me."

"So that you can exploit them for your own gain, Mordo?" said Strange. "No wonder he won't share them with you. All the time you were here, you spoke of your superiority to others, your contempt for those weaker and humbler than you. That Old World snobbery of yours."

"Why serve the common herd, Strange, when you can rightfully command them?"

"And that is the difference between us. Where I would help people, you would rather lord it over them. Magic was never for you. The Ancient One made the mistake of trusting that your better nature would win out. He failed to recognize an unrepentant egomaniac."

"Oh, and you weren't one yourself?"

Strange had to accept the truth of this. He shrugged. "I was, but unlike you, I got better. Now, I need you to back off, so that I can save the Ancient One."

"Back off? Because some jumped-up nobody tells me to? Never!"

"Very well. Then I'll just have to make you."

Strange, in his astral form, took a swing at Mordo.

Mordo ducked. "Fisticuffs, is it?" he snarled. "Trading blows rather than spells? Typical of you Yanks. So barbaric. So unrefined. Well, if we must…"

He hit back. Strange dodged, before delivering an uppercut. Mordo, grunting, launched a vicious salvo of right and left hooks. Strange blocked most of these, but a couple got through his defenses.

It was a peculiar fight, in that both combatants floated in midair as they battled, like astronauts in microgravity. The blows themselves were technically intangible, but each man felt the impacts nonetheless, since both existed in the same state of spirit insubstantiality. Neither of them could directly affect the physical world around him in this form, but he could certainly affect his opponent.

They somersaulted and pirouetted around the room, ghosting through walls, through stone columns, through furniture, grappling and recoiling, a weird elegance to their brutality. Mordo was driven by the all-consuming hatred he felt towards Strange, whom he regarded as responsible for his exile from the Ancient One's retreat. There was pent-up anger behind every punch he threw. As for Strange, his overriding concern was defeating Mordo quickly and soundly so that he would then be free to attend to the Ancient One.

But they seemed evenly matched, he and Mordo. They could fight like this for hours, with no clear victor, while death claimed the Ancient One in the meantime. Strange had to come up with some stratagem to beat Mordo, or at any rate get him to retreat.

The solution came to him in a flash of inspiration.

Use Mordo's conceitedness against him.

"MORDO," STRANGE said, drawing back from his opponent. "I can see neither of us is going to win this bout any time soon."

"The words of a man who knows he is going to lose," said Mordo.

"Perhaps. But somewhere your mortal shell lies inert, defenseless. The Eye of Agamotto can light my way to its location. What's to prevent me racing there and visiting a similar fate upon your body as you have upon the Ancient One's?"

Mordo grinned. "You would not, Strange. Your moral code will not allow you."

"My master hovers at the brink of death," Strange said with bitterness. "The man I respect most in the world. There is nothing I would not do to avenge his murder, even if it means committing murder myself."

"You're bluffing," Mordo said.

"Am I? I should have thought that's a risk you can't afford to take."

"If there's one thing the Ancient One tried to instill in us, it's that magic should only be used to help, not harm."

"You clearly failed to absorb that lesson. It seems only proper I should follow your example."

Mordo scanned Strange's face, looking for some hint that the American was lying. He saw only steely determination.

With a cry that was halfway between a grunt and a curse, he darted away from the room.

Only when he was several miles from the retreat did he look back. He had assumed Strange would give chase, but he could not see him anywhere.

Then he spied him, in the distance. Strange's astral form was, indeed, pursuing his, but for some reason he had delayed setting off.

Mordo chortled. What was the old adage? *He who hesitates is lost.* Well, Strange had hesitated, and now Mordo had a lead over him which he would never be able to make up.

He sped on. Across the deserts and sprawling white cities of the Middle East he went, and over the sparkling blue expanse of the Mediterranean, with Strange lagging far behind. He flew through an electrical storm above Greece and whisked past a jetfighter patrolling the skies of Symkaria. He gave Latveria a wide berth— that nation was not to be trespassed upon, even in astral form—and soon afterwards he was over Transylvania and nearing the thickly forested region of the Carpathian mountains where, in a deep valley, Varf Mandra lay. Castle Mordo was seated atop a crag overlooking the town, a medieval-era cluster of cylindrical towers, buttressed walls and steeply pitched, snow-shrugging roofs, its foundations merging with the selfsame granite from which its masonry had been quarried.

Mordo arrived at his destination and swiftly re-entered his body, spirit and flesh reuniting, the one animating the other like hand in glove.

He barked a triumphant laugh as, moments later, Strange's astral form came to a halt in front of him.

"Too slow, Strange!" he cried. "You can't hope to hurt me now that I have full command of my physical self."

Strange only smiled. "Of course not. But then I never intended to. All I wanted was to get you away from the Ancient One's vicinity. Think about it, Mordo. You enthralled his servant Wong in order to poison him, didn't you?"

"I did. So?"

"So, before I left, I took the liberty of freeing Wong from your influence. He is now awake and already at his master's side, ministering to him. He knows how to restore him to full health. Your plan, in short, has failed."

Mordo was briefly dumbstruck. Then he said, "Oh, very clever, Strange." He gave a slow, ironic handclap. "You never were going to assault my body. That was just a ruse."

"You fell for it. You panicked."

"And now that the Ancient One knows I have attacked him, he will set up various wards around his retreat to stop me trying the same thing again."

"Exactly," said Strange. "And I will assist him in that endeavor. You won't be able to pull this trick twice, Mordo."

"No, true enough," Mordo admitted.

"Nor do I think you are likely to attack *me* now. You have overexerted yourself. Your power is at a low ebb. You need rest."

"That, too, is true. No doubt about it, you win this time, Strange. But that doesn't mean I won't try again. One way or another, I will get what I want. I always do."

"And I," Strange said, "will always be there to stand in your way."

With that, Strange's astral form flitted away, and Mordo was left alone.

Immediately, he fell to brooding again.

Foolish smug American. Stand in his way? Certainly today Strange had proved an obstacle to Mordo. Obstacles, however, were there to be surmounted. Or, failing that, swept aside. And sooner or later, that was what would happen to Strange.

Already Mordo had an idea, a means of trapping Strange and then, at his leisure, destroying him.

Yes. The plan was foolproof.

And once Strange was disposed of, the Ancient One would no longer have his champion guarding him. The selfish old dodderer would be more vulnerable than ever, and Mordo would have no trouble wresting his secrets from him before consigning his soul to join those of his ancestors.

Baron Mordo's scheming cackle echoed hollowly through the castle.

TWO

DOCTOR STRANGE'S phone rang at an ungodly hour.

"Stephen?" said a creaky, English-accented voice. "Is that you? I have the right number?"

"Yes, this is Stephen Strange. Who's calling?"

"Oh, thank heaven! It's Bentley. Sir Clive Bentley. You may remember me."

Strange did. He pictured a prim, well-spoken gentleman in his sixties with thinning hair and an aquiline nose. He looked very much a physician of the old school, right down to his tweed jacket and bowtie.

"We met at a medical conference in Berlin a few years ago," Sir Clive continued, "where I was lecturing."

"Yes, I recall, Sir Clive." Strange glanced at the clock. Three in the morning. He rubbed his eyes and stifled a yawn. "I spent an hour quizzing you about your innovative version of the purse-string suture."

"And then, by all reports, you went on to perfect it."

"I hope you didn't mind."

"Dear boy, I was flattered. But anyway, I was wondering…" Sir Clive paused. "Bless me! I've just realized. It's breakfast time here in the UK, but it's still the middle of the night for you chaps over there. How remiss of me. I do apologize, Stephen. I shall call again later."

"I'm awake now. You said you were wondering…?"

The renowned British surgeon harrumphed embarrassedly. "As I understand it, you no longer practice medicine."

"I don't."

"You have abandoned the field and moved into more, ahem, esoteric pastures. So people are saying."

"Are they now?"

"We're all terrible gossips in the international medical community," said Sir Clive, "and when one of our brethren—one of the foremost surgeons alive, indeed—goes astray, everyone talks about it."

"Your definition of 'astray' and mine may differ," said Strange. "I make no secret of the fact that I have turned from medicine to the mystic arts. At the same time, I don't go to great lengths to publicize it. I have chosen a new direction in life, that's all."

Or had it chosen him? That was a question Strange could never quite answer.

"I'm not here to mock," said Sir Clive. "Or, for that matter, to doubt. I need your help, you see. Specifically yours. Not as a man of medicine but as a man of magic."

"Carry on," said Strange. He could never turn down a plea for assistance, no matter how inconveniently timed. He had pledged himself to the protection and betterment of humankind, much like the costumed super heroes who had lately been appearing all over New York and elsewhere—Spider-Man, for instance, and Iron Man, and the shield-slinging living legend of World War II, Captain America, back after a long absence and as battle-fit as ever. Strange considered himself the magical equivalent of those masked, muscular crusaders for justice. They fought the good fight out in the open, clad in bold, bright primary colors, while he did the same in the shadows. Their opponents were would-be world conquerors and ambitious, super-augmented thieves; his an array of insidious and indefinable, but no less evil, forces.

"It's… It's my daughter Victoria," Sir Clive said. "My only child. My wife Margot died a couple of years back, and since then Victoria is all I have, my only family. And now she—she seems to be developing a knack for… the only word I can think of for it is witchcraft."

"Witchcraft?"

"I know, I know, it sounds absurd. I can hardly believe I'm saying it. But lately Victoria has been having these premonitions which, sure enough, come true. Not like being able to predict which horse is going to win the Grand National." A hollow laugh. "Sadly no. But the other day, for example, she foresaw that my Labrador was going to get run over and killed in the road—this flash of an image in her mind's eye—and lo and behold, he did. Poor old Tarquin. I was out walking him, he slipped the leash, darted straight into the path of a Royal Mail van. Must've caught the scent of a rabbit or something. Never the brightest of sparks, Tarquin, but he was a loyal companion. Then there are the funny turns Victoria has."

"How do you mean, funny turns?"

"Well, she faints, for no apparent reason, and then when she comes round, she says she's journeyed to another world. Says it's all rainbow colors and strange geometric shapes. Gigantic snake mouths in midair, floating orbs with lightning bolts branching off them, doorways within doorways, you name it. Hallucinatory stuff, as though she's been on some sort of psychedelic drug trip, only Victoria doesn't touch that sort of thing. Doesn't even drink. That said, she's always been a solitary, imaginative sort, has my girl, and I suppose this could be some kind of psychotic break. I'm convinced, though, that there's something else going on here, something more. And I thought… I thought, if you are what they say you are, Stephen, then this might be up your street."

"What would you have me do, Sir Clive?" Strange asked.

"Come and see her. It's driving Victoria potty, that's the thing. She's frightened by these bizarre experiences. She thinks she may be going mad. Maybe you can reassure her she isn't, or, I don't know, diagnose what the problem really is, if it is, in fact, magic-related. You'd be doing me a huge favor, dear boy. What do you say? Will you come?"

Strange could hardly refuse. Clearly Victoria Bentley was a psychic sensitive, and was having premonitory visions and inadvertently spirit-voyaging to other dimensions. It was curious because she was a woman in her mid-thirties and only rarely did such abilities manifest so late in life. Most often they were already present in childhood and started to strengthen and solidify around puberty. Possibly they had lain dormant in Victoria all this time, only to be aroused abruptly by grief over her mother's death. At any rate, the matter was worth investigating, and if he could bring her and her father some peace of mind, so much the better.

And so, later that same day, Strange boarded an overnight transatlantic flight to London Heathrow airport. He could have used a spell of physical transference such as the Wondrous Wormhole of Weygg-Kalkuun to get him to England in no time, but the conjuration was draining and he did not want to arrive exhausted and debilitated. Sometimes the everyday magic of a passenger jet, whisking you across thousands of miles in a matter of hours, and in relative comfort, was a perfectly acceptable substitute.

A TAXICAB deposited Strange outside the gates to Denningham Manor, Sir Clive Bentley's mansion in Surrey. Strange took in the rural surroundings with an appreciative eye. Leafy woodland lined both sides of the narrow country lane down which the cab was now fast disappearing. From somewhere far off he could hear a farm tractor groaning across a field, but the dominant sounds were trees rustling and birdsong rippling liquidly. The sun beat down on his head, and the air was pleasantly but not stiflingly hot, summer in England being a far more benign affair than summer on the East Coast.

There was a lodge beside the mansion gateway, a little self-contained one-story cottage. The curtains were drawn in every window. The gate itself stood ajar. Strange passed through and walked up the drive, overnight bag in hand. Sir Clive was heir to a shipping fortune, hence the handsome residence he owned—which he could have hardly afforded otherwise, even on a doctor's salary.

At the large front door Strange operated the old-fashioned bellpull. A chime pealed deep inside the house. No one came. He tried the bellpull again. Still no one.

Sir Clive was expecting him. Perhaps he was out, summoned away on some urgent errand.

Purely out of curiosity, Strange tried the door. It was unlocked. He entered tentatively.

"Hello? Anybody home?" he called out.

No reply.

"Sir Clive? It's Stephen. You know, Stephen Strange, who's just traveled three thousand miles at your request."

Not a sound in response, save for the echo of his own voice.

In a house this size, there would surely be domestic servants present—even if the owner wasn't home. Where was everyone?

Strange's hackles were rising. Something sinister was afoot. Laying down his bag, he ventured further into the building. Briefly he took in the hallway, with its galleried landing and checkerboard floor. A suit of armor stood sentinel at the foot of the winding oak staircase, halberd clutched in one gauntlet. He explored the ground-floor rooms. A library. A billiards room. A drawing room. A dining room. No sign of life anywhere, but he discerned a thin patina of dust on many of the surfaces. It was as though the place had been abandoned, and recently, too, within the past few days.

He prepared a ward of self-defense, just in case—the Shield of the Seraphim. He configured his hands in readiness for casting the spell, each set of fingers assuming an elaborate pattern which mirrored the other hand's. With just a few words and a gesture, he could work the magic.

In a study whose windows overlooked the rear grounds of the house, he found a huge cherrywood desk with a stack of correspondence, documents and newspapers on its leather-inlaid top. Medical textbooks filled the shelves, and there were some fine pieces of decorative chinaware ranged about the room, including a large blue-and-white willow-pattern vase. Oddly, a candle was burning in one corner. A thin plume of smoke spiraled up from its flickering flame.

Strange pondered this anomaly. Why leave a lone candle alight in an unoccupied building? Did it mean something? Was it some kind of tribute?

His eye fell on a newspaper that lay open on the desktop. It was the London *Times*, and the page facing him held the obituary section.

There, in black and white, lay a partial solution to the conundrum of the empty mansion and the candle.

The headline of one of the obituary notices read "Celebrated Surgeon Sir Clive Bentley". Beneath was a photograph of the man, much as Strange remembered him, right down to the bowtie and the earnest, dignified expression.

Sir Clive was dead. Had died, according to the article, a couple of weeks ago, aged seventy-eight.

Someone, perhaps his daughter Victoria, had left the candle burning in the study as a memorial to Denningham Manor's late owner.

What this did not explain, however, was how Sir Clive could have phoned Strange a little over twenty-four hours ago. At least, it did not entirely explain it. In Strange's world, a phone call from a dead man was not an outright impossibility. The spirits of the departed could contact the living in various ways, even through mundane, conventional means such as telecommunications. Often they did this not even knowing they were deceased. Usually it occurred when the soul, only just released by death, was trapped in limbo, unable to move on to the afterlife and very confused about its new state of being. It sent out emanations to the mortal realm that might take the form of writing on a mirror or windowpane, a whispering voice on the radio or the TV, a handwritten letter out of nowhere, a random email, and yes, a phone conversation.

Sir Clive, after death, had wanted Strange to help his beloved daughter. Well, Strange could still do that. He just had to find her.

With the mystery of the empty house solved, Strange felt able to relax his guard. He turned to exit the study...

...only to discover that he was having difficulty moving. His limbs were stiffening. He could scarcely put one foot in front of the other. It was as though the very air around him had grown thick as molasses.

The feeling intensified. Holding his head up was a tremendous effort. He couldn't raise his arms. He certainly couldn't lift his hands to cast a spell. Even his mouth was affected, his lips too heavy to shape words.

Now he was entirely immobilized. Frozen to the spot. He could breathe, he could think, but that was as much as he could manage.

Just at the periphery of his vision he could see the candle, with that little coil of smoke curling up from it.

Of course.

No ordinary candle. The smoke it was giving off was magically infused, containing, Strange suspected, some variant of the Mists of Munnopor.

The whole thing—the phone call, the plea for help, the candle—was a trap.

But who...?

Even as the question was forming in Strange's mind, the answer presented itself to him.

A man entered the study.

Baron Mordo.

THE RIVAL magician halted in front of Strange. His expression was purest gloat.

"What? No words of greeting, Strange?" he said. "Oh no, of course. Silly me. You're incapacitated. Well, well, well. Who would have thought you could be so gullible? Coming all this way on the strength of just a phone call, to help a man you've met only once. I can hardly believe you fell for it." He adopted a voice that perfectly emulated Sir Clive Bentley's plummy British tones. "'Remember me, old boy? I could rather do with a hand. It's my daughter, don't you know?'"

He resumed his normal Central European-accented speech. "All of that is true, by the way. Victoria Bentley has started exhibiting extrasensory powers, to her considerable distress. But she was just the cheese in the mousetrap. She's down at the mansion lodge right now, in case you're curious. That's where she lives. Mourning her poor dead Papa, you won't be surprised to hear. I did wonder whether you might have heard reports of Sir Clive's recent demise, but I gambled that, even if you had, a communication from a deceased person might be as intriguing to you as one from a living person—perhaps more so. At any rate, it all worked out perfectly, didn't it?" He gestured at the paralyzed Strange. "Here you are, and here I am. The candle, of course, does not affect me, as caster of the spell. It does, though, leave you at my tender mercies. Now then, what to do, what to do? Hmmm."

Mordo strolled in circles, hands clasped behind his back, making a great show of musing.

"Assail you with the Rings of Raggadorr? Shock you with the Bolts of Balthakk? Or why not alternately scorch and freeze you with the Flames of the Faltine and the Icy Tendrils of Ikthalon? So many options. So many fates I can visit upon my helpless foe. So many ways to torture him and reverse the ignominy of my defeat. Where to start?"

Helpless? That might be how it looked to Mordo, Strange thought, but it wasn't wholly true. In fact, Mordo himself had provided a potential solution to his predicament.

Strange might not be able to cast any spells at that moment, but he could still send out a mental distress signal on a magical wavelength that could be picked up by anyone with some degree of psychic sensitivity. Under normal circumstances he would have aimed it at the Ancient One, but his teacher was far away and still recuperating from the poisoning Mordo had inflicted on him.

There was, however, someone much closer to hand who would be receptive to the signal.

Strange projected his psychic mayday, hoping against hope that it would be heard and heeded. Hoping, too, that Mordo would not hear it, being too preoccupied with plotting his demise.

EVENTUALLY MORDO came to a decision.

"I shall begin by binding you in the Chains of Krakkan, Strange. Their constricting embrace can, I understand, be exquisitely painful," he said.

Suiting deed to word, Mordo conjured up the mystical restraints, wrapping them around Strange's stationary body from shoulders to ankles. Face contorted with glee, he instructed them to tighten, then tighten yet further.

Had he been able to, Strange would have woven the counterspell that traditionally combated the Chains of Krakkan, namely the Fangs of Farallah. As it was, all he could do was writhe and grimace as the Chains dug their mauve links into him ever more agonizingly, squeezing him like the coils of some giant python. A scream rose in his throat, but his mouth could not open to vent it.

Mordo looked on, exultant. "You humiliated me last time we clashed, Strange. Now it's my turn. I'm going to make you suffer.

I'm going to make you regret you ever heard the name Baron Mordo. I trust you will not pass out from the pain. I want you conscious throughout this whole ordeal, which is, let me tell you, going to last a long time. A very long time."

The Chains of Krakkan were now digging in so hard Strange could hardly draw breath. Practically every muscle in his body was afire, and every bone felt ready to crack.

Mordo was focused solely on his enemy's anguish, deriving a sick, sadistic pleasure from it. His hands bunched into fists as he willed the Chains to increase the pressure that little bit more. Strange did not think he could withstand it much longer.

Then came a crash—the sound of crockery smashing.

Someone had brought the willow-pattern vase down on Mordo's head, hard.

Mordo crumpled to the floor, out cold.

Instantly, the Chains of Krakkan relinquished their grip, vanishing. The relief, for Strange, was immense. This must be how someone drowning felt upon suddenly, at the last minute, being plucked from the water to safety.

His rescuer was a woman who resembled Sir Clive Bentley in certain ways, especially the gray eyes and the forthright patrician nose.

"I… I don't pretend to know what's happening here," said Victoria Bentley. "All I know is I felt this strange urge to come up to the house. Someone was in trouble." She pointed at Strange. "You. And it had something to do with him." Now she pointed at the unconscious Mordo. "And that." She approached the candle. "Why is it even lit? The staff have been laid off. An unattended candle is a fire hazard in an old place like this." She pinched out the flame between her fingertips.

Just like that, Strange was released from the effects of the Mists of Munnopor. Control over his limbs reasserted itself. He was able to speak again, albeit hoarsely.

"Miss Bentley," he said, "I cannot thank you enough. I was in dire straits and might have died, if not for you. Forgive me—I should introduce myself. Dr. Stephen Strange. An acquaintance of your father."

"I know the name," said Victoria. "Dad mentioned you once or twice. He had a high regard for you, Doctor Strange."

"And I him. My condolences on your loss, by the way."

"Thank you."

"I suppose I should explain all this." Strange motioned at the candle, then at the prone Mordo with the scatter of ceramic shards around him.

"I suppose you should," said Victoria. "But first, how about some tea? You look like you could do with it."

"I undoubtedly could."

Victoria made to leave the study, but just then Mordo let out a groan.

"He's coming round," Strange said. "I must do something to restrain him."

"I could fetch some rope, if that'll help," Victoria said.

"In this instance, it won't. He could get out of rope easily. Something rather more exotic is required."

Strange was about to conjure the Crimson Bands of Cyttorak to fasten Mordo, but all at once, showing a surprising turn of speed, Mordo sprang to his feet.

"Oh no you don't!" he cried, and with an intricate wave of his hands, he disappeared. A flash of light, a burst of smoke, and he was gone.

"Curse me for a novice!" Strange said, clenching a fist in anger. "If only I'd been quicker off the mark."

"Did that man just vanish?" said Victoria, astonished. "In a literal puff of smoke?"

"The fumes that erupt when someone uses the Wondrous Wormhole of Weygg-Kalkuun aren't, strictly speaking, smoke," said

Strange. "They're closer to brimstone. But yes. That is more or less what happened."

"My goodness. This is all very bewildering. I really do need that tea. And an explanation."

<hr>

OVER STEAMING cups of tea in Denningham Manor's kitchen, Strange told all. There seemed no point concocting some elaborate cover story that asked Victoria to reject the evidence of her own eyes. For saving his neck, he owed her nothing less than the truth.

She took it well. "I must say, ever since I started having these peculiar episodes of mine—the predictions, the visits to other worlds—I've been receptive to the idea that there's more to life than meets the eye."

"A great deal more," said Strange. "The question is, how best to help you adjust to your newfound psychic senses?"

"Perhaps," said Victoria, "you might be willing to teach me? That is, after all, why you came here. Admittedly, it wasn't actually my father who asked you to, it was that Mordo fellow masquerading as my father. But since providence has brought you to my door, why not?"

Strange considered it. "I'm sorry, Miss Bentley," he said, "I don't think that's going to be possible." He spoke sternly but with genuine reluctance. "I simply don't have the time to offer the level of counseling you require. My work keeps me extraordinarily busy. Occult threats loom constantly over the world. I can't relax my vigilance for a moment."

She looked disappointed but accepting. "Too bad."

"However," Strange said, "there is someone I can suggest. Better still, he doesn't live as far away as I do. He's an Irishman, Anthony Ludgate Droom, although these days he goes by the name Doctor Druid. He used to be a monster hunter, but since then he's trained under certain lamas, swamis and yogis, honing his innate arcane faculties. I'll put you in touch with him. I'm certain he will be a wise and useful mentor for you."

"Thank you," said Victoria. "And I'm sure Dad, wherever he is, thanks you too."

THREE

ON THE flight home from England, Strange ruminated on his encounter with Victoria Bentley. He was in no position to take another person under his wing and be responsible for them, at least not yet. But it put him in mind of the man who had nurtured and fostered *his* talents and, moreover, brought him hope and purpose when he'd believed he would know neither ever again.

That man was the Ancient One, and as the airplane flew westward through the brilliant blue of the lower stratosphere, Strange's thoughts drifted back to the time before the mystic arts entered his life, back to when he was a surgeon—one of the country's most acclaimed and successful. He had breezed through his undergraduate and medical degrees, and his years of residency, passing every exam with flying colors and receiving nothing but praise from his professors and supervisors, all of whom remarked on his phenomenal powers of concentration and focus.

In the operating theater he wielded scalpel, forceps and suture needle with the steadiest of hands. He was quick, efficient and fearless. He performed procedures other surgeons might balk at, sometimes taking huge risks with his patients' welfare but never faltering or failing. His fees grew commensurately large, meaning he was able to indulge his taste for fast cars, tailored clothes, expensive wristwatches and vintage wines.

He was also one of the most arrogant and self-centered individuals to ever live. If a patient in recovery asked to see him so that they could thank him for saving their life, he was not interested. He wanted to know only if his bill had been paid yet. If colleagues enquired whether he would help with a research project or carry out some *pro bono* work for the underprivileged or uninsured, he dismissed the notion with contempt. Doctor Strange did not do charity. If someone came to him in dire need of his skills but could not meet his fees, he turned them away. He did not care whether they lived or died. He cared only about his bank balance.

Women came and went. The relationships never lasted long. A handsome, wealthy physician was an attractive proposition, no doubt, but not one as cold, aloof and egotistical as Stephen Strange. For a while his lovers could convince themselves he loved them, and so could he, but it was obvious his greatest love was himself.

It shamed Strange now to think of the man he had been. Sometimes people like that went through their entire lives without being held to account. They never realized their own unpleasantness or the consequences their callous behavior had on others. There was no comeuppance for them. They died unchanged and unrepentant.

Not so for Stephen Vincent Strange.

He could barely remember the near-fatal car crash. His mind had drawn a veil of amnesia over the event. He knew he had been out on a weekend jaunt in his sports car, driving too fast on a country road upstate, reveling in the feel of performance tires as they clung to the asphalt and the thrum of several hundred horsepower churning beneath the hood. Beyond that, everything was a blur. He learned subsequently that he must have misjudged a hairpin bend, taking it at too great a speed. The car hurtled off the road and headlong into a tree. It was a write-off and so, too, was its driver… almost.

He suffered a dozen different fractures, severe concussion and widespread internal ruptures and bleeding. Paramedics at the scene had to restart his heart twice, and he underwent a total of forty hours in surgery, followed by weeks of intensive care and physiotherapy. He recovered well, but there was one area of nerve damage which no surgeon—except perhaps Doctor Strange himself—could have repaired.

His hands.

Those hands, once able to wield surgical instruments with unparalleled delicacy and precision, no longer functioned as they used to. They felt clumsy and numb, as though he was wearing mittens. Strange knew the damage was irreversible: he would never be allowed to operate again. He practiced and practiced, but he found he could not even thread a sewing needle with a piece of cotton. His hands' fine motor skills were shot. In a single moment of recklessness, he had destroyed his career.

Colleagues rallied round. He was offered jobs as a consultant, a lecturer, a professor. He rejected them all. He was a doer, not an adviser. For a time he wallowed in self-pity, drinking too much, consumed with bitterness. Such friends as he had drifted away. With no income, his funds dwindled and his glamorous lifestyle faded. While not quite falling destitute, he came close.

Still unable to give up on the idea that his hands could be mended, Strange visited every neurology specialist he knew of. Each time the answer was the same: *sorry, nothing to be done*. Finally accepting that there was no conventional remedy for his condition, he began pursuing less orthodox cures. He submitted himself to acupuncturists, herbalists, homeopaths and other similar practitioners of alternative therapies. He tried a faith healer, a naturopath, an Ayurvedic guru, someone who purported to be the reincarnation of a Paleolithic shaman, and someone who claimed that any ailment could be alleviated through a special diet. He expected little from these treatments and got less.

It was during this dark, desperate period of his life, when he was at his absolute nadir, that Strange first heard of the Ancient One. Even now, he wasn't quite sure who initially mentioned that name to him. Within the twilight world of occultism and spirituality he had descended into, it just seemed to crop up in conversation from time to time, almost of its own accord. Usually it was couched in the same hushed, reverent tones people might use at church. From what Strange heard, or overheard, the Ancient One was an exceptionally enlightened being, possessed of unearthly talents and abilities. He was known as the Sorcerer Supreme, and there was nothing, people said, that he could not do. Those who sought him, and were fortunate enough to gain an audience with him, returned from the encounter with their lives forever changed for the better.

Strange saw no option but to visit this supposed miracle worker. He asked around, he conducted research, until at last he was pretty certain he'd pinned down the Ancient One's whereabouts. Feeling both foolish and oddly optimistic, he flew to Tibet.

○——————○

FROM LHASA to Kathmandu and onward, into the Himalayas, Strange traveled. By bus, taxi, moped, even on foot, he ventured higher and higher into the mountains, into ever remoter regions and ever more rarefied climes. The locals were among the friendliest people he had ever met, many of them inviting this wild-eyed, weary American stranger into their homes, offering him food and assistance and a bed for the night. Onward he went, driven by an overriding compulsion to reach the Ancient One's retreat.

The place, however, proved elusive. Most Tibetans had heard of the Ancient One but were unsure exactly where he dwelt. Strange chased down several false leads. One time, he met a wizened old man who claimed he was the Ancient One, although he turned out to be a money-grubbing charlatan, eager to defraud hapless Westerners.

He almost abandoned all hope of ever finding his quarry and resigned himself to failure.

Then, seemingly by accident, he strayed into a valley where he came across a goatherd who, at the mention of the words "Ancient One," pointed to a temple-like building halfway up the mountainside. Strange was convinced the goatherd had either misunderstood his question or was bamboozling him. Nevertheless, it seemed worth a shot. *One last try*, he told himself. *This, and then head home.*

He toiled up a long, meandering footpath to the building. He reached it exhausted, short of breath, a starveling, half-mad scarecrow figure with stubbled chin and gaunt cheeks. He barely had the strength to knock on the arched, iron-banded door, and no sooner did it open than he collapsed in a dead faint.

* * *

DAYS LATER, Strange was ushered into the Ancient One's presence.

In the interim, he had lain in a narrow bed, being tended to by a genial, shaven-headed Tibetan called Wong. He had been weak and dazed, running a fever. Only when Wong deemed him well enough was he allowed to meet the man he had come so far and endured so much to see.

Strange was still having trouble believing his quest had come to an end, right up until the moment Wong showed him to the Ancient One's private quarters.

Though short, slender and scrawny—physically unimpressive— the Ancient One nonetheless radiated an air of immense authority. He sat cross-legged on a dais, dressed in robes and furs and surrounded by tapestry-swathed walls and statuettes of weird, inhuman gods and goddesses.

"Dr. Stephen Strange," he said gravely through his white beard, which hung halfway down his neck. His eyes, embedded in countless wrinkles, shone with a still-youthful luster. "I know why you have come. I know what you seek."

"Wong has told you everything, I'm sure," Strange said.

"Even if he had not," said the Ancient One, "it does not require great insight to see a man in need."

"My hands. Can you fix them? Can you make them work like they used to?"

Smiling, the Ancient One shook his gleaming hairless head. "Would that that were in my power."

Strange was crestfallen. "You mean, after all I've been through to get here, I've wasted my time?" Anger suffused his words.

"Not necessarily, Doctor. It may be the case that what you want is not what you thought you want."

"Oh, for heaven's sake," Strange snapped. "What's that supposed to mean? Are you trying to annoy me? Everyone says the Ancient One is this almighty sage who's capable of superhuman feats. All I see is a little old man spouting pseudo-profound nonsense."

He took a step towards the Ancient One, brandishing a fist. He wasn't going to hit him. He was just infuriated, and keen to see the other man flinch.

Calmly, the Ancient One gestured, and all at once Strange was floating two feet off the floor. He windmilled his arms and kicked with his legs, but to no avail. He remained suspended in midair, like a puppet hanging from invisible strings.

"What—what is this?" he spluttered. "What are you doing? Stop it! Put me down!"

"I will," said the Ancient One, "on condition that you promise not to assault me."

"Yes. I promise. No assaulting. Now please…"

The Ancient One nodded, and slowly Strange came down to rest on the floor. He felt dizzy and flummoxed. What had just happened? Had the Ancient One really levitated him somehow? It must be some trick. He had drugged him. That or maybe used hypnotism.

"You came to me for help, Doctor Strange," the Ancient One said. "You wish to have your old life back. That, my friend, is lost to you permanently. And be honest, do you really want to be that man again? That self-important, condescending fool who had everything the material world could offer him but still felt empty inside? Tell me, why did you become a doctor in the first place? Was it solely for the glory and the money? Or was there some part of you, deep down, that saw it as your mission to help your fellow man? Where did that impulse go? When did you lose it?"

"I... I don't know what you're talking about."

"Oh, but you do, Doctor." The Ancient One narrowed his pouchy, wrinkled eyelids. "Look into your heart, as I am looking now. What do you see? I see an essential spark of goodness that has grown dim over the years but still glows. It is at present a mere ember, but with the right guidance, the right training, I believe it can be fanned into a mighty flame."

"Training?"

"You have huge potential, Stephen Strange. With an inner drive, a willpower like yours, you could become so much more than you are. You could even one day stand in my stead as Earth's Sorcerer Supreme. Let me mold you. Let me channel your energies into new, productive ends. I have been looking for a worthy pupil, and I believe I have found one."

"Pupil," Strange echoed. "Thank you, but I've done enough learning for one lifetime."

The Ancient One shrugged. "Very well. The offer stands. In the meantime, you are free to stay or leave, as you see fit—although it may be some days yet before you can go. It can't have escaped your notice that snows have fallen while you were lying prostrate in bed. The pass into and out of the valley is closed to all traffic."

"Then I'll wait," said Strange, "and as soon as the pass is clear, I'm gone."

"Absolutely. That is your prerogative." The Ancient One clapped his hands. "Mordo!"

Strange turned to find a Westerner like himself entering the room. Mordo offered the Ancient One a low bow. "Master?"

"Show Doctor Strange around, would you, Mordo? He is our guest and has the run of the place."

"Of course, Master."

IN THE ensuing days, Strange learned that the Ancient One's retreat was a hospitable community whose residents, led by Wong, worked tirelessly at their domestic duties and rubbed along uncomplainingly. Life was plain and monastic. Young Tibetans came there as acolytes, to acquire habits of discipline and self-restraint under the Ancient One's aegis—he the tranquil sun around which they orbited, and the twinkly-eyed ascetic role model whose example they tried to copy. It was like a cross between a kibbutz and a seminary, but without any overt religious aspect. Strange fell into its simple rhythms of existence and found this, somewhat to his surprise, soothing.

Mordo was the only fly in the ointment. Surly at the best of times, he seemed particularly sullen around Strange. Strange had no idea why this might be, other than that the European aristocrat had a superiority complex and this did not endear him to someone who, like Strange, equaled him in that respect. Mordo feigned humility well enough and managed polite conversation when required, but beneath that, something simmered. Something dark and ugly.

The snows didn't thaw. In fact, more fell. At first Strange felt trapped, but as time wore on, he minded less and less. There were worse places to be stuck. And what did he have to return to back in America anyway? Nothing much. The withered husk of his former life. The dregs in a once-full glass.

Not once did he see any indication of strange powers or supernatural feats, aside from that moment when the Ancient One had appeared to lift him off the floor with just a flick of the wrist. He became convinced he'd imagined it. He had still been feeling unsteady on his feet, hadn't he? Lightheaded. Surely that accounted for it.

All this changed when, one evening, he chanced to pass Mordo's room. The door was ajar, and Strange couldn't help peering in.

Mordo stood hunched over a small brazier, in which an uncanny green fire blazed. Lit from below by the flames, Mordo's face was a mask of intense concentration. Sweat beaded his forehead.

"Hail to you, Dormammu," Mordo said, "Lord of the Dark Dimension. The Ancient One is withholding true power from me, I can feel it. He does not trust me. He calls me his pupil but of late his lessons have seemed lacking, as though his heart is no longer in it. He is looking favorably on the newcomer, the accursed American called Strange, for whom he evidently harbors great hopes. This cannot stand. Hear me, Dread Dormammu, and aid me. I beseech you, for I would be your true servant, ever and always. Grant me what the Ancient One will not, the magics I need to do your bidding."

As Strange watched, a face began to form in the heart of the flames. It was practically featureless, just a suggestion of eyes and mouth, yet for all that it conveyed clear, diabolical malice.

Unable to suppress his astonishment, Strange gasped aloud.

Mordo swiveled about. His gaze fell on Strange. His brow furrowed.

"You!" he said.

At the same moment, the green-hued fire in the brazier winked out of existence, as quickly as if someone had turned a gas burner off.

Mordo jabbed an accusatory forefinger at the interloper. "How much did you see? No, never mind. Whatever you have witnessed here just now, you shall not breathe a word of it to anyone."

So saying, he executed a series of complex movements with both hands.

"There. That should fix you."

"Fix me how?" said Strange, with a scornful sneer. "All I saw was an overweight chump waggling his stubby fingers in the air."

"You try telling the Ancient One, or anybody else, about this." Mordo motioned to the brazier. "See how far you get."

Strange chuckled. "All right then. Challenge accepted."

He hurried off to the Ancient One's quarters. Until now, he had not been bothered overmuch about the friction between himself and Mordo. He had thought it more Mordo's problem than his own. But if the guy wanted to make things personal, then okay. Strange would denounce him to the Ancient One. What was it Mordo had said? *He does not trust me.* If that was the case, then Strange was about to give him another reason not to. He would bring up, too, the face he had seen in the green fire. He definitely had not imagined that, and it was something that merited an explanation.

The Ancient One looked up quizzically as Strange came in. "Yes, Doctor?"

"I want to—"

"Yes?"

"I'd like to—"

The old Tibetan raised a hoary eyebrow. "Like to what?"

For some reason Strange could not seem to get the words out. Try as he might, his tongue wouldn't obey him. He could start the sentence; he just couldn't finish it.

Mordo appeared behind him. "Master," he said to the Ancient One, smiling obsequiously, "I must apologize for Strange's intrusion. Clearly some sort of mental aberration has overcome him."

"That's not true," Strange declared. "You know you—" But again, his mouth was stopped. He couldn't say what he wanted to say. There was a kind of barrier between brain and lips.

"What's the matter, Strange?" Mordo said, sounding solicitous. "You seem very confused. Perhaps it's the altitude. It can have quite a sapping effect, if one isn't careful. The weather has turned and the snows have begun to melt. It might be best for you to depart as soon as you can. This place obviously isn't for you."

Strange flailed for a few moments more, but it was no use. Mordo had done something to him. He couldn't reveal what he had witnessed. He couldn't even hint at it.

Turning on his heel, Strange stalked agitatedly out. He found Wong and tried the same thing with him as with the Ancient One. Again, his speech was impeded. He could ask Wong what was for dinner and make small talk, but he could say nothing connected with Mordo's furtive doings.

Baffled and a little bit frightened, Strange headed to his room. On the way he passed a mirror and had a shock.

His reflection showed a bulky iron gag clamped over his mouth.

He knew the gag wasn't there. For one thing, he'd have felt it. More to the point, the Ancient One and Wong would have mentioned it.

The mirror, however, insisted it was. He patted his face just to double-check. His fingers found nothing but flesh.

What in God's name was going on?

<hr />

ALL NIGHT, sleepless, Strange thought about it. Had Mordo worked some kind of magical charm on him? Was that possible? And if Mordo was the Ancient One's pupil, as he had heard him claim, from the sound of it he was unhappy in that role, and his teacher was unhappy about it as well. The Ancient One thought Strange himself a more suitable candidate. Strange could understand Mordo feeling envious of him for that. But the envy seemed to stem from something else, as though Strange might prevent Mordo from achieving his goals, even though he had no need or urge to do so.

Or did he? Strange had developed a liking for the Ancient One, and he knew now that Mordo was not all he pretended to be. As a pupil, Mordo did not have his teacher's best interests at heart.

Come the morning, Strange's mind was made up. If, as it seemed, Baron Mordo had placed a magic spell on him, there was one way to deal with that. Fight magic with magic.

Going to the Ancient One's quarters this time, Strange felt a strong sense of rightness. It was almost as though the decision was out of his hands. Events had conspired to bring him to this moment, this choice, this willingness to commit himself. He was a paper boat on a stream, being borne along by the current.

"Ancient One," he began, "the offer you made some days ago. I wish to take you up on it. I will be your student."

The elderly Tibetan merely nodded, as if he had expected nothing else.

"Teach me magic," Strange went on. "There are people who seem to want to use magic for their own selfish purposes. I would like to use it to help others. When I was a surgeon, I lost sight of what helping others meant. I won't make the same mistake twice."

"I know you won't," said the Ancient One, adding, "And you don't have to worry about Mordo and the gagging spell he has cast on you, either."

"What? You know about that?"

"I sensed it on you as soon as you walked in here yesterday. It stood out a mile." He thrust both hands forward, as though miming a shove. "There. A minor cantrip. It is banished. Why, though, did Mordo feel the need to muzzle you?"

"In order to protect himself," said Strange. "I caught him in the act, doing something he clearly didn't want me to tell you about." He described the scene with the brazier and the ominous face in the green fire. "He was addressing someone called... the Dread Dormouse? Something like that."

The Ancient One's face darkened. "Dormammu?"

"Yes, that's it. Said he was his true servant."

The old Tibetan's frown became a scowl. "It's worse than I thought, if Mordo has allied himself with that embodiment of all that is evil. When he first came to me, I could tell that he had some considerable aptitude for magic and I believed I could, with patience and diligence, steer him in the right direction. Clearly I was misguided. Well, in light of what you have told me, I have no choice but to cast him out. The decision is made easier, now that I have a new pupil, one who I feel will be a more than adequate substitute. Mordo must go. You, Stephen, will take his place."

MORDO DEPARTED the premises that very same day, and not graciously. He slouched away muttering about ingrates and dolts and vowing that the Ancient One would pay for rejecting him. The last thing Strange heard him utter was a series of phrases in his native tongue, which he spat out in such a way that they could only have been oaths.

Then began Strange's apprenticeship.

It entailed…

- poring over countless dusty, leatherbound volumes of magical lore, including *The Book of the Vishanti*, *The Tome of Zhered-Na*, *The Scrolls of Watoomb*, *The Krakoan Grimoires*, and even the dreaded *Darkhold*
- fathoming the alphabets, syntaxes and vocabularies of several long-dead and largely forgotten languages
- memorizing the wording of a host of spells until they were ingrained in his brain
- getting to grips with a sprawling cosmology of deities and demons
- understanding how eldritch forces could be channeled and shaped through technique coupled with sheer willpower
- mastering the intricate finger formations needed to enable spellcasting

The last of these was especially tricky for Strange at first, because of his injuries. Magic, however, required a lesser degree of manual suppleness and dexterity than medicine. His hands might no longer be able to perform delicate surgery but they were nimble enough for his new vocation.

Overall, it was hard going, but the Ancient One was a patient pedagogue and Strange a diligent disciple. There were moments of stymied frustration and moments of breakthrough joy. Soon, surprisingly swiftly, Strange felt as comfortable with his newfound abilities as he had with medicine. Just as he knew the myriad ways in which the human body worked and could fail, now he knew the myriad ways in which magic worked and could fail.

Eventually it was time to leave the Ancient One's household and put his suite of freshly acquired mystical talents to good use. A new home awaited him, an early-1900s townhouse on Bleecker Street which the Ancient One suggested would suit him perfectly. It had been built on a confluence of dragon ley lines, at a spot on Manhattan Island which in past times had been used for Native American shamanic rituals and vision quests, and subsequently pagan sacrifices. Now it lay vacant, having garnered a bad reputation over recent decades as a haven for beatniks, satanists and drunks. Its last owner had died in mysterious, gruesome circumstances, and several property developers had since tried refurbishing it and selling it on but, for one reason or another, failed to make any headway with their plans.

Strange, by selling his apartment and his last remaining stocks, had just enough money to purchase it. He moved in and embarked on a new career as a master of the mystic arts.

Magic, he quickly discovered, was not just a second chance.

It was redemption.

FOUR

THE DREAM Dimension was created long, long ago by the collective unconsciousness of all the sentient beings in the universe, amassing out of the chaotic stories people told themselves in their sleep, the reveries they had while awake, the aspirations that kept them going through life, the fictions that brought them comfort. It had innumerable component realms—some pleasant, some less so—but the darkest, dreariest and most dismal of them all was the one ruled over by Nightmare.

Here, the backdrop was a field of constant roiling purple, shot through with streaks of inky black and greasy green. There was no such thing as solid ground, just isolated patches of landscape that were in perpetual flux, forming and re-forming all the time but never evolving into anything scenic. The various native fauna were a more repellent-looking bunch of creatures than even Bosch or Brueghel could have imagined—skulking, creeping things with slimy hides and mismatched eyes, patchy fur and odd numbers of legs.

Nightmare's palace, likewise, was monstrous, architecturally speaking. It resembled nothing so much as a fusion of specter, cobweb and storm-blasted tree. There was not a single straight line in it, or right-angled corner, or level floor.

In its throne room, Nightmare sat upon a bulbous floating chair that was like some unholy union of turtle and turkey, all scaly protrusions and wattled textures. A member of his personal guard stood to attention beside him, a hulking figure whose head was fully masked like an executioner's. Kneeling before him, a lowly serf with manacled wrists and tattered tunic held up a chalice in which a thick, moss-green liquid swirled turgidly.

"Sire," said the serf, "your alchemists have labored long and hard, and at last the potion you demanded is ready. Any mortal sleeper who sups it in their dreams will become your hapless thrall. Their soul will remain trapped here at your leisure, to be dealt with however you wish."

A grisly grin split Nightmare's pallid face. "Good. All these many eons I have lived off the unhappiness of sleeping mortals. That has been my meat and drink, the source of my power. It has occurred to me, however, that even after so much time, I know precious little about these beings. I have regarded them as cattle, yet not so long ago one of them dared to challenge me. Here, in my own domain!"

"Aye, sire," said the serf, "the sorcerer known as Strange. But his defiance was short-lived. One glimpse of your majestic might, and he turned tail and fled."

"It won't be the last time Strange meddles in my affairs, I'm certain of it," Nightmare said. "Especially since I am resolved to conquer the mortal realm and have it for my own. No more waiting for tormented slumberers to find their way here by chance. Why put up with scraps from the table when I can have the entire supply?"

The manacled serf groveled harder. "Oh yes, sire! Why indeed?"

"But, for that purpose, I have decided I must learn all I can about human beings before embarking on my conquest. The better informed I am, the easier it will be to exploit their weaknesses when I attack their world." Nightmare gestured at the serf dismissively. "Go. See to it that you bring me a good sampling of mortals. And should you fail..." He nodded at the masked guard, who cracked his knuckles meaningfully. "You know the penalty."

Quailing, the serf scurried off, careful not to spill a single drop from the chalice.

———o———o———

DOCTOR STRANGE was perusing the *Daily Bugle* over breakfast when the doorbell rang. He had been home from England a little over a week, and during that time his thoughts had turned again and again to Victoria Bentley. He knew he had made the right decision, refusing her request to teach her how to control her psychic abilities, but he still felt guilty.

The guilt had been alleviated somewhat thanks to a phone conversation with Doctor Druid the previous day. Druid had called to say that, even after just a couple of sessions with him, Victoria was flourishing. Her powers were not great but under his guidance she was learning the extent of them, and already found them less troubling. Druid was confident that, in due course, she would be able to lead a normal, productive life.

"I'm grateful to you for recommending me to her, Doctor Strange," Druid said. "Flattered, too, that Earth's pre-eminent mage is even aware I exist. Perhaps one day you and I might work together."

"The ways of fate are unknowable," said Strange, "but doubtless our paths will cross, Doctor Druid, and I look forward to it."

When he heard the doorbell, he sensed that whoever this visitor was, they had come in connection with the content of an article on the *Bugle*'s front page. The paper's main, above-the-fold story concerned a bank robbery which Spider-Man had apparently foiled, although an editorial sidebar clearly implied that the "wall-crawling menace" had somehow been complicit in the heist. Beneath that was a shorter piece headlined "Another 'Sleep Victim' Reported", with the subheading "City's Fifth Unexplained Coma Patient In As Many Days".

On the doorstep of the Sanctum Sanctorum stood a former

colleague, Dr. Harlan Warren, medical director of the New York–Presbyterian Hospital, where Strange used to work. Warren—bespectacled, bald on top, with a fringe of close-cropped hair around his lower scalp—was an agreeable sort, good with coworkers as well as with patients. He had been one of Strange's staunchest supporters not only during his career but also in the aftermath of the car accident, and the last to give up on him when he began his descent into alcoholism and despair. He was also the only person Strange knew with a golf handicap lower than his own, which he had always found a little aggravating. Warren's appointment as medical director of the hospital was one Strange viewed as both commendable and inevitable.

Sure enough, Warren had called to discuss the so-called "sleep victims".

"It's not just in New York, Stephen," he said. "There've been reports of patients exhibiting the same symptoms as far afield as Moscow, Beijing and Mumbai."

"Those symptoms being sudden-onset, fully unresponsive somnolence," said Strange, "which none of the standard methods of stimulation can counteract. That, at least, is what I've been able to gather from the news."

"Correct. But what's really strange—no pun intended—is the fact that these people are asleep with their eyes wide open. I've never seen the phenomenon before."

"Coma patients can sometimes open their eyes spontaneously, usually if there's brain stem injury involved."

"But keep them constantly open? No. Besides, we're not talking head trauma. It isn't persistent vegetative state, either, or catatonia. The patients are asleep and can't be woken, that's what it comes down to."

"Could some form of pathogen be involved?"

"We've run every form of test and found no sign of external cause. This isn't some epidemic, in the conventional sense, and yet it's happening all over the planet. I've consulted with peers on four continents, and we're stumped, Stephen. Completely at a loss."

"You know this sort of thing was never my area of expertise," Strange said. "More to the point, I'm not practicing medicine anymore. My license expired last year and I haven't renewed it."

"I know," said Warren. "I also know you dabble in occultism these days."

"It's not occultism, and I don't dabble in anything. But apart from that…"

"Well, whatever you like to call it. The thing is, I think we could really do with… a different approach. Science is failing us, and at this stage I'm willing to try anything. Even…"

"Even magic?"

With an apologetic smile, Warren said, "Even that."

STRANGE HADN'T ever expected to be back at New York–Presbyterian in any official capacity. The place was unchanged. Still the same atmosphere of fragile serenity, a barely contained tension ready to erupt at any moment into a sudden emergency—alarm buzzers sounding, pagers beeping, doctors and nurses rushing to the ER or someone's bedside. Behind every door, hidden suffering and the potential for tragedy. The smells of floor polish and antiseptic masking worse odors.

In the ICU wing, Warren showed Strange the sleep victim.

"Thirty-two-year-old male," he said, "in otherwise good health. No history of narcolepsy or other sleep disorders. Vitals all normal. Went to bed the evening before last, never woke up. He's been like this for over forty-eight hours. The nurses irrigate his eyes with saline drops regularly. We've tried closing the eyelids manually but they just spring back open."

It was, Strange had to admit, rather uncanny the way the man lay there, just staring into space.

"Leave this to me, Harlan," he said.

"You're going to try your hocus-pocus on him?"

Strange suppressed a sigh. "Yes, I'm going to try my hocus-pocus on him."

"Okay," said Warren. "It's probably a good idea I'm not around for that. The board of directors would have my hide if they knew I'd even brought you in."

When he was alone with the patient, Strange leaned over him and invoked the power of the Eye of Agamotto. The amulet emitted its beam of truth-infused light, instantly disclosing a mystical aura that surrounded the sleep victim. The aura glowed dark green and throbbed in a sickly, arrhythmic fashion, like the pulsing of a diseased heart.

The Eye of Agamotto's light probed further, deeper, revealing an emptiness within the supine figure. An essential, intangible part of the man had been scooped out.

"Some form of sinister enchantment," Strange murmured to himself. "His body functions but his soul is absent."

The combination of a sleeping man and a missing soul suggested only one thing to Strange.

Nightmare.

BACK AT his Sanctum Sanctorum, Strange slipped into a self-induced trance and projected his astral form into the Dream Dimension.

As he ventured into Nightmare's realm, he took the precaution of generating a floating path infused with the protective power of Hoggoth. The path unfurled ahead of him like a carpet unrolling, curving this way and that. As long as he remained on it he would be immune from attack, and its winding course would conduct him homeward once his mission was done.

The further Strange traveled into the kingdom of Nightmare,

the more garish and phantasmagorical his surroundings became. Strings of fleshy, globular blobs hung in the air, some looking like planets, others like molecules. Gigantic tentacles reached across gulfs, tangling sinuously and sensuously with other tentacles. Sparking comets streaked overhead, leaving multihued trails. A thing like a gargantuan bacterium propelled itself past him with rippling wafts of its cilia. Strange kept his head down and his eyes on the path. A place like this distorted your sense of what was real and what was not. It could drive you mad if you let it.

He was working on the theory that Nightmare had captured the souls of the sleep victims and was holding them prisoner. He could not think why, but then that was of less concern than rescuing them. The Hoggoth-blessed path would lead him to them.

As he trod the path, Strange was unaware that he was being observed.

Lurking behind a thorny thicket, one of Nightmare's many minions gazed on him with cold, unblinking eyes.

○━━━━○

THIS SERVILE entity had, like his brethren and sistren, been created by Nightmare for no other purpose than to do his master's bidding and fawn over him at all times. His particular job was to spy at the borders of Nightmare's realm, keeping an eye out for enemies and also for errant, troubled dreamers whose pain might serve as nourishment for Nightmare.

Now, seeing the infamous Doctor Strange walking through the realm, the minion was appalled. The impudence of the fellow! He skulked off, making for Nightmare's palace. There were routes he knew that Strange could not know, little shortcuts and back-channels along which he could scuttle like a rat within the walls of a building. In no time he arrived in his master's presence and prostrated himself before him.

"Wondrous Lord Nightmare," he said, "pardon the intrusion."

Nightmare was, at that moment, presiding over the handful of human souls he had so far collected from the mortal realm. Each of these sleepers, while dreaming, had been offered the chalice with the green potion and been unable to resist taking a sip. Each, as a result, had found their route back to waking barred and had drifted inexorably into Nightmare's waiting clutches.

The souls stood huddled inside a corral made of thick, coiling strands of an ectoplasm-like substance, and Nightmare had mesmerized them so that their wills were entirely subject to his. He had begun interrogating them about the ways of their world and, numbly, dazedly, they were supplying answers. His understanding of earthly politics, geography and customs was growing. The impression he had of humankind's strengths and defenses was that they were poor. This gladdened his infernal, greedy heart. Feeble beings. It was almost like they were asking to be subjugated.

"What is it?" he snapped at the minion, ready to kill him for his intrusion.

"Oh sire, look kindly upon your unworthy underling. I come bearing important news. Doctor Strange is again trespassing in your territory."

Nightmare reared up in outrage. "Is this true?"

"Would I dare lie to you, sire? I saw him with my own humble eyes. He treads a path of his own making."

"He has come for these pathetic things." Nightmare waved a hand at the captive souls. "The pitiful fool. Does he not realize that in my kingdom, I am supreme?"

"Sublimely supreme, sir," said the minion.

Nightmare concentrated for a brief moment, then grinned. "There," he said. "That will detain him while I saddle up and ride out to greet him. Thinks he can just stroll in here with impunity, does he? I'll show him!"

OUT OF nowhere, a vast reptilian head made of stone appeared in front of Strange. The path he had conjured veered into the head's gaping maw, which was sealed with a rivet-studded iron door.

Strange smiled wryly. He was not surprised. Sooner or later, Nightmare or some spy of his would have detected his presence. Now Nightmare was attempting to intimidate and obstruct him. It wouldn't work.

He cast the spell known as Azrael's Doorbell. The door submitted to his magical ministrations and opened wide.

Beyond lay an immense yawning chasm, infinitely deep. The path continued, traversing this abyss, but now it forked into three.

Strange's smile lost some of its wryness. Nightmare had been a little cleverer than he thought. Only one of the paths was the original. The others doubtless led to doom. Either they would crumble underfoot, sending him plunging eternally downward, or they would draw him astray into the furthest, most labyrinthine reaches of Nightmare's realm from which he would struggle to find his way out again. His mortal body could not survive indefinitely without his astral self inhabiting it. Left untenanted for too long, it would waste away and perish.

The Eye of Agamotto, however, would be his salvation. He invoked its light, and the true path showed itself as solid. The other two crumbled to nothingness.

Strange strode onward, and shortly heard a familiar far-off thundering: the sound of hooves, which could belong to no other animal than Nightmare's horse.

Here came the horned, night-black steed, hurtling along with its fiendish rider at the reins.

"Doctor Strange!" Nightmare cried. "I see my trap did not deter you."

"It'd take a lot more than that, Nightmare."

"Perhaps. At any rate, I know why you've come and I know what you want."

"Then let's dispense with the formalities, shall we?" said Strange. "Lead me to where you're keeping the souls you've stolen."

"Better yet, I'll bring them to you." Nightmare snapped his fingers, and an airborne platform materialized behind him, a lumpen gray disc seemingly made of pumice, atop which the sleep victims' souls stood in a docile cluster.

Strange's path immediately, of its own accord, snaked towards the platform, attaching itself to one edge.

"There you are, Strange," Nightmare said. "They're all yours. And don't think I'm unaware that I cannot harm you as long as you're on that path. Even I have to admit that the power Hoggoth exerts over it trumps my own."

"All very accommodating of you," Strange said. "I'm sure there's a catch."

"None whatsoever." Nightmare offered him a look of wounded innocence. "It's wisdom to know when you've been outplayed and to concede victory to whoever has outplayed you."

"Still, it seems like you're giving them up rather easily."

"Oh, I'm done with them," Nightmare said airily. "Their usefulness is at an end."

"Usefulness?"

"As teaching tools. I have learned much about your world and its ways from close study of these souls, information which will prove of great value when I come to take over Earth."

"That's it, is it?" said Strange. "You're graduating from dream-vampire to aspirant planet-ruler?"

"It seems…" Nightmare shrugged. "Inevitable."

"To you, maybe."

Keeping a wary eye on the dream-lord, Strange followed the path's upward slope. Stopping just short of where it joined the platform, he beckoned to the souls.

"Come this way," he said. "Keep to the path and it will guide you back to where you need to go."

One after another, obligingly, the souls filed off the platform and traipsed down the path. They moved with robotic stiffness, their expressions glazed. Strange felt assured that they would reach their destinations unscathed, waking up in their bodies with perhaps a vague recollection of a very peculiar dream they had had.

As the last of them marched off the platform, he allowed himself a moment of self-congratulation. It had all gone more smoothly than he could have hoped.

Only then did he realize he had made an error. A potentially fatal one.

IT WAS literally a misstep. Strange had, without noticing, put one foot on the platform.

All at once, he was no longer under Hoggoth's protection.

Nightmare had been waiting for just such a lapse in concentration. He had deliberately made things easy for Strange, in hopes of catching him off-guard.

He fired a bolt of eldritch energy that smashed the section of platform the path was attached to. Strange lost his balance and instinctively lunged forward, just about managing to gain the safety of the platform.

Crouching on all fours, he barely had time to recover from this sudden turnabout before Nightmare destroyed the platform beneath him. With nothing to support him, Strange tumbled through space. It took him a few seconds to realize he was falling not down but up. The laws of physics didn't apply in the Dream Dimension, least of all in Nightmare's private corner of it.

He plunged headlong through space until he landed with a bump on a patch of grass whose blades shattered like crystal beneath his weight. He got unsteadily to his feet, brushing off tiny, glassy shards of the grass. Normal gravity had reasserted itself, at least, and he looked around him to find he was in the middle of a verdant plain where every plant glittered and looked as brittle as spun sugar.

And here was Nightmare, still on horseback, looming over him. He was carrying a long rod in one hand. The other end sparkled and crackled with whatever the Dream Dimension's equivalent of electricity was.

"Behold the spinybeast!" Nightmare said, using the rod to goad a large, insect-like creature towards Strange. "His touch is death, even to a spirit form. And look, he wants to meet you, Strange. He wants to snuggle up close."

The spinybeast was the size of a large dog and had the combined physical attributes of scorpion, crab and porcupine. As its name might suggest, it was covered in spines, which protruded from its carapace in all directions. Venom dripped from their pointed tips.

The thing did not, in fact, seem to want to meet Strange. It seemed to want to be left alone, but Nightmare kept jabbing it with the rod, which delivered hefty shocks like an earthly cattle prod. Thus provoked, the spinybeast grew irritable and fixed its multitude of dead little eyes on Strange. Clearly someone had to pay for this mistreatment. It might as well be the figure who apparently lacked any means of hurting it.

The spinybeast shuffled across the fragile, crystalline grass, which crunched to pieces beneath its clawed feet, and Strange began edging backwards. Nightmare followed the creature, giving it the odd poke every time it looked as though it might be losing enthusiasm. The whole situation would have been absurd, Strange thought, if it wasn't so serious. He didn't question Nightmare's assertion that the spinybeast could kill him in his astral form. The rules of this realm were Nightmare's own. That was the risk you took when entering an other-dimensional plane presided over by a vain despot with absolute control over every aspect of life—and death.

Strange retreated until he could go no further. He had reached the brink of a precipice, and directly below him a monster awaited. The spinybeast was a worrisome gnat compared with this sprawling orange-brown leviathan, part earthworm, part whale, with dozens of mouths, each lined with serrated teeth all the way down the gullet. The mouths gaped ravenously, seeming certain that one of them would soon be enjoying Strange as a tasty snack.

No way forward, no way back. Strange was running out of options.

The Eye of Agamotto, however, had yet to fail him.

He chose his moment carefully. The spinybeast was almost at his feet, with Nightmare right behind.

He closed his eyes, muttering the words, "Seven Suns of Cinnibus, lend me your light."

The amulet opened *its* eye, all the way.

Pure, blazing incandescence shot forth. It was the power of a god, a beacon of shining truth, boosted by energies from a dimension of brilliantly radiant wisdom. It shone for no more than a millisecond, but that was enough.

Nightmare's steed reared up, whinnying in fright.

Nightmare himself was briefly blinded.

In his startlement, his hand reflexively stabbed the rod down. The action was so forceful that he didn't just give the spinybeast a jolt, he skewered the creature all the way through its abdomen.

Strange, seizing his moment, made his getaway.

GRADUALLY NIGHTMARE'S vision cleared. He blinked around, but there was no sign of Strange. There was just him, his skittishly prancing mount, and the impaled spinybeast, now twitching its last on the ground.

He knew where Strange must be. He tossed the rod aside, jerked his horse about, and galloped off towards the Hoggoth-protected path.

Too late.

Strange had already found his way back to the path and was escorting the sleepers' souls the final few steps along it to the far end, where it adjoined the waking world. Even as Nightmare arrived, the last of the souls slipped from one realm to the other and was gone.

Nightmare let out a howl of vindictive rage. "Strange! Enjoy your triumph while you can! It won't be long before we meet again, and next time, I shall be victorious."

Strange turned round just long enough to offer Nightmare an ironic salute, before exiting the Dream Dimension and re-entering his body.

FIVE

IN CASTLE Mordo, the brooding seldom ceased, and when it did, it was only because the owner had brooded until he could brood no more and was now implementing his latest scheme—the outcome of the brooding.

In this instance, post-brood, Baron Mordo was in his spell chamber, putting the finishing touches to a replica of Doctor Strange's house in Greenwich Village. The scale model of the Sanctum Sanctorum was small enough to fit in his hand and was made out of a chunk of wood from a sacred cedar tree which Mordo had purchased, at great price, from a Shinto priest in Kyoto. He had done the carving himself and, in his own estimation, made a pretty good job of it.

Laying the model on a table, Mordo got to work wreathing a spell over it, a blend of the Mists of Munnopor and the Vapors of Valtorr, with elements of Satannish's Hex of Translocation and the Denak Duplication Charm thrown in. It enveloped the model in an eddying, shimmering cloud.

The spell took a few moments to understand its own purpose. The model was a fetish, there to instill it with an objective and a location. When the magical cloud stopped swirling and came to a standstill, Mordo knew the spell had absorbed the information it needed and was now ready.

With a sweep of both arms, he dispatched it out through an

open window. The little cloud scudded swiftly out of view.

Mordo hurried to a scrying mirror, which he had configured beforehand to show him Strange's actual house. Via the mirror, he had seen Strange leave the Sanctum Sanctorum an hour ago. Strange hadn't come back in the interim, or the mirror would have alerted Mordo to that fact.

As Mordo looked on, his spell settled over the building and began seeping in. Swiftly, imperceptibly, it penetrated every brick, every window, every layer of mortar, every roof tile, until it was fully absorbed. Mordo had wrought the spell so that it would be undetectable even to the mystically attuned senses of someone like Strange.

The snare was set. All he had to do was wait.

It was after midnight in Transylvania and late evening in New York. It surely wouldn't be long before Strange returned home. The man had to sleep, didn't he?

Mordo waited and waited, doing his best to rein in his impatience.

He thought of how Strange had got the better of him, first when he tried to extract knowledge from the Ancient One, then when he attacked Strange at Denningham Manor. Twice the man had thwarted him—three times, if you counted the way he had been instrumental in getting Mordo ousted from the Ancient One's retreat with his magical training still incomplete. The impertinent commoner! He was embroiled in a game whose magnitude he just could not comprehend, and Mordo needed to deal with him once and for all, before matters proceeded much further. This wasn't just what he himself wanted; it was what Dormammu decreed, and you did not disobey Dormammu, not if you had any sense. Dormammu had vast, sweeping plans; Mordo, as his agent on Earth, was duty bound to help bring them to fruition, not least by disposing of anyone who might oppose them. His desire to see Strange brought down was a satisfying combination of the professional and the personal.

At last the mirror showed Strange strolling along the neon-lit street, approaching his front door.

Mordo leaned forward in anticipation.

Blithely, Strange unlocked the door. Without betraying the least suspicion, he went inside.

As soon as the door closed behind him, the spell enacted the next phase of its magic. The building began to shudder, to waver, to fade from sight.

Within seconds, the Sanctum Sanctorum had vanished, as though erased from the face of the earth.

Next moment, it reappeared.

This, though, was not the building itself but a perfect simulacrum, an illusory Sanctum Sanctorum with little more substance than a stage set. Passersby would not notice the difference. While the enchantment held, it would appear as though nothing had changed. Doctor Strange's house was where it always was.

Meanwhile, the real Sanctum Sanctorum, with all it contained, including Strange himself, lay...

Elsewhere.

○———○

IN THE Mirror Dimension, to be precise. A place of planes and reflections. Of reversals and deceptions. Of images, and images of images, and images of images of images.

The Sanctum Sanctorum floated in the midst of that dimension's infinitude of replication. Thousands upon thousands of identical copies surrounded it, canted at every conceivable angle. They folded and divided, merged and separated, an ever-shifting mass of mimicry.

Within the actual, original Sanctum Sanctorum, Doctor Strange struggled to overcome his disorientation.

He had already been feeling drained and off-kilter in the wake of his visit to Nightmare's realm. Interdimensional travel in astral form took its toll, leaving both body and soul weakened. Nonetheless, after reinstalling himself in his physical frame, he had managed to contact

Dr. Warren and give him the glad tidings. Warren said he had been on the point of calling Strange anyway, to inform him that the sleep victim at New York–Presbyterian had just come round.

"The others," Strange said, "will soon be waking too, if they haven't already."

"I won't ask what you did, Stephen," Warren said, "and I probably don't want to know. I'm just grateful you did it."

After the call was finished, Strange, with some urgency, headed out for food. His favorite sushi place was just a short walk away in the Bowery, and he left it with a belly fully of maki rolls and his vigor somewhat restored. It was a nice evening and he decided to wander around the neighborhood before going home. He had cast a glamor over himself so that he appeared to be wearing street clothes and wouldn't draw unwelcome looks. That being said, his magician's garb wasn't much more outlandish than the outfits some Greenwich Villagers wore. It was one of the many reasons he felt at home there.

By the time he got back to the Sanctum Sanctorum, he was looking forward to a well-earned rest.

And now this.

A glance out of a window had told him the entire house had been transported to the Mirror Dimension. That was some powerful magic and would take time and effort to reverse.

It would be simpler to find who had woven the spell and persuade them to unpick it.

He could not just step outside the house, not unless he wanted to get lost amid a horde of replica selves—a multiplicity of Doctor Stranges, all of whom believed they were the genuine article.

His astral form, however, cast no reflection. It could navigate through the dimension unduplicated and therefore unhindered. Sending it out again so soon after the last time required effort and would put a strain on his already depleted reserves of energy, but needs must.

As his astral form sprang forth from his body, Strange said, "Eye of Agamotto, guide me to the source of this ominous occurrence."

A narrow finger of light emerged from the amulet. It probed this way and that, like a bloodhound seeking a scent, until all at once it locked on to its target. All Strange had to do now was follow the beam, which was as straight as a ruled line, to its destination.

That proved to be—no great surprise—Castle Mordo.

GLIDING INTO the castle, Strange didn't have to look far to find its owner.

He was passing through a spacious flagstoned hallway that was lit by an enormous chandelier, when he unexpectedly butted up against an invisible mystical barrier. He wheeled round, only to find a barrier behind him too, and also on either side. He was fully hemmed in.

A door opened, and Baron Mordo stumped into the hallway.

The aristocrat mage had been waiting for Strange.

More accurately, lying in wait to ambush him.

"Trapped not just once but twice in one night, Strange," Mordo said. "You're really slipping."

Strange cast a spell of emancipation, invoking the aid of the ageless Vishanti.

It was no use. In astral form, his powers were never at full strength, and they had been at low ebb to begin with. He didn't have the wherewithal to counter Mordo's spell.

"It's an old but good one," Mordo said. "A bottle of containment. If it can hold a genie or an imp for centuries on end, it can surely hold you."

"What do you want this time, Mordo?" Strange said.

"What I wanted before. Only one man knows more about the mystic arts than you or me. He is going to fill in the missing pieces of my education, or else."

"The Ancient One."

"Who other? And now he doesn't have you to protect him, as he did before. So it's a double victory for me. The Ancient One at my mercy, and you, my mortal enemy, securely captive. With your astral form sundered from your physical self, how long do you think you'll last? Twenty-four hours at most." Mordo shook his fists in elation. "You have no idea how good it is to see you helpless like this. I could stand here all day, just looking at you. But my private jet awaits. I shall be in Tibet by nightfall. Enjoy your stay at Castle Mordo, Strange. Try not to get too comfortable."

"The Ancient One will never give you what you ask," Strange said as Mordo turned to leave. "He'd rather die."

"If that is his choice," said Mordo over his shoulder, "so be it."

And then he was gone.

○——○

EIGHTEEN HOURS later, Baron Mordo was walking up to the Ancient One's retreat. His jet had taken him to Lhasa, with stopovers in Azerbaijan and Pakistan to refuel. A chartered helicopter had carried him the rest of the way.

As he approached the main door, he stooped his shoulders and put a heaviness in his tread. To look at him trudging along like that, you might have thought he was there as a humble penitent, full of regret.

Wong let him in, with every appearance of great wariness.

"Mordo. I must say this is a surprise."

"Wong," said Mordo. "Dear, loyal Wong. Little wonder you look askance on me. I deserve it. But I am not here to do your master harm. Or you, for that matter. On the contrary. I come begging forgiveness."

"Do you now?"

"That suspicion in your voice—how it pains me! But it's perfectly understandable. Why should you trust me, after all I've done? Please, just hear me out. I have seen the folly of my ways. I wish to be the

Ancient One's pupil again. Take me to him, so that I can plead my case."

Wong wavered, then came to a decision. "Very well. But I shall not leave your side, and if I suspect for one moment that you mean my master ill, you'll regret it. I may not know magic but my arm is as strong as anyone's. If you even look like you're starting a conjuration, I'll have you flat on the floor and crying for your mother in no time."

"Colorfully put, Wong, and I have no doubt you'll be as good as your word."

"I can't forget how you made me poison the Ancient One. He could have died. You used me, and I've been itching for an opportunity to pay you back for that."

"And who could blame you? Certainly not I."

Shortly, Mordo was in the presence of the Ancient One, with Wong hovering within arm's reach, tense as a coiled spring.

"Master," said Mordo. "At least, I hope I may call you that again, for I would like to resume my magical studies. I am unworthy of your clemency, and I would understand if you were to throw me out without listening to another word. I… I have changed. That's all I can tell you. I know I have done wicked things, unpardonable things, but now I just want to be better. I want to be *good*. If my run-ins with Stephen Strange have taught me anything, it's that the light of virtue far outshines the darkness of evil."

"And what of Dormammu?" said the Ancient One, sitting serenely on a heap of cushions. "I was under the impression you had pledged yourself to him and were at his beck and call."

"Pfagh!" Mordo spat. "Dormammu! I have turned away from him. I renounce him and his works. I forswear any allegiance I ever had to him. That was just another of my many mistakes, the indiscretions of a man who lusted after power for its own sake rather than power for the benefit of others."

"Very interesting," said the venerable old mage. "And Strange himself? What has become of him? Do you know?"

"Why do you ask? I should have thought you would have a better idea about that than I. Presumably he is at home in his Sanctum Sanctorum, or on some mission to protect the innocent and save the endangered. The kind of mission I myself hope to discharge someday if, by your grace, I am permitted to finish what I started here."

"I ask," said the Ancient One, "because you left him at your castle, inside a bottle of containment."

"What? No! What are you saying? I would never."

The Ancient One stood. "I'm saying that because Strange is in fact no longer there." He waved a gnarled hand from left to right, and his body seemed to split apart along a seam, like a cocoon opening. Flesh dissolved into thin air, evaporating like dawn mist in the sunlight.

Where the Ancient One had been, there stood Doctor Strange in astral form.

<hr />

MORDO GAWPED. "No," he breathed.

"I'm afraid so," said Strange.

"But… But how…?"

"How did I escape? Easy. You were sloppy, Mordo. Your bottle of containment was unbreakable, yes, but also incomplete."

"Incomplete?"

"It had sides and a top, but like an idiot, you neglected to give it a base," said Strange. "It was child's play for me to sink down through the floor, then make my way here and warn the Ancient One you were coming. One glamor later, and the Ancient One you thought you were talking to was actually me."

Mordo's look of astonishment soured into a scowl. "Oh-ho! You think you are so very clever. But I know you are weakened, Strange. It will be a trivial thing to eliminate you here and now, then turn my attention on the Ancient One."

He rounded on Wong.

"And don't *you* go getting any funny ideas, Wong," he said. "After all your threats, I'll have no hesitation reducing you to a pile of smoldering ashes with the Bolts of Balthakk."

Wong held up both hands in a pacifying gesture. "Don't worry, Mordo. I won't lift a finger against you."

He pointed behind Mordo.

"He, however, will."

Mordo spun round, to see the Ancient One emerging from behind a wall-hanging, where he had been hiding all along.

Mordo's former teacher shook his head sadly. "You came here with deceit in your heart, my former pupil," he said. "It seems only fitting to have met your trickery with trickery."

"Why you—"

Furiously, Mordo began crafting a spell. He didn't quite know what it would be, only that it would blast the Ancient One into a million pieces.

But the Ancient One had anticipated this. Not only that but, despite his great age, he was defter, faster. He had decades of experience to draw on. He was, above all else, the Sorcerer Supreme.

Blackness enfolded Mordo, and he was buffeted by winds, hurled this way and that as though caught in a maelstrom. He could see nothing. There was only a roaring vortex of titanic forces around him.

Then, as abruptly as it had begun, it ceased. Mordo was back at his castle, lying crumpled on the floor in his spell chamber. Bewilderedly, he picked himself up.

"No," he murmured.

A flash of light. A *whump* of detonation.

"No!" he cried.

His scale model of Strange's Sanctum Sanctorum had burst into flames. It was consumed within seconds, shriveling down to a few charred remnants.

"No-o-o!" he wailed.

Again.

Defeated again.

How much more of this could a man take?

His pang of self-pity didn't last long. Baron Mordo was not someone who dwelled on setbacks.

One way or another, he would vanquish Doctor Strange and the Ancient One.

For the sake of his own pride, mainly.

But, more importantly, for Dormammu's sake. Because Dormammu did not look kindly on failure.

"IT PAINS me, Master," said Strange, "that Mordo keeps attacking us, and every time he seems stronger and more dangerous. I wish there were some lasting way of dealing with him."

"You mean kill him?" said the Ancient One. "You know, Stephen, that that is not our way. Not the way of the kind of magic we espouse. We must simply remain vigilant and counter his threat whenever it rears its head. Now, you must be tired, and your mortal shell awaits the return of your astral form, which is long overdue. Go."

Strange did as bidden.

Once more his Sanctum Sanctorum was in its proper place on Bleecker Street, and once more his astral form was in its proper place within his body.

When would Mordo strike again? It was inevitable that it would happen, and sometime soon.

But that was a concern for another day.

For now, all Doctor Strange could think about was crawling into bed, which he did, falling into a deep and blissfully dreamless sleep.

SIX

IN THE weeks that followed, Strange fought off an invasion of body-possessing ethereal beings in a remote Bavarian village; rescued a pair of crooks who had fallen foul of a magical gem, been sucked into the sinister Purple Dimension and ended up as slaves of its tyrannical ruler Aggamon; and saved a team of TV ghost hunters from a supposedly haunted house in Poughkeepsie which turned out to be an entity from some far-flung corner of the spacetime continuum that had come to Earth and adopted the form of a Dutch Colonial cottage in order to study the human race.

More often than not, it was the Orb of Agamotto that alerted him to supernatural threats like these. The scrying sphere was a reliable tool of divination and he could count on it to identify where a danger was arising and assess the severity. The Orb was not, however, infallible, for there were methods evildoers could use to shield themselves against observation by it.

One evening, close to midnight, Strange consulted the Orb. He had been filled with a sense of apprehension all evening, but the sphere's lambent depths revealed no source for this feeling. All seemed right with the world, for once.

Then his phone rang.

"Help me, Doctor Strange!" said a man's voice on the other end, ragged with anxiety. "Help me! You must come at once!"

The caller gave an address, then hung up.

No specifics. No name. No clue as to why Strange's help was needed. Just an urgent plea for aid and that address: a meat processing plant in New Jersey.

Strange knew he couldn't ignore the call. There had been a bit of a brouhaha recently about the meat processing plant, which had been shut down by the Food and Drug Administration due to health and safety violations. It was possible the closure might have had unreported supernatural underpinnings that the anonymous caller felt he should investigate. Equally, the whole thing might be a trick, some jokester playing a prank. It might also be a trap. After his recent adventures, Strange could not discount that possibility. All the same, he could never ignore a cry for help.

Leaving his body behind at the Sanctum Sanctorum, Strange flitted out across Lower Manhattan and over the Hudson River in astral form. He reached New Jersey in a matter of moments, swooping towards the meat processing plant.

The place was empty. All the machinery had been stripped out, leaving just a series of cavernous industrial spaces with rusting girders, graffitied walls and bare concrete floors dotted with puddles where rainwater had leaked in through the roof. Strange could sense no magical residue anywhere. Nothing sorcerous or paranormal had occurred there recently.

A wild goose chase.

Swiftly, he about-turned and headed back to Greenwich Village. If the unknown caller had gone to the trouble of luring him out from the Sanctum Sanctorum, there had to be a reason for it.

No sooner did he arrive home than the reason became clear.

His body was gone. The chair he had left it sitting in was vacant.

As was his habit, Strange had set various protective wards and mystical tripwires around his body before he went. These should have prevented anyone getting close to it, and alerted him if it was being menaced or interfered with. Apparently they had all been circumvented.

That meant the person responsible for making off with his mortal shell must be a skilled magician. Whoever it was, they had managed to carry out the deed—break in, disable Strange's defenses and remove his body—in under a couple of minutes.

Strange could think of only one likely suspect, and even as the culprit's name formed in his mind, there was a sudden dazzling burst of light and an oversized head loomed before him, floating in midair.

A mental projection by Baron Mordo.

"I thought so," said Strange coolly. "You."

"Why wouldn't it have been me?" replied the floating head, as bright and bloated as a full moon. "Who else would take the time and effort to abscond with your physical self? Who else, for that matter, boasts the mystical prowess to do so?"

"What is it this time? Blackmail? I give you something in exchange for my body's safe return?"

"Oh no, Strange," said Mordo. "Nothing nearly so mercenary. I've transported your body elsewhere and hidden it away. It is sheathed in numerous enchantments of concealment. All you have to do is find it." A ghastly grin spread across his face. "But of course, you have only twenty-four hours. Body and soul can stand to be separated for no longer than that before both wither and perish. If your astral form is not reunited with your physical form by midnight tomorrow, Eastern Standard Time, it's curtains for you."

"Wouldn't it be easier just to have destroyed my body? Same result, less fuss."

"Perhaps, but nowhere as satisfying as knowing that you will hunt in vain for it, becoming ever more frantic and desperate as the hours tick away. The thought of your suffering is something to savor, more so than your mere death."

Strange heaved a sigh. "Demons of Denak! Why do you persist with these schemes, Mordo? You strike at me; I defeat you. It's futile. Won't you ever learn?"

"I can fail countless times but only have to succeed once. And this is that once, Strange, I'm sure of it. You haven't a hope!"

With a leering chortle, Mordo's head vanished.

○————○

THERE WAS no time to waste. Strange's life hung in the balance.

He activated the Orb of Agamotto and invited it to search for his body.

No good. Mordo hadn't lied about the enchantments of concealment. The Orb didn't know where to begin to look. It couldn't find Mordo himself, either, suggesting that Strange's enemy had hidden himself magically too.

Strange remained calm. Twenty-four hours. Plenty of time, when your astral form could travel round the world in mere minutes.

There was a mystical link between soul and body, a kind of incorporeal thread which nothing could truly sunder. Strange cast a spell over himself to augment that link, invoking the Benign Visage of Vandularr to lend it power. Now, when his astral form was in proximity to his body, within a mile or so, he would feel a resonance, a psychic tug. Using this as a sort of homing beacon, he could zero in on his target.

The first place he tried was Castle Mordo. Baron Mordo surely wouldn't be that obvious, but Strange thought he should at least eliminate the possibility.

His body was not there. Neither was Mordo.

Over the next few hours he crisscrossed the globe, visiting every major city on the planet. In none of them did he feel the slightest tingle to indicate that his body was close by.

He paused to take stock. He had seen several dawns and nightfalls during his worldwide peregrinations, but he knew that, on the East Coast, it was currently nine a.m.

He decided to explore less populated areas. He hurtled over desert and rainforest, mountain and plain, volcanic slope and ice floe. He circled above cave systems, veldt villages, and coral atolls. Hidden valleys. Lost temples. Secret lagoons.

Nothing.

Three p.m. EST.

He scanned war zones and farmland. He checked favelas, projects and suburbs. He investigated sites of magical significance— the Egyptian pyramids, Stonehenge, Easter Island, Mount Wundagore, and the Nexus of All Realities in the Florida Everglades, to name but a few.

Still nothing.

Eight p.m. EST.

He was not quite despondent, not yet. But he could feel his momentum starting to dwindle. That and his will to carry on. There was only so much searching he could do before it began to seem pointless. The world was so big, and his body could be practically anywhere.

Was this it? Would Mordo triumph at last?

He flew to Tibet, to consult the Ancient One.

His aged mentor nodded concernedly as Strange explained his plight.

"I can't hope to locate your body if you yourself can't, Stephen," he said. "I can, however, offer you this advice. Try to think as Mordo does. Ask yourself what you would do, if you were he, to prevent your body being discovered."

Strange pondered this as his astral form flew away from the Ancient One's retreat.

If he was Baron Mordo, he wouldn't just hide the body, he would ensure that Strange would have difficulty gaining access to it in the event that he did find it.

In other words, he would guard it magically.

"I've been coming at this from the wrong direction," Strange said to himself. "I've been looking for the buried treasure when I should have been looking for the X that marks the spot."

He returned to his Sanctum Sanctorum and commanded the Orb of Agamotto to pinpoint areas of increased magical activity across the world.

There were several, but one stood out.

It was only a few miles away.

Strange had to admire Mordo's sheer chutzpah. The whole of the Earth to choose from, and where had he opted for? Somewhere practically on Strange's doorstep.

A wax museum in Coney Island.

○————————○

STRANGE WASN'T completely sure he had guessed right. He wasn't even sure his theory about magical activity was on the money. It was gone eleven p.m. EST, less than an hour before the division of his soul from his body became final and fatal.

This was a last roll of the dice. A Hail Mary pass. All or nothing.

Below him, the rainbow lights of the Coney Island boardwalk glittered and flared, even though the amusement parks were closed for the day, the Ferris wheels and carousels stilled, the rollercoasters silent. Across the bay lay a promontory—a thin strip of Queens—and beyond that, the dark rolling expanse of the Atlantic.

Strange began his descent towards the wax museum, and in that moment his doubts were dispelled.

A trio of wraiths soared from below to greet him. They were pale semblances of men, garbed not unlike ninjas, and they homed in on Strange as a flock of crows might on an encroaching bird of prey.

Strange flung the Flames of the Faltine at them. Each wraith burned to a cinder, becoming a tumbling handful of ashes.

Bright red spiked balls veered at Strange out of nowhere, like the heads of giant maces being swung at him. He deflected them with the Shield of the Seraphim before blasting them to smithereens, one after another, with Bolts of Balthakk.

The Crimson Bands of Cyttorak shot up from below, tangling around him, doing their best to ensnare him. Strange repelled them with rays of light from the Eye of Agamotto.

Encountering all these defensive measures confirmed that he was on the right track. Mordo was trying to keep him away from his destination.

Trying, but not succeeding.

Before further attacks could come, Strange darted down into the wax museum. It was one of those fading old-time attractions, well past its prime, with rooms full of effigies that more or less resembled notable personages, past and present. Their clothing looked motheaten, and some of them seemed to sag where they stood, as though even sculptures could get tired.

In the midst of an exhibit labeled *Famous Warlocks and Wizards*—which saw the likes of Merlin, Morgan Le Fay, John Dee, Marie Laveau and Rasputin rubbing shoulders—there was one figure which looked fresher and much more lifelike than the rest.

Dr. Stephen Strange, no less. Gazing sternly into the middle distance, fist on hip, with a placard at his feet describing him as a "New York-based charlatan whose career was short-lived and ignominious."

This was no waxwork, of course, but the real thing, in the flesh.

His body.

The placard was a typical Mordo touch. The man really did have an inferiority complex.

Strange prepared to re-enter the body.

But Mordo, as it turned out, had surrounded it with a powerful barrier. It was as though a suit of unbreakable glass armor encased it. Strange knew he would be able to penetrate the barrier, if he had the time and the strength. He was running low on both, however. Zooming around the planet for so long, then fighting the aerial battle, had used up almost all of his energy. He was down to his last reserves. Not only that, he could feel his astral form starting to lose cohesion. The twenty-four-hour deadline was close to expiring, and so was he.

From a shadowy corner of the room, Mordo emerged, strolling into the dim light coming in from outside through the windows.

"This couldn't have gone any better, Strange," he said. "I hoped you would make it here eventually, so that I could watch your final moments at first hand. I can see how weak you've become. Your astral form grows more blurred and translucent with every passing second. Not long before it disperses altogether. How will you spend this last brief gasp of your life? How will you use your dying breaths? Begging for mercy perhaps? Pledging loyalty to me if I let you return to your body so that you may live? Or…"

Strange stumbled away, vanishing through a wall.

"I have my answer, it seems," said Mordo. "Fleeing like a coward. Well, you won't get far, Strange. Not in your current condition. Meanwhile, I shall stay put and look on as your body slowly disintegrates."

Strange overheard these words even as, unbeknownst to Mordo, he doubled back through a different wall, sneaking into the room behind Mordo. Between them stood the waxwork of Merlin, which was clad in a floor-length robe and conical hat with a matching stars-and-crescent-moons pattern.

Strange's astral form slipped inside the effigy.

Mordo was right, he *was* weak. He didn't know whether he had strength left to perform this next feat. But it was his best—his only—hope.

With a huge mental effort, Strange animated the waxwork. Stiffly, unsteadily, the artificial Merlin began to walk. Strange was inhabiting the sculpture as though it was his actual body, although moving around in it felt like wading along the seabed in a diving suit made of lead. Every step required intense concentration. His balance was off and he feared he might fall over before he got to his intended destination.

Mordo continued to gaze at Strange's body, reveling in its imminent demise. He had no idea that Strange was creeping up on him, inside the Merlin waxwork, until the very last instant. He heard a scraping footfall behind him. He turned. His face registered shock and alarm as he beheld the effigy of the Arthurian wizard lunging for him. A heavy waxen fist whistled through the air. Then blackness.

———o————o———

MORDO CAME round a quarter of an hour later with a ringing headache and a bruise tightening the skin around his jaw. He was bound all the way from ankles to nose in the Crimson Bands of Cyttorak, like a corpse in a winding sheet. He couldn't move nor speak.

Strange stood over him, astral form occupying body once more. It was past midnight. Mordo's scheme had failed.

"I'll say this for you, Mordo," Strange said, "you did your best. You actually came quite close to getting your way this time. But no one, not even the greatest magician on Earth, can stand up to a good, solid roundhouse right."

Mordo would have come back with a sharp, angry retort if he'd been able to. Instead, he did what he thought Strange would least expect. He thrust his astral form out. His spirit self was still a match for Strange, undoubtedly. The other man might have the advantage of being fully embodied, but he was exhausted and couldn't have much left to offer in the way of resistance.

A spell tingled at Mordo's fingertips—the Curses of the Fiends of Fungol Thopa, which covered the recipient in a fast-growing, life-draining mold. Just as the words of the spell formed on his lips, however, Strange summoned a Conjurer's Sphere.

Mordo's astral form was caught amid a swirling, dark gray fog. He knew better than to attempt to free himself. Any spell cast within a Conjurer's Sphere was reflected back on the spellcaster. Nor could he return to his body. The Sphere clung to him like thick glue and would only let go of him on Strange's say-so.

He was trapped like a fly in amber. All he could do was hang limply in that nebulous mystical miasma, at his opponent's mercy.

"I think I'll put your body over there," Strange said, "where mine was. I won't bother with a placard like you did. Anyone visiting the museum will just have to wonder who the tubby middle-aged man with the ostentatious goatee is supposed to be. Perhaps they'll assume you're a Las Vegas turn, or maybe the 'Great Satan' himself, Aleister Crowley."

"So you're going to do to me exactly as I did to you," said Mordo. "Leave me cut off from my body until the inevitable end."

"Turnabout is fair play, as they say. And don't think I'm not tempted to kill you. But I'm not you, Mordo. Your astral form will remain in that Conjurer's Sphere, invisible to the untrained eye, for the next twenty-*three* hours. Just so you experience something of what I had to go through. Then you'll be released."

"Of course. You lack the guts to finish me once and for all, Strange. Has it ever occurred to you that that will be your undoing? I won't rest until I have rid the world of you."

"I know," said Strange. "And *I* won't rest until you grow tired of trying."

SEVEN

STRANGE TOOK the F train back to Greenwich Village. At this late hour the carriage he was in was sparsely occupied: just a handful of subway-goers dotted around the seats, quiet and careworn, lost in their own thoughts. None of them could have the slightest inkling that the man with the cloak, amulet and wearily sagging shoulders had just won a desperate struggle with his very life in the balance. To them he was simply a fellow traveler, another member of the city's nocturnal flotsam and jetsam.

But then maybe, Strange thought, some of these people had fought a battle of their own today. Maybe they were fighting it right now, secretly, inside, with a foe every bit as insidious as Baron Mordo: their own inner demons. They might not show it, the strain might be less visible than it was on him, but that didn't make their conflict any less important. Not all heroes wore masks and spandex, and not all battles saw the Earth imperiled by some cackling super villain. Sometimes what was at stake was simply a person's happiness.

Strange found this idea both saddening and consoling.

He arrived back at the Sanctum Sanctorum feeling faint with exhaustion. His bed beckoned, but he didn't even make it that far. Slumping into the first armchair he came to, he let sleep swamp him like a tidal wave.

He woke up innumerable hours later, feeling stiff-limbed and groggy.

In front of him stood a robed figure, carrying a scythe. A skull peeked out between the folds of its hood. The hands holding the scythe were skeletal.

Death.

The grim reaper himself.

Strange's immediate thought was that this was some mystical illusion. It had to be. The image of Death as a scythe-wielding skeleton was pure folklore, a way of personifying that terrible unknown and thus making it a little bit more knowable. It had no existence outside of iconography.

Instinctively he lashed out with the reversed version of the Images of Ikonn spell, to dispel the grisly phantom.

Death, unaffected, grinned his bony grin at Strange.

Next thing Strange knew, the scythe came hissing towards him. The blade passed straight through his midriff.

He was dead.

He was in a void. Featureless grayness all around him. No sense of up or down. No horizon.

Limbo.

What came next? Was he here forever? Was this the answer to the great mystery of the afterlife? Just an eternal twilight oblivion?

No.

He was dreaming. That was the only explanation. All he needed to do was wake himself up.

Strange woke up.

He was in his armchair, as before.

In front of him stood a robed figure, carrying a scythe. A skull peeked out between the folds of its hood. The hands holding the scythe were skeletal.

Death.

The grim reaper himself.

Again!

Strange summoned the Whirling Winds of Watoomb, which should have sent the hooded figure spinning helplessly into the distance.

Death remained unmoved.

The scythe whispered its lethal message.

Strange hung in the void again.

A dream. Still a dream.

He forced himself to wake up.

Before him, yet again, stood Death.

Strange attacked.

The scythe swung.

The void.

Wake up.

Death.

Spell.

Scythe.

Void.

And again.

And again.

The scenario repeated itself, endlessly, remorselessly, and whatever Strange did, he could not alter the outcome.

It was like some…

Some recurring…

"Nightmare," Strange growled.

○———○

AND WITH that utterance, he found himself in Nightmare's throne room, face to face with Nightmare himself.

"Took you long enough, Strange," said the Dream Dimension's resident troublemaker and connoisseur of misery. "My dream-loop of death and awakening—I thought you'd see through it several iterations before you did. It's good to know you're not infallible.

Good to know, too, that you don't always protect yourself in your sleep. Even you have your careless moments."

Strange gritted his teeth. He *had* been careless. He had neglected to set up various guards and protections, as he usually did, before dozing off, to prevent something exactly like this from happening. He'd just been too tired.

"I admit it, you caught me on the hop," he said to Nightmare. "But I'm ready for you now. Do your worst."

"Oh, I shall! You forget, you're in my realm. Here I am master of everything. My will is the only will. See?"

All at once, Strange was the size of a child's action figure. Nightmare was holding him in the palm of his hand.

"I can shrink you," Nightmare said, "or I can do this."

Now Strange was a stone statue, frozen from head to toe, immobile.

"Or this."

Strange was back in the endless void.

"How about it, Strange?" Nightmare's voice rang in his ears, seeming to come from everywhere and nowhere at once. "How long do you think you can remain here, alone, surrounded by pure nothingness, with only your thoughts for company, before you go stark raving mad?"

Suddenly, Strange was falling.

Falling.

Falling.

"Feel that?" he heard Nightmare say. "That sickening uprush in your belly? That sense of abject helplessness as you plummet through space? Not knowing when or if it'll ever stop, and if it does stop, if there is solid ground below you, or what the impact will be like. Now imagine feeling that feeling *forever*! Ha ha ha!"

And now a dizzied, disoriented Strange was in Nightmare's throne room again. He crouched on all fours, peering up at his tormentor.

"What—what is all this supposed to prove, Nightmare?" he said.

"That I can toy with you to my heart's content, Strange. I can visit any number of dire fates upon you. Anything my mind can think up, I can inflict."

"And all in aid of what?"

"Teaching you a lesson, obviously. Showing you what happens to those who interfere with my plans."

"But this is just dreamstuff," said Strange reasonably. "I know it's not real, and you know I know it's not real. Sooner or later I'll wake up and you'll no longer have any power over me."

"Maybe, but between now and then I have plenty of time with you as my plaything. What is just a few short hours in your realm, I can make seem an eternity to you. When I'm finished with you, you'll have become completely deranged. Your brain won't have a coherent thought left in it. You'll be a gibbering, drooling wreck. And, as a bonus, throughout your ordeal I shall get to feed off your suffering. I wonder what the mental anguish of a master of the mystic arts tastes like. I imagine it will be delicious."

Nightmare smacked his lily-white lips.

"But anyway," he continued, "while I ponder what to do with you next, why don't you stick around?"

With a gesture, he formed a gigantic spider's web out of nothing. Strange hung spreadeagled in its thick, gluey strands.

"There you are," Nightmare said, "as powerless as the fly that awaits the venomous fangs of its captor. Just hang there and think about what's coming."

Settling back in his throne, he drew up his legs, put an elbow on one of the throne's arms, placed his chin on his fist, and half closed his eyes. The very picture of pensive contemplation.

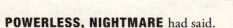

POWERLESS, NIGHTMARE had said.

But that was not quite true.

Strange had done some homework on Nightmare since their last encounter. He knew the Dream Dimension entity had a certain vulnerability.

Nightmare intended to terrorize Strange. But two could play at that game.

Strange's arms were bound by the spider's web, but his hands were free, his fingers capable of motion and articulation. His mouth was free, too, so that he could murmur under his breath.

A section of the throne room floor began to bubble and churn. It was as though magma was boiling up through it from below.

Nightmare's eyes widened. "What's this?"

The patch of turmoil spread until it covered half the throne room floor.

Then, in the midst of it, a head appeared. Huge, spiked, orange-brown in hue, it rose slowly, mightily, revealing a lugubrious face and a pair of empty, pitiless eyes.

A thick neck followed, and a bulky set of shoulders, and a torso as broad and weathered as a sequoia trunk.

A whimpering moan escaped Nightmare's lips.

Yet more of the fearsome apparition emerged, until at last the whole of it was clear of the heaving chaos in the floor. It stood twenty feet tall, and it glowered down at Nightmare with all too evident enmity.

"The—the Gulgol," Nightmare stammered. If his face were not already chalk-white, it would surely have paled. Suddenly he wasn't a swaggering, domineering despot anymore. Suddenly he was like a terrified, quaking child.

"Yes, the Gulgol," said Strange. "The creature who never sleeps."

"But I have erected barriers to keep him out of my realm. He can't have broken through them. It's not possible." Nightmare shot a look of hatred at Strange. "You."

"Guilty as charged."

"But why? He has the power to destroy us both."

"Maybe, but it'll be you first," said Strange. "You're his main target. I'll just be collateral damage."

The Gulgol began to lumber towards Nightmare, reaching out his arms to grab him. Strange recalled seeing news footage of the being known as the Hulk. The shaky camerawork had shown the Hulk advancing on a platoon of soldiers in the Arizona desert, head down, impervious to their rifle fire. The Gulgol moved in much the same way as that marauding green-skinned man-monster, with a similar stolid, imperturbable gait.

Nightmare threw up a portcullis-like shield between him and it, but the Gulgol barged through the obstruction as easily as if it were made of tissue paper. Nightmare transformed the floor between the Gulgol's feet into quicksand, but the creature was barely impeded, trudging onward like someone knee-deep in water. A wall of flame proved no more effective; neither did a dense sheet of ice.

"Nothing," Nightmare said desolately, trembling all over. "Nothing I do can stop it."

Which was, Strange knew, precisely why the Gulgol was the perfect countermeasure to Nightmare. It was soulless, heartless, speechless, and sleepless. It was a mass of seething primal urges, with no interior life, not one subconscious sensitivity that Nightmare could tap into and exploit. Since the dawn of time, so the books of magical lore said, Nightmare and the Gulgol had been mortal enemies, each the other's nemesis. They were pure polar opposites, yin and yang. The Gulgol was perhaps the only foe Nightmare could not defeat, and thus the only thing he truly feared.

"*I* can," said Strange.

Nightmare blinked at him.

"I can stop the Gulgol," Strange said. "I can banish him back to where he came from. But you have to release me."

Nightmare looked from Strange to the Gulgol and back again. The Gulgol was now only a few paces away from him, still implacably bent on his destruction.

"You lie," he said.

"Fine," said Strange. "I'm lying. I'll happily just hang here and watch as the Gulgol rends you limb from limb. Ringside seat."

Even as Nightmare shrank away from the oncoming Gulgol, Strange could tell he was weighing things up, making a mental calculation.

"All right," Nightmare said at last. "All right! Save me, Strange."

"Are you sure? I mean, I don't mind seeing you snivel like this. It's very entertaining."

"Yes, I'm sure!"

Nightmare waved a hand. Just like that, the spider's web was gone and Strange was free.

Strange interposed himself between Nightmare and the Gulgol. He raised one hand and snapped his fingers.

The Gulgol vanished. The throne room was back to the way it had been before, as though the creature had never even appeared.

Nightmare gaped at him. A sly expression crept over his face.

"I see," he said. "Very cunning. Damn you, Strange, it was nothing more than an illusion."

"The Images of Ikonn spell comes in very handy at times, and the mirages it generates can be utterly convincing, particularly when they draw on the subject's deepest, darkest fears."

"Nonetheless, this changes nothing. I still have you in my realm. There's nothing to stop me torturing you, as planned, until I break you."

"And there's nothing to stop me conjuring up the Gulgol again," Strange retorted.

"But if I know it's not the real Gulgol..."

"That's it, though, Nightmare. That illusory Gulgol was only for show. I'm perfectly capable of bringing the real Gulgol here if I want to. All I need do is shatter your mystic barriers—and I can."

"I don't believe you."

"Try me." Strange raised his hands, arranging his fingers in readiness. "A tenth-level unraveling spell, and the Gulgol will come. I suspect your demise at its hands will be neither swift nor pleasant."

"But you'll surely perish too. After me, the Gulgol will make short work of you."

"The sacrifice will be worth it, if it gets rid of you once and for all."

Nightmare glared at him. His scarlet eyes were full of skepticism, but in their depths there was a distinct glimmer of fear.

The truth was, Strange had no idea whether he could bring down the barriers keeping the Gulgol at bay. He thought probably not. But Nightmare didn't know that.

"So let's call this a stalemate, why don't we?" he said. "I go back to the waking world, you leave me alone, the Gulgol stays where it can't get at you, everyone happy."

Nightmare gave vent to a sound that was both a cry of rage and a groan of frustration. He pivoted on his heel and flounced out of the throne room.

"I'll take that as a yes," Strange said to his departing back.

STRANGE WOKE up in the armchair. For one brief moment he expected to see the grim reaper in front of him, scythe poised to swing.

But no. It was just his Sanctum Sanctorum. The chair was just a chair, the room just a room.

He made a mental note: *never, ever fall asleep without protecting yourself properly beforehand.*

Nightmare would not catch him napping again.

EIGHT

A BRUSH with the Asgardian god of mischief.

A trip back in time to Ancient Egypt.

All in a day's work for Doctor Strange, Master of the Mystic Arts.

But whether he was foiling an attempt by Loki to get his hands on Mjolnir, the magical hammer that belonged to his half-brother Thor, or saving Queen Cleopatra from the vengeance of a corrupt high priest whose affections she had spurned, Strange remained preoccupied with other concerns.

Mordo.

Nightmare.

These two were constant thorns in his side, seemingly competing to be the one who brought him down. Mordo coveted the Ancient One's power and the role of Sorcerer Supreme. Nightmare had designs on Earth, wanting to annex it and bring it under his sway. Strange kept frustrating them in their goals. It was only a matter of time before one or other of them struck at him again.

But which would it be?

THE ANSWER came one afternoon as Strange was studying the *Book of the Vishanti* and learning more about Oshtur.

Companion to Hoggoth and mother of Agamotto, Oshtur came into being as one of the Elder Gods of Earth, created by the Demiurge, the sentient biosphere from which all life on the planet stemmed. When internecine war broke out among the Elder Gods, Oshtur fled to the outer darkness in order to escape the carnage. There, while exploring the further reaches of the cosmos, she met Hoggoth, last survivor of an ancient mystical race.

After several millennia had passed, Oshtur travelled back to Earth with Hoggoth in tow, to find that only two of the Elder Gods remained, the very worst of them, Chthon and Set. Humankind was in its infancy then, and that sinister duo were busy steering people towards anarchy and evildoing. Oshtur gave birth to Agamotto, and together with Hoggoth, the three of them, as the Vishanti, applied themselves to countering the malevolent influence of Chthon and Set, and demonstrating the path towards goodness and enlightenment.

Oshtur was famous for her wisdom, her nobility and her compassion, and spells cast in her name were traditionally related to strength, protection and alteration. The Tripartite Hex of Transmogrification was one. Another of them, Flamel's Lasso of Retrieval, was said to work very effectively in conjunction with the Wand of Watoomb, a prodigiously powerful artifact of which Strange possessed half. Many millennia ago, the Wand had been broken in two by its creator, the wizard Watoomb, so that it might not be misused by others. The half Strange owned was stored in a locked cabinet in his Chamber of Shadows. The whereabouts of the other half were unknown, and it was widely believed lost for good.

Strange was refreshing his memory on the Lasso of Retrieval spell, in the unlikely event he might need it someday. This involved deciphering passages of sometimes very faded runic script, and he was devoting his full attention to the task.

That was when the home invasion occurred.

THEY CAME in through the walls—a band of wraiths, their faces half-masked, scarves trailing in their wake as they flew. Their movements were swift and purposeful, their eyes blank and mournful.

They slipped into formation around Strange, surrounding him on all sides. A wraith was a wandering evil spirit, one that any magician worth their salt could easily capture and manipulate to do their bidding. Wraiths were used as spies, as a means of intimidation, and perhaps most commonly as attack dogs. Among ordinary men and women, unversed in the ways of magic, they could sow terror and disruption. Their touch brought soul-chilling horror, insanity, and in some instances death. They were, to put it mildly, not nice.

To Doctor Strange, however, they were little more than a pest. Vermin needing to be exterminated.

It was quick and it was brutal. One by one he blasted the wraiths out of existence with a salvo of destructive spells. Soon nothing remained of them but a few, faint vaporous wisps that lingered momentarily in the air before vanishing.

Strange recalled that an enemy of his had sent wraiths against him not too long ago. Had these ones been emissaries of Baron Mordo too? If so, what did Mordo hope to gain by assaulting him with them? He must know that Strange could dispatch them without even breaking a sweat.

Unless…

"A distraction," Strange muttered grimly to himself.

As to what Mordo was trying to distract him from, there was surely only one answer.

Strange hurried to the Chamber of Shadows in order to confirm his suspicions.

He opened the Orb of Agamotto and harmonized with its inner vibrations. An image appeared: the Ancient One's retreat. Strange invited the Orb to probe inside the building, seeking out his mentor's private quarters.

The Ancient One was not there.

The Orb conveyed further images, widening its scope to show a worried-looking Wong as he combed the retreat's corridors, calling for his master. There was consternation throughout the place, an atmosphere of mounting panic. Acolytes rushed to and fro, scouring every inch of the premises and searching the surrounding mountainside.

Unexpectedly, inexplicably, the Ancient One was missing.

Strange deactivated the Orb of Agamotto and stepped back, stunned. Had the Ancient One been kidnapped? It wasn't possible. Who had the power to do such a thing? More to the point, who would dare?

A loud knock at the front door interrupted his fretful musings.

A visitor? Strange tutted irritably. Whoever it was could come back later. Finding the Ancient One was his priority.

The knock came again, louder this time, and Strange had an inkling that the presence of a caller, at this moment of crisis, could be no coincidence.

He went to open the door.

On the doorstep stood someone he was both surprised—and yet also somehow not surprised—to see.

"**MAY I** come in, Strange?" said Baron Mordo. "Or are you just going to leave me standing out here like the ill-mannered lout you are?"

"You have some kind of nerve, Mordo," Strange said, "showing your face like this."

"Yes, yes, my temerity knows no bounds." Mordo brushed past him, entering the hallway. "Doubtless you're by now aware that your beloved master has taken an, ahem, unscheduled leave of absence."

"I am."

"And doubtless you've also divined who is responsible."

"Your wraith attack was a fairly broad clue." Strange shut the door. "I thought misdirection was a technique only stage conjurers employed."

"Don't bother goading me, Strange. It won't work. The simple fact is, the wraiths were meant to keep you occupied in case the Ancient One was able to send you a mental distress signal. While you were handling them, I penetrated his retreat, overcame him and transported him elsewhere. It took mere moments. Could scarcely have been simpler."

"Forgive me if I have a hard time believing that."

Mordo shrugged. "Believe what you like. It's true."

"You, going toe-to-toe with the Sorcerer Supreme and winning? You aren't nearly powerful enough."

"Things have changed, Strange. My magical abilities grow daily."

"If you have him," Strange said, "prove it."

"Fair enough."

Mordo conjured up a vision of the Ancient One, bound and shackled by various spells: the Manacles of Mokarr, the Clamp of Containment, the Rings of Raggadorr, and the Bandages of Banebtumtet—all of them reinforced with the strongest and least escapable binding enchantment of them all, the Crimson Circle of Cyttorak. Strange was appalled. The revered old man—kneeling, shoulders slumped, head bowed, weighed down by numerous magical restraints—looked humbled and humiliated, a pitiful sight.

Mordo dispelled the vision before Strange had a chance to study it closely. "Ah, ah, ah!" he said, wagging a forefinger. "No, you don't. I'm not letting you scan the backdrop for hints as to where I might be keeping him. Just know that the Ancient One is mine to do with as I please. I am giving him one last opportunity to share his secrets with me. If not... well, he knows the penalty."

"Even if you do manage to extricate the knowledge you want from him, it won't make you Sorcerer Supreme, Mordo. You realize that, don't you? There's a lot more to the role than just magical ability. It requires integrity, honor, a sense of duty, altruism—the last things you think of when you think of Karl Amadeus Mordo."

"Bah! Sorcerer Supreme! It's just a title. I'm no longer interested in any of that. I have greater aims, and I'll achieve them with or without the Ancient One's assistance. It'll just happen quicker if it's *with*."

"Or," said Strange, "it might not happen at all."

He adopted a primary fighting stance, knees braced, hands aloft, with thumbs extended and middle and ring fingers bent.

"A magical duel?" said Mordo. "Is that what you're hoping for, Strange?"

"Not hoping for. Feeling obligated to do. Tell me where the Ancient One is, or so help me, I'll annihilate you."

"Excellent." Mordo broke into a grin and shook out his fists like a boxer limbering up for a title bout. "But for the record: if anyone is doing any annihilating today, it's me."

THE HALLWAY of the Sanctum Sanctorum resounded with the sizzle of spells being initiated, the hum of magical shields being summoned, the crunch of those same shields being shattered, the crackle of eldritch energies being manipulated, and the low thrumming buzz of forces being unleashed—the kind only the boldest and most accomplished of mages might dare command.

Interspersed with these sounds were oaths from the two combatants, the shouting of which functioned both as a means of focusing concentration and as a taunt to the opponent.

"By the Hoary Hosts of Hoggoth!"
"By the Demons of Denak!"
"In the name of Omniscient Oshtur!"
"For Dread Dormammu's sake!"
"By the Shades of the Seraphim!"

"By the Suppurating Tentacles of Shuma-Gorath!"

Now and then, there was a searing hiss as a magical bolt went astray and scorched a section of the floor or some item of furniture.

Mordo fought with a ferocity Strange had not seen in him before. His skills, moreover, seemed to have been augmented. As the two of them circled each other, firing off spell and counterspell, Strange had the impression that his opponent had been holding back in their previous clashes. Or else he had tapped into some new mystical power source which he was channeling adroitly. Either way, he was more formidable than in the past. Until today, Strange had been confident he could win any battle with Mordo. Now, he was not so sure.

But if he lost, there would be no one to come to the Ancient One's rescue. His mentor would be Mordo's hapless prey.

There had to be some way he could beat Mordo *and* save the Ancient One. Ideally, both at the same time.

Then inspiration struck.

Cowardice.

That was the solution.

Swathing his body in a multilayered protection spell, Strange slipped free of it in astral form.

Mordo spotted Strange's spirit self as it departed the scene. Abandoning his assault on the defenses Strange had erected, he gave chase in astral form too.

"Fleeing, eh?" he said. "Not a surprise, given how badly you're losing. Rest assured, you can't escape. There's nowhere you can go where I can't follow."

That, as it happened, was what Strange was counting on.

THEY ROSE above the Sanctum Sanctorum, soaring high into the Manhattan skies, invisible to the city's inhabitants. Mordo shot deadly zigzagging bolts at Strange, any of which could have reduced his astral form to ashes if it struck home. Strange parried with shields, then retaliated with offensive spells of his own, which Mordo in turn deflected.

Out across the Atlantic they flew, passing a cruise liner coming into New York Harbor and a trawler hauling in its catch on the Grand Banks. Within seconds they were over the rolling countryside of southern England and then the white cliffs of Dover, still dogfighting, like a strange parody of Spitfire and Stuka planes during the Battle of Britain. Following that, in the blink of an eye, they were in Paris, weaving under the Arc de Triomphe, and in and out of the iron struts of the Eiffel Tower. Next it was Cairo, where the Great Sphinx gazed impassively into the distance as the two magicians waged war overhead. Onward through the countries of the Middle East they went.

Throughout, Strange led the chase, Mordo in hot pursuit. The former appeared to be fighting a rearguard action, the latter harrying him from behind.

"This is a useless maneuver, Strange," Mordo called out as they crossed the Arabian Sea. "Utter madness. All you're doing is tiring yourself out. Honestly, I expected better of you."

Strange did not reply. He was too busy protecting himself...

And searching.

What Mordo failed to perceive was that the Eye of Agamotto on Strange's chest was open and aglow. Its owner had commanded it to scan the landscape below him, on the lookout for any deep concentration of magical energies. Magical energies at a level that could sustain the Crimson Circle of Cyttorak and the various other spells currently holding the Ancient One prisoner.

The Eye swept its gaze around even as Strange raced across the world, fending off Mordo's attacks. It was primed to alert him the instant it detected what it sought.

Then it did.

Strange and Mordo were in the Madhya Pradesh region of India when the Eye sent Strange a psychic flash.

Beneath him lay sprawling green jungle interspersed with writhing veins of brown river. Somewhere down there, the Eye told him, was a small but fiercely intense locus of magical power.

Immediately, Strange broke off from combat with Mordo and dived to earth, following a course indicated by the Eye. The amulet steered him towards a half-ruined temple, built several centuries ago by the indigenous Gond people but long since abandoned. It was constructed from granite slabs, with stepped, ziggurat-style tiers and a host of intricate carvings. Vines now crawled over it and ferns sprouted from cracks in the stonemasonry, while a troop of baboons called its high, conical roofs home.

Strange's astral form swept in through the temple's main entrance, beneath a lintel that depicted animalistic gods frolicking. Within the shadowy, cobwebbed interior he found the Ancient One, who was seated in the midst of those numerous binding spells, just as Mordo's vision had shown.

Strange's eyes locked with the Ancient One's, and he had just enough time to give his mentor a consoling, reassuring look before Mordo's astral form came darting in after him.

He wheeled round and saw, with some satisfaction, a severely chagrined expression on Mordo's face.

"Curse you, Strange!" the aristocrat mage declared. "I should have known you weren't simply running away."

"On the contrary, Mordo," Strange said. "I was leading you a merry dance. Two can play at misdirection, you know. It just so happens that I can play better."

With a guttural, impassioned oath, Mordo loosed off a volley of dark magical shafts at Strange. They shot at him across the temple like jet-black ramrods.

Strange's riposte came in the form of light from the Eye of Agamotto. Opened to its maximum, the amulet radiated such pure brilliance that Mordo's shafts were shattered to pieces.

Mordo sent out the Vapors of Valtorr in a roiling, bruise-purple cloud that enclosed Strange, blotting him out of sight. Then, clearly having come to the conclusion that discretion was the better part of valor, he turned around and made for the temple entrance.

Light began to seep through the seething mass of vapors. The next instant, beams of coruscating radiance shot out in all directions, reducing them to useless tatters and ridding Strange of their occluding embrace. The Eye of Agamotto had once again come to his aid.

Before Mordo could escape, Strange summoned the Crimson Bands of Cyttorak to ensnare Mordo's astral form. The twisted sorcerer strained and squirmed within the Bands' churning, overlapping coils but couldn't break free. The harder he fought against them, the tighter Strange wrapped them around him. It was a battle of wills, and Strange's will was greater than Mordo's. After several minutes of struggle, Mordo gave up and resigned himself to his fate.

"The day is yours, Strange," he sighed. "Again."

"Release the Ancient One," Strange said, "and I'll release you."

Mordo ground his teeth but consented. He performed the necessary gestures, and the spells fastening the Ancient One fell away, one after another, like the tumblers of a safe unlocking. Soon the venerable Tibetan was free. He rose stiffly to his feet and offered his former pupil a nod of gratitude.

"And what of me, Strange?" said Mordo. "I've kept my side of the bargain. Now keep yours. Let me go."

"In a moment," said Strange. "Master, are you all right?"

"Cramping up in places," said the Ancient One, "but I'll live. You did well, Stephen. Mordo caught me unawares. He was able to overwhelm me and bring me here before I could stop him. His power has grown and I was unprepared for it."

"I've noticed that too. He's much stronger than he used to be. There must be some reason for that."

"We shall discuss the matter later, when I'm home again and rested."

"You'll be able to get back to your retreat without help?"

"I'm not so old and feeble, Stephen, that I can't muster up a spell of physical transference when necessary."

"What should I do with Mordo, though?" Strange said. "I can't let him keep on harassing us like this. There must be some way of neutralizing him for good."

"I wish there were an easy solution," said the Ancient One. "As a physician, you swore the Hippocratic Oath, pledging that you would not harm your patients. As a magician following the righteous path, you must abide by a similar principle."

"I've no great wish to harm him. Just... incapacitate him somehow."

"The fact that you keep trouncing Mordo must sink in eventually. He must come to realize that it's futile to carry on."

"I'm right here, you know," groused Mordo. "I can hear everything you're saying."

"I'll think of something to do with you, Mordo," Strange said. "In the meantime, just sit there and keep quiet."

He waited at the temple until the Ancient One had collected himself and had called upon a Wormhole of Weygg-Kalkuun to convey him to his retreat. Then, with a scowl at Mordo, he set off back to New York. Mordo cried out in protest as he departed, but Strange ignored him. Only when he was in his Sanctum Sanctorum again did he remotely undo the binding power of the Crimson Bands of Cyttorak. And that was only after he had removed Mordo's mortal shell from the house and put it elsewhere.

Somewhere Mordo would not like.

It was a petty act of retribution but, under the circumstances, Mordo ought to consider himself fortunate. Strange had been quite restrained. He could—perhaps should—have done a lot worse.

NINE

AS BARON Mordo's astral form homed in on his body, he cursed inwardly. Had Strange put it where he thought he'd put it? Damn the fellow, he had!

Mordo had no choice but to re-enter his physical self, for all that it now sat inside a trash-filled dumpster. The dark, confined space reeked foully. Spluttering and retching, he thrust up the lid and scrambled out.

He was in one of Manhattan's narrower, grimier side alleys. With his hair disheveled and his clothes soaked with garbage seepings, he looking anything but a dignified, patrician figure. Out of the corner of his eye he saw something move, something small and brown, and looked round to find a cockroach as big as his thumb perched on his shoulder. It must have clung to him as he clambered out of the dumpster. It eyed him up familiarly, waggling its antennae at him, as though to imply they were brothers-in-scavenging. With a shudder of revulsion he brushed the insect off.

Strange would pay for this indignity. Oh, how he would pay.

Before any of that, however, Mordo had to consult with his master.

He transported himself home, using a Wormhole of Weygg-Kalkuun much as the Ancient One had done. On arriving at his castle, he discarded his filthy clothes and had a long, hot bath, after which he spent the next few hours recuperating and gathering his strength.

Only then did he feel able, both physically and mentally, to face Dormammu.

○━━━━━○

GREEN FIRE erupted from the brazier. Tongues of flame licked upward, casting an eerie emerald glow over Mordo's face.

"Dormammu," Mordo intoned. "I call upon you. Answer your faithful servant, I beg you. Speak with me."

The flames guttered and subsided, and for a moment Mordo was relieved. Perhaps Dormammu was unavailable, meaning he would not have to deliver the bad news just yet.

Then the fire sprang back into full life and a face formed in its midst.

The face of the Dread Dormammu.

"Baron Mordo," Dormammu said. His voice sounded like the crackling of a funeral pyre. "You failed. The Ancient One is at his home, safe and well. Doctor Strange has beaten you again."

"O great Dormammu, Lord of the Dark Dimension, I beseech you, look mercifully upon me. I did my best."

"Your best is not good enough, Mordo. I lent you a fragment of my power to help you in your task. Still you did not succeed."

"Perhaps if you had given me more power."

"More?" said Dormammu. The flames flared angrily. "More?"

Mordo quivered inside. "A tiny bit more, maybe?"

"Why would I squander yet more power on a nonentity like you, who does not get results? It would only be a waste."

"Because you have, in me, the staunchest ally you could ask for, my lord," Mordo replied. "Because you need a representative on Earth to pave the way for you, so that your plans for conquest may be brought to fruition more easily. Because there is no one better qualified than me for that role, and no one more willing to do what it takes."

"You mean no one as keen to pursue power," said Dormammu. "No one like you who will do anything to attain it, even joining forces with a being who regards him as not much more than a lowly insect."

Mordo bowed in obeisance and acknowledgement. "I remain humble enough to admit that I am your inferior. I'm honored that you look favorably on me at all. I exist only to do your bidding, Dormammu, and strive to please you at all times and in all ways."

"Then why are the Ancient One and Doctor Strange still alive?" Dormammu barked. "Their deaths would please me greatly, and you assured me you could arrange that."

"I almost beat Strange this time," Mordo said. "Were I able to discover the Ancient One's last few secrets, there is no way he or his toadying sidekick would ever overcome me again."

"More excuses. Tell me why I shouldn't destroy you where you stand, Mordo."

Mordo gulped. "Sooner or later, I swear, Strange will be gone. I'll stop at nothing to get rid of him. Even now, I am recruiting aides—magic-wielding individuals who are happy to sell their services to me. Where alone I may not be Strange's equal yet, bolstered by these others I will easily surpass him. Once he is out of the way, the Ancient One will prove no problem, and then your path will be clear of potential obstacles, Dormammu. The only two people who might stand against you, the only two with any hope of defending Earth against you, will be no more."

"You talk as though I would have difficulty eliminating Strange and the Ancient One myself. I would not."

"No, no, my lord, of course not. But if you crave a straightforward, seamless victory, this is how to go about it. No Strange, no Ancient One—I can still make that happen for you."

"And all you want in return is a portion of Earth to rule over."

"The great majority can be yours, Dormammu. I simply wish dominion over the nations of Central Europe. Mine to do with as I please, while the rest of the planet falls subject to your glorious majesty. That and sufficient magical might to enforce my reign. That was our agreement, the pact we made, and I trust you'll stand by it."

"Only as long as you uphold your end of things," Dormammu said. "So far you have not, and I am rapidly losing patience."

"Have faith in me, my lord. That's all I ask."

"There will come a time, Mordo, when you let me down once too often. Your punishment then will be terrible and everlasting."

Dormammu's face faded from the flames and the green fire dwindled, extinguishing itself.

Baron Mordo stood by the brazier for several minutes, trembling so hard he could not move. Eventually the shakes subsided, and he hurried off in search of wine. Castle Mordo boasted a well-stocked cellar, and he guzzled down an entire bottle of vintage Fetească Neagra, which helped soothe his nerves.

Sometimes he wondered why he had ever sworn allegiance to Dormammu. He was in league with the most vile being in all the Multiverse. It was like being tethered inextricably to a man-eating shark, being towed along in its wake, never knowing when the beast might turn around and consume him. At first he had found it exciting, offering himself as an earthly thrall to Dormammu. It had promised power of the kind the Ancient One was steadfastly refusing to grant him.

He had failed to foresee the price of such power. If you weren't careful, you could lose more than you hoped to gain. Mordo understood that he remained alive only because Dormammu considered him marginally more useful that way than dead. On a whim, the Lord of the Dark Dimension could snuff him out, and his plans for conquering Earth would proceed anyway. Mordo scarcely dared think about the "terrible and everlasting" punishment Dormammu might mete out on him. All he knew was it would take every ounce of wheedling and ingratiating he could muster to stay in his demonic master's good books.

Which was just one more reason why Doctor Strange must die.

DORMAMMU HIMSELF was more concerned, at that moment, with someone other than Baron Mordo.

He knew there was another contender for the position of ruler of Earth. It was time to put this rival in his place.

He sent out a thought impulse through the membrane between his home dimension and an adjacent one. The thought impulse, like a trained pigeon, sought out a specific entity, and having found its quarry, opened an interdimensional channel so that the two of them, Dormammu and this other, might communicate.

"Nightmare," said Dormammu, in a tone of voice somewhere between salutation and sneer.

The darkest denizen of the Dream Dimension returned the greeting with a hoarse laugh. "The Dread Dormammu. To what do I owe the honor of this visitation?"

"I'm calling to offer you a polite warning."

"It sounds more like a threat," said Nightmare.

"Take it how you wish. Leave Earth alone. That world is mine."

"I didn't realize it had your name on it, Dormammu."

"Don't be facetious. I'm well aware you have designs on the planet."

"Who would not?" said Nightmare. "It has such abundant resources. All those billions of humans, riddled with fears and anxieties that plague them in their sleep." He licked his pallid lips. "A banquet of angst. Of course I want it."

"I want it more," said Dormammu. "I've seen you hatching your schemes, only for Doctor Strange to thwart them."

"Strange? Hah! Strange is nothing but a nuisance."

"A very persistent nuisance, whom you seem unable to deal with effectively. I'm telling you, Nightmare, Earth is not for you."

"So I am to back down?" said Nightmare. "Abandon my plans, step aside and give you free rein?"

"That would be wise."

"And were I to refuse?"

Dormammu laughed mirthlessly. "I will raze your kingdom to the ground, obliterate all that you have created, and expunge you from existence so completely that the universe will forget you ever were."

Nightmare did his best to look unimpressed. Both of them, however, were aware that what Dormammu had said was true. Nightmare's power was considerable, but Dormammu's dwarfed it the way a hurricane dwarfed a storm. Nor was there any question that the Lord of the Dark Dimension would do exactly as he had stated, if provoked.

"Having given it some thought," Nightmare said eventually, "I shall accede to your request, Dormammu."

"Splendid."

"On balance, I feel you have a stronger claim on Earth than I."

"I am delighted you see it that way. For what it's worth, I'm going to make a point of disposing of Doctor Strange and his master before anything else."

Nightmare grinned ghoulishly. "It pleases me to hear that."

"I thought it might. I dislike mortals who practice magic, especially ones who practice it to a high degree of expertise. Those two shall perish first."

"Painfully, I hope."

"You may count on it," said Dormammu.

———o———o———

AFTER THE conversation with Dormammu was over, Nightmare sat on his throne with his thin, bony fingers steepled, their tips pressed to his nose.

A minion who was in the throne room with him coughed discreetly.

"Yes?" Nightmare snapped.

"Sire, I was wondering…"

"Yes?"

"Well, surely you were bluffing," said this underling, who looked like a humanoid insect grub—bloated white body, segmented legs, mandibular mouth parts, compound eyes. "Perhaps you are thinking, sire, that while Dormammu is preoccupied with conquering Earth, you might take advantage and launch an assault on the Dark Dimension, snatching it from him while his attention is diverted."

"Of course I was thinking that," Nightmare said, when in fact the idea had not occurred to him. "I was also thinking how that would be a very unwise thing to do. Idiotic, even."

"But sire…"

"Dormammu would not leave his realm entirely defenseless. Would you have me attack it, knowing I might well not succeed? Do you want to see me crushed, you pathetic little nonentity? Is that it?"

"Sire, no!" cried the grub-like minion. "That's not what I meant at all. I was simply expressing—"

"Treason!" Nightmare thundered. "Treason was what you were expressing."

The minion shrank away from him. He feared what was coming next. He had aroused Nightmare's ire. Whenever that happened, someone inevitably suffered.

Nightmare rose to his feet. "I will not abide perfidy in my court."

The giant hooded guard who stood beside his throne grunted. The message was clear. He was volunteering to deal with the minion.

Nightmare shook his head. "No. Leave this to me."

He aimed a forefinger at the minion.

The terrified underling promptly exploded, disintegrating into a thousand wet globs of flesh.

Satisfied, with much of his frustration exorcised, Nightmare resumed his seat.

No. There would be no attacking Dormammu. Dormammu was all-powerful—practically a god. Much though he resented it, Nightmare had to accept that Earth was off-limits to him. For now. Perhaps for all time.

There was, however, one silver lining to this cloud.

Earth, under Dormammu's cruel governance, would be hellish. Its mortal inhabitants would know little but misery and suffering. Their dreams, accordingly, would be fretful, riddled with pain and sorrow.

Which meant that, in their sleep, they would gravitate towards his realm, and Nightmare would grow fat on their torment.

Nightmare chortled and rubbed his belly in anticipation of the feasts to come.

TEN

AT THE Ancient One's retreat, Doctor Strange ate a frugal meal with his master.

The Ancient One was in an unusually somber mood. The conversation was stilted, and he barely picked at the food in front of him. Strange, for his part, relished the dishes Wong had prepared, especially the sha phaley—semicircular parcels of bread stuffed with cabbage and seasoned meat—and the soft, fluffy dumplings known as tingmo. However, out of deference to the Ancient One, he didn't gorge himself as he would have liked, instead just nibbling discreetly.

After Wong cleared the plates away, the two diners drank jasmine tea. The Ancient One remained uncommunicative, so that in the end Strange felt compelled to inquire what the matter was. "You asked me to come," he said. "I wormholed my way over. I think now's the time you told me why."

"Stephen," said the Ancient One, setting down his teacup, "since leaving here to go out into the world, you have excelled yourself. You have shown yourself worthy of the trust I placed in you."

"Thank you, Master."

"When you first came to me, you were a man who had been consumed with hubris and brought low by it. You were desperate and arrogant. Others might not have considered you promising material."

"Thank you, Master," Strange repeated, this time somewhat questioningly.

"I gave you a chance because I saw that there lingered a fundamental decency within you. My instinct was that you could be a great magician and even, one day, Sorcerer Supreme. I am glad to have been proved right. Over the past few months you have faced severe challenges and dire adversaries, and shown yourself equal to the task every time. People come to you in crisis and you bring them succor and resolution."

"Yes, it somewhat reminds me of my physician days. Greet the patient, hear the symptoms, diagnose the problem, provide the cure."

"Just so," said the Ancient One, with a nod. "And if only such a state of affairs could continue. Unfortunately, events are conspiring against that. If Mordo's latest offensive action has taught us anything, it's that we can no longer afford to be complacent. His power has increased."

"I'm all too aware."

"How do you think that might have come about?"

"He's been studying hard?"

"Mordo is too lazy for that, too eager for shortcuts. No, it was borrowed power, bestowed on him by another."

"Who?"

The Ancient One heaved a deep sigh. "It can only have come from one source. Mordo has forged a full-blown alliance with Dormammu. I sensed as much in the magics he used to bind me. They carried the unmistakable taint of the Dark Dimension, Dormammu's realm. He is Dormammu's thrall, and that can only be bad news—for you and me personally, but perhaps also for the whole world. Why would Dormammu need a human servitor unless it were to further any aims he has regarding Earth? An agent, a collaborator, an infiltrator—someone here to help him enact his nefarious plans."

"Maybe he just likes husky Central Europeans with goatees. And if so, who are we to judge?"

The old man clucked his tongue. "This is no time for flippancy,

Stephen. Dormammu has long coveted our world. He sees Earth as a fruit ripe for plucking. The place teems with magical resources which he would like to add to his own, and humankind are nothing more than an inconvenience: there to be subjugated or obliterated, whichever takes his fancy. One of the purposes of the Sorcerer Supreme is to act as a deterrent to all such putative demonic dictators. As long as there is someone with sufficient power and ability to repel them, the planet is safe. I know, now, that my time as Sorcerer Supreme is nearing its end. You will soon take the mantle from me."

"Don't talk like that, Master," Strange said with sincerity. "You have plenty of years left."

A wan smile from the Ancient One. "You're kind, but we both know that isn't true. I am ageing, weakening. The stamina I once had, I no longer have. My bones creak. My fingers are gnarled and stiffening and cannot form the spellcasting shapes as fluidly as they used to. There is no shame in admitting these things. We all grow old. We all decline."

"Beats the alternative."

"Too true, although death is nothing to be scared of. If there were a choice in the matter, then I could understand fearing it, but since it is inevitable for all of us, why worry?" The Ancient One's eyes glittered shrewdly within their wrinkled sockets. "But back to the subject at hand. Dormammu, Stephen. He has to be confronted sooner or later. There's no getting around it. He, like death, is inescapable. Which is why I asked you here."

"Finally, we come to the point."

"We do. I'm going to send you on a mission. A very perilous one. I would not make this request if I didn't think it necessary and didn't think you were up to it. But be in no doubt, should you go, you will be putting yourself in grave jeopardy. There is every chance you may not return."

Strange squared his shoulders and clenched his jaw, serious now. "What mission? Tell me what I have to do."

"Simply this," said the Ancient One. "Travel to the Dark

Dimension. Find Dormammu. Deliver him an ultimatum. Warn him to abandon whatever he's planning."

A beat.

Strange blinked.

Then he said, with airy irony, "Oh. Is that all?"

○———○

OVER THE next few days, the Ancient One did his best to prepare Strange for what lay ahead. He put him through a series of rigorous training exercises, to ensure his spellcasting was at peak proficiency. He also schooled him in all the potential dangers the Dark Dimension had to offer, or at least as many as were mentioned in the scholarly texts—although the books' authors tended to be rather hazy on the subject, relying more on inference and guesswork than hard data.

When at last he thought Strange was ready, his final piece of advice was this: "Remember, Dormammu is like no entity you have encountered before. His power is beyond description. By all means avoid direct magical confrontation with him. Merely deliver your message and leave."

"Understood," said Strange.

"I wish I were going with you."

Strange arched an eyebrow. "Do you? Really?"

The Ancient One gave a dry chuckle. "Not really. I am concerned for you, though, and you should be concerned on your own behalf. Once, many years ago, I fought off an attempted incursion by Dormammu. I was young and at the height of my powers, but even so I barely succeeded. I was lucky to escape with my life."

"What did people call you back then? The Youthful One?"

The Ancient One disregarded Strange's quip. "I can't imagine he has grown any weaker since that time. I pray for your safe return."

"Well, let's not put this off any longer," Strange said. "Dark Dimension, here I come."

○━━━━━━━━○

ASTRAL FORMS could slip between planes of existence with relative ease, but Strange wouldn't be traveling to the Dark Dimension that way. He had to go as his physical self, so that he would have access to the full panoply of his magical powers.

It was the Ancient One's job to conjure up a portal for him to step through.

Candles were lit. Incense was burned. A hush fell over the room as the elderly Tibetan adopted the lotus position atop a bank of cushions, focused his inner energies, aligned his chakras, and concentrated on opening a way between the dimensional planes. Strange waited, fighting down the surges of nervousness that kept threatening to undermine his resolve. He had never been frightened in the operating theater. For one thing, the life at stake had always been his patient's, not his own, and his confidence in his surgical skills had been absolute. Now, he was venturing into the unknown, into a world of unpredictable, possibly lethal dangers, and there was no guarantee his magic would protect him.

The Ancient One let out a gasp. "So be it!" he cried. "By the Shades of the Seraphim! In the name of the All-seeing Agamotto!"

He brought his hands together, palms up, and raised them as though lifting a huge, invisible weight. Then he brought them together and slowly parted them.

Titanic forces were swirling around Strange. Winds tugging at his clothes and hair. Bursts of incandescent light. Shocks like earth tremors. A hole was being punched through space. The fabric of reality was bending, warping, ripping.

An oval aperture appeared in the air before him, at first no larger than a mousehole but swiftly dilating until it was the size of a hatch in a submarine.

"I'll maintain the portal for as long as I am able," the Ancient One said. "Now go, Stephen. May the wise Vishanti watch over you and may the Hoary Hosts of Hoggoth guide you on your way."

With a nod to his master, Strange ducked into the portal, emerging the other side into…

MADNESS.

Bedlam.

Pandemonium.

A place where geometry and geography had no meaning.

Where perspective shifted constantly.

Where scroll-like pathways wound from nowhere to nowhere, some of them folding into unending Möbius strips.

Where puddles of liquid hung in the air, oozing and re-forming into new shapes.

Where doorways opened to reveal other doorways, which opened to reveal yet more doorways, and so on, seemingly infinitely.

Where bubbles floated in clusters, bursting into showers of sparks that coalesced into snowflakes, which in turn became bubbles again.

Where staircases and ladders wrapped around one another, circling in endless Escher-esque loops.

Where smoke was solid and stone gaseous, water like fire and fire like water.

Strange reeled, assailed on all sides by bizarre phenomena and mind-bending impossibilities. Nothing made sense here. Nothing was logical. His psyche strained at its moorings, wanting to tear itself loose, to succumb to the insanity rather than have to try to accommodate it.

He commanded himself to adjust. Inwardly be still. Focus. The Dark Dimension was a place like any other. It had rules. It had reason. What appeared to be chaos was just a different form of order.

Gradually things settled into a semblance of sensicality. Strange oriented himself, discovering that he was standing on an enormous, twisted tree trunk which stretched horizontally towards a huge, fortified gateway like the barbican of a medieval castle. Presiding over the gateway was an immense statue of a monstrous entity with six arms, a pair of batlike wings and a single, large hexagonal eye.

He recalled the Ancient One telling him that the Dark Dimension was a reflection of its ruler's twisted psyche. He also recalled him saying that all roads in that realm led eventually to Dormammu's lair.

Behind him, the tree trunk spread into an impenetrable tangle of bare branches. That clinched it. No choice but to go forward.

As Strange approached the gateway, the statue began to move. Bracing itself on the ground with four of its six arms, it bent its head down and brought its monocular gaze to bear on him from above. All at once he was bathed in a column of light emanating from the eye. It was like being immersed in intangible fire. Strange's body was unhurt but his brain seethed. His thoughts were water boiling in a cauldron. He clutched his head, staggering.

A test.

This was some kind of test.

The statue was assessing his strength of will, his ability to endure, to prevail. If he passed, he would be allowed through the gateway.

He steeled himself. The pain wasn't real. It was an illusion. A figment of the imagination.

All in the mind. Literally.

He told himself this, repeating the words like a mantra, until it became true and the pain abated.

The column of light receded. The statue resumed its previous position. The gates—a pair of angular doors carved with sinuous patterns—parted.

Strange walked through.

He came to a vast space crowded with oblong platforms of various sizes and colors, all suspended above, below and alongside one another, each as thin as glass. Together they seemed to form a three-dimensional labyrinth, whose solution must entail stepping from one to the next until you reached the far side. There, he presumed, lay the exit, but the labyrinth was easily three or four miles long and the same again in height and breadth. If there even was a way out, it was too distant to be seen.

Before Strange could begin tackling the labyrinth, a figure burst up from the ground at his feet. It was the size of a small child, as featureless as a shop-window mannequin, and fashioned from a gleaming, gold-like substance.

A Golden Golem. Inorganic matter, animated by magic and granted rudimentary intelligence.

Dormammu knew Strange was there. The statue guarding the gateway must have relayed news of his presence to the realm's ruler. This Golden Golem was the next line of defense.

Without uttering a word, the golem hurled a spell at Strange, a simple little cantrip which he deflected easily, almost by instinct. He answered with a counterspell, just a low-grade destructive hex, in the hope that this was all it would take to incapacitate the golem. The spell hit home, undefended, and that should have been that.

But instead, the golem shuddered and grew. Now it was teenager-sized, and the next spell it cast was proportionately stronger. Strange shielded himself and delivered a robust response in the form of a Bolt of Bedevilment.

That really ought to have put paid to the golem's efforts, but as before, the uncanny, faceless thing simply received the magical blow and swelled up further. Now it stood a head taller than Strange. It lashed out with a blistering eldritch blast from both hands which he only just managed to ward off. He struck back with all the force he could muster, and the golem became a towering figure, twenty-five feet from top to toe, as big as the super hero Giant-Man at his maximum height.

Given that the golem's power seemed commensurate with its size, Strange knew its next attack might quite easily be too much for him to withstand. By now, however, he had figured out how the thing operated. He berated himself for not realizing sooner.

His magic was feeding the golem. It absorbed and was enhanced by every spell he cast at it.

The answer, then, was not just to starve it of nourishment. He should put it on a crash diet.

He summoned the Rains of Raggadorr, and the Golden Golem was engulfed in a sudden mystic deluge that washed it clean of all magic. It shrank rapidly, squirming and flailing, until it was no higher than Strange's ankle. He trod on it, squashing it flat. The tiny mangled golem twitched a few times and lay still.

Brushing his palms together, Strange turned his attention to the labyrinth of platforms. He assumed all he had to do was head across it, keeping in roughly the same direction all the time, and he would eventually gain the other side.

He assumed wrong.

STRANGE BEGAN hopping from platform to platform, but the third one he came to, although it appeared as solid as any of its neighbors, was not. He fell through it as if it were an open window. He plummeted for a split second, landing with a bump on a patch of ground made of steel cables, thick as a freighter's hawsers, that slithered and coiled like a nest of snakes. He got to his feet, but it was hard keeping his balance on such unsteady, ever-changing terrain.

That wasn't his main worry, though.

His main worry was the half-dozen metallic figures closing in on him. They moved like automatons, stiffly and mechanically, and each carried a net woven from some sort of silvery thread. Lurching at Strange, they sought to wind their nets around him, pinning him in place.

"A catch!" one of them cried in a voice like a rusty hinge.

"Look at the size of it!" said another, each word an electric buzz.

"We won't throw this one back!" declared a third, sounding like a chainsaw.

As the nets encircled him, Strange fought back. The Eye of Agamotto emitted a beam of light. Before its blistering brilliance the robotic "fishermen" recoiled in bedazzled distress, dropping their nets and sinking to all fours. They squawked and shrieked in their panic.

Keeping the Eye's beam trained on the automatons, Strange looked up to see the underside of the platform he had fallen through—a rectangular gap in space. It lay just too high to reach. Unless, that was, he could find something to climb on.

Such as a crouching, cowering automaton.

He leapt onto the back of the one nearest him and grasped the inner edges of the platform with both hands. Hauling himself up and through, he sprang onto the next platform along, with every hope that this one would not turn out to be false too.

It wasn't. He ignited the Eye of Agamotto again, this time inviting it to show him which platforms were safe to tread on and which were effectively trapdoors, with potentially deadly fates lurking below. Perhaps he should have done something of this sort to begin with, but he hadn't known at the outset that the labyrinth was littered with hazards.

Live and learn, as the saying went. Or perhaps, in this instance, narrowly escape dying and learn.

Strange strode on, up, down, left, right, using the platforms like stepping stones, with the Eye warning him which of them to avoid.

In due course he reached the other side. Ahead, he saw a vast city that sprawled all the way to the horizon. Mostly it was a warren of narrow streets and low, flat-roofed buildings. At its heart, however, there rose a citadel—a collection of shining needle-sharp towers, each seemingly trying to outdo its neighbors in height and cast them in its shade, like trees in a forest.

Dormammu's den. His stronghold.

Strange set off towards the city.

The gates were unguarded and wide open. He strode through, and soon he was passing along winding streets, between those low buildings that huddled close to one another, some leaning skewedly on their neighbors as though for consolation as well as support. The roadways were filthy and debris-strewn, with flies buzzing over heaps of garbage, cadaverous carrion birds rooting through the refuse for scraps of dead flesh, and huge, glowing-eyed rat-like things scurrying along the gutters with prize morsels clutched in their teeth.

Strange was not the only pedestrian, but others were few and far between. Nobody showed the least curiosity about him or any kind of sociableness. Rather, people hurried to avoid him. Sometimes a lean, hungry face peered at him through the grime-caked panes of a window, vanishing the moment their gazes met. These were Dormammu's subjects: a furtive, timorous lot, clothed in rags and eking out miserable, deprived existences. Their lord and master seemed not to care about them, to judge by the sordid conditions they lived in. Perhaps he valued them only for the sense of superiority they must give him.

Strange walked on through the grubby, semi-deserted city, while the shining citadel, his destination, loomed ever larger ahead.

IN THAT citadel, from a balcony on one of its tallest towers, a pair of eyes looked down. They had been watching Strange since he entered via the city gates, following his progress with interest.

They were extraordinary eyes, their icy blue irises shot through with veins of silver, and they were set in a perfectly oval face beneath a pair of determined eyebrows. The face itself was framed with hair which was silvery white and arranged in thick curls, two of which rose above its owner's forehead like horns.

The woman to whom the eyes belonged had observed Strange with curiosity at first. She had had no difficulty identifying him as an outsider. His clothing, his demeanor, his deportment—everything spoke of a mortal from another realm. But who was he? And why was he entering Dormammu's city, where no outsider in their right mind dared to tread? She marveled at his intrepidity, and at his foolhardiness too. He was on an important errand of some sort, judging by his purposeful air. Did he think Dormammu would simply ignore him? Did he assume he could wander through the city unopposed?

If so, he was in for a rude awakening.

One he was unlikely to survive.

OUT OF nowhere, a storm elemental appeared.

It flew at Strange, the torso of a man atop a blazing, twisting tail of lightning.

It launched a firebolt at him.

Strange retaliated with a spell of banishment.

Just like that, the storm elemental was gone.

An easy victory.

Too easy.

The storm elemental had simply been a feint, an exploratory attack.

Strange walked on, braced for the next challenge.

A warlock appeared at a junction ahead: probably the person who'd sicced the storm elemental on him. He was garbed garishly, with chunky, multilayered body armor and an elaborate headdress that was somewhere on a spectrum between ceremonial and street carnival.

Arms outstretched, the warlock sent a host of hollow green blobs scudding through the air at Strange. They swarmed around him, latching on like leukocytes attacking a virus. For every one he got rid of with a magical blast from his fingertips, two more took its place.

In no time the blobs were all over him, restricting, suffocating.

He invoked the power of the Eye of Agamotto, and a narrow-focused, laser-like beam pierced the encrustation of blobs, lancing through to strike the unsuspecting warlock beyond. The warlock staggered and collapsed, insensible.

Then all Strange had to do was summon the Vapors of Valtorr. The green blobs, with no one to keep replenishing them, were dispelled in seconds.

Stepping around the fallen warlock, Strange entered a plaza. Mossy cobblestones surrounded an ornamental fountain that had long since ceased to function. Its basin was full of dust, and the fountain structure itself, a simple set of rising tiers, was liberally smeared with bird droppings.

Elsewhere he had noted a marked hush hanging over the city. Here in this plaza it seemed deeper than ever, doubtless because what should have been a busy meeting place was utterly empty, devoid of activity and life.

The shutters on a nearby window slammed shut, the sound echoing in the stillness. Inside one of the buildings that overlooked the plaza, he heard someone call out to someone else, telling them to stay low and keep quiet.

Strange thought of a scene in a Western movie: the lone gunslinger arriving for his main-street showdown with the bad guys, the townsfolk sheltering to avoid getting caught in the crossfire.

And here they came.

A half-dozen more warlocks, all dressed as extravagantly as the last one.

They materialized in a circle around Strange.

A pitched battle ensued. Strange deftly fended off assault spells left, right and center, responding in kind whenever an opening presented itself. One by one his opponents caved and crumpled. Their magic was strong and they had the advantage of numbers, but they were overconfident and that made them clumsy. Strange, by contrast, was alone and on his mettle. His spellcasting was correspondingly accurate and well-calibrated, because it had to be; he could not afford a single mistake. He picked off his adversaries with a precision that was pinpoint. Surgical, even.

Soon enough he was the last mage standing. The warlocks lay either unconscious, or magically bound and impotent.

He sensed a presence behind him, and wheeled round, raising his hands in a standard offensive-ready posture.

"No," said the new arrival softly. "I'm not one of them. I mean you no harm."

Strange was looking at a silver-haired woman in a form-fitting, wing-collared bodice—purple in color and decorated with overlapping circles—and similarly-patterned lilac leggings to match. She was strikingly beautiful, but in spite of this, and her mollifying words, he did not lower his guard. Beauty could be deceptive, and the woman's aura radiated magical ability. There was every chance she was just the next challenge he had to face before he got to Dormammu, the latest stage in this gauntlet he was running.

"I came to tell you not to go any further," she said. "Turn back now, while you still can."

Strange stayed wary. "Who are you?"

"I think I'm the one that should be asking *who are you*? You've come from elsewhere, outside this dimension, and you seem determined to bring Dormammu's wrath down on your head. If it's conflict with him you're looking for, then don't. You're obviously very adept in magic, but nowhere near powerful enough to beat him. No one is."

"Listen, I appreciate the advice, whoever you are. Fact is, I'm here to give Dormammu a message."

"And you reckon walking up to his front door means he's just going to let you in and hear you out?"

"I seem to have got his attention, haven't I? And," Strange added, gesturing at the defeated warlocks around them, "I've dealt with everything he's thrown at me so far. All in all, I feel I've earned an audience with him."

The woman gazed at him with bemusement and, he thought, a hint of admiration—or perhaps he was imagining that. Her eyes, with their glints of silver, were like none he had ever seen before, and utterly beguiling.

"You're either phenomenally sure of yourself," she said, "or an imbecile. I can't make up my mind which."

"You wouldn't be the first woman to tell me that."

"Well, I've said my piece, and risked a lot in the process. If Dormammu were to find out what I'm doing…" She shuddered. "It doesn't bear thinking about. Go on then. Go to your certain doom. You can't say I didn't try to warn you."

The silver-haired woman wove a spell around herself and disappeared.

For several moments, Strange stared at the space where she had been standing. He had a peculiar feeling of destiny, as though this woman was more than just some concerned, well-meaning stranger, as though she had a far larger role to play in his life. It was a conviction so deep, it was almost visceral.

He shook his head. Focus on the job at hand, he told himself.

He started walking again, but had gone only a few paces when everything suddenly went blank.

An instant of pure whiteness.

Then he was no longer in the plaza but somewhere else.

A chamber with a high vaulting ceiling, marble floors, long colonnades, and a parade of windows that showed a view of the city he had just been in, far below.

At the center of the room sat an imposing figure, robed in shades of red and purple, with a head made of burning flames.

Strange, after all the trials and tribulations he had endured, was at last in the presence of the one he sought.

The Dread Dormammu.

ELEVEN

EYES OF pale fire glared at Strange. A mouth, likewise of pale fire, moved.

"Rather than waste any more time beleaguering you with underlings," said Dormammu, "I thought I'd bring you to me. I'll dispose of you myself."

The Lord of the Dark Dimension raised a hand, readying a spell. Deadly energies crackled at his fingertips.

"Wait!" said Strange. "Wait just a moment!"

"Quiet!" Dormammu barked. "Did I ask you to speak?"

"You didn't forbid it," Strange pointed out.

Dormammu paused. What looked like a quizzical grin appeared on those fiery features, but only for a moment, briefly there then gone.

"You have some effrontery, mortal," he intoned. "Nobody talks to me in that manner and lives."

"You were just about to kill me anyway," said Strange, "so it really doesn't make much difference how I talk to you, does it?"

At that, Dormammu laughed, but it was far from a pleasant noise. It was how the rising flames must sound to a martyr being burned at the stake.

"Dr. Stephen Strange," he said. "The Ancient One's disciple. Sorcerer-Supreme-in-waiting. Your reputation for audacity is not, it seems, undeserved."

"If you know who I am, you can surely guess why I'm here."

"I don't care why." Dormammu shrugged. "What I do care about is that you managed to get as far as you did. I despise many things, but incompetence I despise most of all. Let me show you what I do to those who dissatisfy me."

He clapped his hands, and all the warlocks who had attacked Strange were suddenly in the room with them. They looked around, dazed, and as it gradually dawned on them that their master had transported them there, their expressions turned to horror.

They began pleading with him to spare them, kneeling down, abasing themselves before him.

Dormammu yelled, "Silence!"

The plaintive hubbub petered out.

"I should destroy you all where you stand," he said. "But I would rather punish you, in such a way that you never forget it. I am going to send you to the Pitiless Pit of Neverness."

There was a collective gasp of dismay.

"Yes, that dire desert wilderness," Dormammu continued, "where winds blow constantly, blasting you with sand, and there is no shelter and nothing to eat or drink. You will be there for just a day, but as you are doubtless aware, time is relative in the Pitiless Pit of Neverness. A day here is a subjective lifetime there. You will emerge only a few hours older but with the memory of decades' worth of misery to look back on, and you will, I expect, be truly penitent."

Now the warlocks turned on one another. There was mutual denunciation, everyone blaming everyone else for their collective failure.

Dormammu, with a flick of one hand, sent them hurtling into a shimmering portal, which swallowed their screaming, flailing bodies before snapping tight shut.

"Talk," he said to Strange.

"I come with a message from the Ancient One," Strange said.

"He does not dare deliver this message himself?" asked Dormammu

"I speak with his full authority."

"I do not deal with subordinates. The Ancient One should be here in person."

"Well, he isn't. You've got me instead. Take it or leave it."

Dormammu laughed again, this time with a touch of incredulity. "Your impudence is astounding. It's as though you're courting my wrath. Out with it, Strange. What does the Ancient One want me to know?"

"He has tasked me with telling you to leave Earth alone."

"Leave Earth alone? How amusing. I recently delivered the same polite warning."

"To who?"

"Nightmare."

"Oh. Him," said Strange, feigning nonchalance. "Yes, come to think of it, he does have designs on my world."

"Not anymore. Earth will be mine. You would be well advised not to try and stop me."

"If I'm not mistaken," Strange said, "you staked a claim on Earth once before, which the Ancient One denied you. What makes you think you have a better chance this time?"

"I am even stronger now, and the Ancient One is weaker."

"But he has me by his side. Between us, we're more than a match for you."

"Indeed?" said Dormammu. "Let's put that to the test, shall we? Defeat me, here, now, and I'll agree to your demands."

"Just me alone? Versus you?"

"Scared, Strange?"

"I just want to establish the parameters. A one-to-one duel…"

"To the death."

"To the death," Strange echoed.

"Yes," said Dormammu. "You must be aware that your magical skills are no match for my own."

"Knowing the odds are against me has never stopped me in the past."

Even as he said this, Strange recalled the Ancient One's warning about Dormammu. *His power is beyond description. By all means avoid direct magical confrontation with him.* But direct magical confrontation was exactly what was being discussed here, and Strange didn't see how he could refuse Dormammu's challenge. If he did, he would lose face, for one thing, and thereby confirm Dormammu's low opinion of his capabilities. More importantly, he would be turning down an opportunity to stop the Lord of the Dark Dimension in his tracks before he could develop his plans any further. If there was a chance of beating Dormammu right now, while the stakes were at their lowest, then however slim it was, he had to take it.

"Well?" said Dormammu. "What's it to be?"

"Okay," said Strange. "You're on."

"Excellent. I shall give you some time to prepare yourself. Gather your thoughts. Devise a strategy. I don't want things to be too easy for me. There is no sport in that."

"That's very generous of you."

"Return when you feel ready. And if you should reconsider your decision to fight me and attempt to flee my realm…"

"Yes?"

"I shall hunt you down and destroy you."

"I see," said Strange. "Persuasively put."

"Quite," said Dormammu. "Now begone!"

STRANGE EXITED the room into an adjoining antechamber, where he halted and took a moment to chastise himself.

"Stephen, Stephen, Stephen," he murmured, pounding fist against brow. "What have you done? Are you mad?"

He didn't mind being the underdog, but in the forthcoming battle he wouldn't even be that. He would be a flyweight first-timer entering the ring with the undisputed heavyweight champ.

David, when he went up against Goliath, at least had his slingshot. Strange wasn't sure he had a pebble to aim at Dormammu, let along something to fling it with.

Despair, however, was the refuge of the weak-willed. It was not in Stephen Strange's nature, and he did not wallow in it for long. There must be some way to get the better of Dormammu. He just had to find it.

As he began racking his brains for a solution to his predicament, a patch of air in the antechamber shimmered. The next instant, the silver-haired woman appeared.

Without a word, she beckoned to him.

"What?" said Strange, a little more testily than he meant to. "What do you want?"

"Come with me," the woman said.

"I'm busy."

"You have agreed to face Dormammu in mortal combat."

"How do you know about that?"

"I keep an eye on things. I've worked out ways of watching Dormammu without him knowing. I want to show you something. Something that might make you rethink."

"It can't wait?"

"It can't," she said determinedly. "It's important."

Strange deliberated, then said, "All right. Quickly. Dormammu's waiting next door."

The woman conjured a portal, ushered Strange into it and dived through after him.

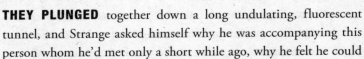

THEY PLUNGED together down a long undulating, fluorescent tunnel, and Strange asked himself why he was accompanying this person whom he'd met only a short while ago, why he felt he could trust her. It helped that he found her incredibly attractive, but there was an undeniable sincerity to her, too. She emanated pure honesty.

On top of all that, she seemed not to be on Dormammu's side. A classic case of "my enemy's enemy." She might be of help to him.

Not that he was going to drop his guard around her. Not until he was one hundred percent convinced she was on the level.

"What's your name?" he said as they continued to hurtle along the tunnel, whose sides shimmered and shifted around them like a kaleidoscope.

"Clea," she replied.

"Hello, Clea. I'm Stephen. Stephen Strange."

"I know."

"Tell me, why do you not seem intimidated by Dormammu, the way everyone else here is?"

"My attitude towards him is complicated, as is my relationship with him," Clea said. "That's as much as I'm prepared to tell you for now. And here we are."

The tunnel ended, disgorging them onto one of the weirdest prospects Strange had ever laid eyes on—and he had laid eyes on some very weird prospects indeed.

"We're at the outskirts of the Dark Dimension," Clea said. "The borderlands, where reality becomes fragile."

It was a place of unfinished things. A place of fragments and snippets. Landscapes that dwindled into frayed edges. Half-made clumps of terrain, like discarded ideas, hovering in space.

Beyond the point where these tenuous scraps of solidity were at their thinnest and most scattered, there was only fog. Nebulous, tenebrous, grayly swirling fog.

And within that fog, figures moved. Dark, humanoid and lumbering.

Strange recalled reading about the ominous creatures who dwelled at the fringes of the Dark Dimension. The magical books had given them no name, just hinted at the existence of a race of primordial beings who skulked around with nothing but malignancy in their hearts.

Now, as he watched, there was a break in the fog, revealing two of them clearly. They were large, man-shaped and lumpy, their hide pachyderm-thick and the color of charcoal. For facial features they had only a postbox-like slit where eyes might have been, illuminated from within by a sickly yellow glow.

The pair were, for no obvious reason, fighting. Each hammered the other with slow, clumsy punches and the occasional thudding kick. For a while they seemed content to settle their differences this way, but then one of them escalated the dispute by striking its opponent with a beam of energy from the eye-slit in its face. The other returned the compliment, and so the battle continued, with an exchange of these energy blasts, which delivered enough of an impact to stagger the recipient but not stun or slay. Then the pair resorted to punching and kicking again, with some added wrestler-style grappling too.

As the fight wore on, more of the creatures came into view, lumbering out of the fog to stand around and watch. Several of them shook their fists or nodded their heads, as though urging the combatants on. Two of the spectators got into a fight themselves, after one accidentally bumped the other with an elbow.

These brutish, troglodytic individuals were, Strange thought, both terrifyingly stupid and at the same time stupidly terrifying.

"We call them the Mindless Ones," Clea said in a low voice. "They're primitive, savage, totally lacking in love or kindness or any type of intelligence. Engines of destruction that live only to fight and to destroy. Dormammu once persuaded my grandfather to attempt to expand the boundaries of the Dark Dimension. He inadvertently broke through to the region where the Mindless Ones dwell. They have plagued our realm ever since. These you see here are just a tiny fraction of their number. There are millions, and all they want is to attack us and kill us."

"Then why don't they?" Strange asked. "What's preventing them?"

"That."

Clea motioned towards the Mindless Ones. Several of them, having heard her and Strange talking, had begun moving in their direction. Instinctively, Strange readied a defensive spell.

But there was no need. Abruptly, the Mindless Ones drew up short, as though they had encountered a wall of reinforced glass. They milled about, bumping into the unseen obstacle and tottering back. One fired an optic blast. The energy beam ricocheted off nothing, or so it seemed, and lanced backwards straight into the chest of another Mindless One, knocking it onto its rear end.

"A barrier," Strange commented. "Invisible, impenetrable, built to keep the Mindless Ones out."

"Precisely," said Clea. "And who do you think created and sustains the barrier?"

"Dormammu."

"And what do you suppose might happen if, by some miracle, you beat Dormammu today? Render him powerless somehow? Kill him, even?"

"The barrier would fall," said Strange, "and the Mindless Ones would come storming through."

"And that would be the end for everyone who lives here."

Strange watched the crowd of Mindless Ones as they thumped vainly at the barrier, desperate to lay their paws on him and Clea, whom they viewed as prey.

"I've seen enough," he said to Clea. "I'm heading back to Dormammu's citadel."

He re-entered the kaleidoscopic tunnel, with Clea alongside him, and moments later he was in the antechamber once more.

"Well?" she said. "Now do you understand what's involved? You can't fight Dormammu. You mustn't."

Strange shook his head somberly. "I don't have a choice. Someone has to nip his plans for Earth in the bud."

"You'd protect your own race, at the possible expense of ours?"

He bowed his head. "If that's how it has to be, then yes. It's not what I want, believe me."

"I thought..." Clea glared at him. "I just thought you'd understand."

"I do. That's what makes the decision so difficult."

"And you won't change your mind?"

"No."

"Then damn you, Stephen Strange," Clea said, her lip curling bitterly. "Damn your arrogance and your lack of empathy."

"It's not arrog—"

But Strange was talking to thin air. She was gone.

He sighed. Clea, through no fault of her own, had just made his job significantly harder by muddying the moral waters.

Then a thought occurred to him.

Or had she?

Had she possibly just handed him the key to victory?

STRANGE TOOK a few minutes to collect himself, then left the antechamber for the room where Dormammu awaited.

In the interim, the room had been miraculously restructured so that it now resembled, more than anything else, a stadium. There was an arena and raked rows of seats around it filled with Dormammu's peons, who formed a ragged, petulant audience several thousand strong. They were there to support their ruler, but only because they had no choice in the matter.

Dormammu himself stood expectantly at the center of the arena.

And he was not alone.

Beside him, encased in a spiky crystalline mass like a butterfly in amber, was Clea. She was held in stasis, alive but immobilized. Her expression was frozen in shock.

"What's she doing here, Dormammu?" Strange demanded.

"Why is she trapped like that?"

"Why ask what you already know, Strange?" the Lord of the Dark Dimension replied. "My niece has betrayed me."

"Your… niece?"

"Did she not tell you that? Yes, Clea is my sister Umar's child. Umar and I are estranged, and her daughter has always had an ambivalent attitude towards me. It appears that that has evolved into outright sedition."

"All she did was try to convince me not to fight you," Strange said. He was finding it difficult to believe that Clea and this grotesque, malevolent monstrosity could be related by blood. "Her motives were pure."

"I should tolerate betrayal? No! Her fate is linked with yours, Strange. You lose, you die, and lovely young Clea dies too."

"But if I win, you'll free her?"

"You're not going to win!" Dormammu scoffed.

"*If* I do, you swear no harm will come to her?"

"Very well." Dormammu nodded. "I am not without honor. You have my word that, *if* I should lose, I shall let Clea go. Now, enough of this prattling." He raised his arms and his voice, addressing the crowd. "Hear me, one and all. I have challenged Doctor Strange to a duel to the death. He has accepted. Now, let battle commence."

At this announcement, a desultory cheer went up from the audience, some of them managing to muster up more enthusiasm for the imminent event than others. Whatever their feelings towards their lord and master, the fight wasn't much cause for excitement; its outcome was a foregone conclusion.

Dormammu gathered his power. The air crackled electrically, as though at the advent of a summer storm.

Strange stood poised, ready to withstand whatever the Lord of the Dark Dimension threw at him.

This wasn't going to be about winning or losing. This was going to be about surviving.

DORMAMMU'S FIRST few attacks were tentative, gauging Strange's resistance, testing his abilities. Strange gave a good account of himself, meeting each spell head-on with an appropriate counterspell.

Then Dormammu escalated his assault, using various techniques to dazzle and confound an opponent—enmeshing coils of light, darting tongues of flame, booming sonic detonations. Strange held his ground and endured, before deploying a barrage of similarly bewildering effects.

Dormammu brushed them off as though Strange had merely pelted him with feathers. Hunching down, he generated a pulsating fireball between his hands and bowled it across the arena at Strange.

Strange deflected the fireball straight back at its creator, who dispersed it into harmless flickering shreds. Dormammu's fiery face registered condescending approval, seeming to acknowledge that Strange was not unskilled.

Then came a thunderously devastating blast. Strange only just succeeded in raising a Shield of the Seraphim in time, and was rocked back on his heels by the sheer concussive impetus of the force Dormammu unleashed on him. The shield remained intact, but only just.

Smoke swirled. Dust settled. Dormammu evinced surprise when the air cleared and the Earth magician was still alive. So did the audience. There were a few intrigued murmurs. Had the Dread Dormammu found a near-equal?

Dormammu tried to melt Strange into sludgy ooze. Strange resolidified himself.

Dormammu struck at him with a flock of winged daggers. Strange repelled them like a batter driving off multiple pitches at once.

Dormammu surrounded him with a many-faceted prism that folded Strange in on himself. Strange, briefly turned into human origami, looking like a Picasso portrait, was able to restore his form.

With every attack that Strange nullified, Dormammu grew

more irritated. The audience, meanwhile, grew more impressed by the outsider. They did not at all mind seeing their cruel ruler being given a hard time. One or two of them even decided to root for Strange, albeit quietly, celebrating with a surreptitious clenched fist or an under-the-breath "Yes" each time he emerged unscathed from Dormammu's latest assault.

Dormammu redoubled his efforts. All Strange could do now was manage whatever came his way. It was taking everything he had just to hold his own against such a formidable adversary. His stamina was waning. He didn't know how much more of this he could stand.

What he did know was that Dormammu was using up his power and having to draw on his deepest reserves. And the more power he expended on combat, the less of it he had to support the barrier which kept back the Mindless Ones. Sooner or later those blundering, aggressive creatures would break through. Strange prayed it would be sooner. Later, for him, might just be too late.

IN TIBET, the Ancient One was also feeling the strain.

The effort of maintaining the portal to the Dark Dimension was taking its toll. When he was young, he could have kept a magical gateway like this open for a day or more. Now, barely a couple of hours after Strange had stepped through it, he was succumbing to exhaustion. The portal wavered, threatening to collapse in on itself. If it went, he doubted he could conjure up another any time soon. Without it, Strange would be trapped and might never find his way back to Earth.

The Ancient One's mystical senses told him that his disciple's mission had reached its crux. More than that, Strange had gone against his advice and was challenging Dormammu personally.

"That hotheaded streak of yours, Stephen," he muttered. "I fear it will be the death of you."

He prayed to the Vishanti, begging them to grant him strength and to look kindly upon Doctor Strange in his hour of need. It was all he could do. That, and not let the portal fail.

———o———o———

STRANGE WAS on the ropes. He felt dizzy and nauseous with fatigue. It was getting harder and harder to repel Dormammu's attacks. His whole body seemed as heavy as lead. He didn't think he could last another minute.

Dormammu, meanwhile, was unrelenting. He pounded away at his opponent, not letting up, offering no quarter. He was aware that, among the audience, there were those giving Strange their tacit approval. He could not permit that. He could not allow a scintilla of disloyalty to flourish in his subjects. It must be crushed, and that would be achieved by crushing Strange comprehensively, demonstratively, uncompromisingly.

"Submit, Strange," he said. "This can only end one way. Surrender to the inevitable."

"Never," Strange gasped. "Not… while there's breath… in my body."

"As you wish."

The onslaught persisted, but Strange noticed a certain lack of focus creeping into Dormammu's attacks. Or was that just wishful thinking? No, the Lord of the Dark Dimension seemed distracted, he was sure of it. His spells had started to lack form and cohesion.

Could it be…?

"No," he heard Dormammu say. Then, louder, "No!"

"What's the problem, Dormammu?" he enquired. "Getting tired? Not me. I can keep this up all day."

Dormammu fired off a blast of the Flames of the Faltine at him, but it felt perfunctory to Strange, as though his mind was on other things.

"Something bothering you?" Strange went on.

"Enough!" Dormammu barked. "This contest is hereby suspended. I shall deal with you later, Strange. There is a more pressing matter requiring my attention."

"Might it have something to do with the Mindless Ones?"

"How do you know about that?"

"They've broken through the barrier, haven't they?"

Consternation erupted amid the audience at these words. There were gasps of horror and howls of dismay.

"How long before they reach the city, Dormammu?" Strange said. "Not long, I'd imagine. You'd better get out there and stop them before they besiege the place. Your subjects are counting on you."

"I can," Dormammu said. "I can stop them."

"You don't sound very confident. You've already used up a lot of your power fighting me. Do you really have enough left in the tank for the Mindless Ones?"

"That's immaterial. I have to try. If I cannot repel them, we are all doomed."

Dormammu conjured a tunnel, as Clea had done.

"Wait!" Strange called out.

Dormammu paused at the tunnel's threshold. "What now?"

"I'm coming with you."

"You?" Dormammu sneered. "Why? What possible use do you think you can be?"

"You need help. I can give it."

"Your magic is as depleted as mine. More so."

"Any help's better than none, don't you think?"

The Lord of the Dark Dimension wavered. Then, with a brusque shrug, he indicated that Strange should follow him.

In seconds, they were at the borderlands. Mindless Ones were shambling purposefully through the fragmentary, haphazard geography of that region. Any lifeforms they encountered, be it fauna or flora, they either trampled underfoot or incinerated with optic energy blasts.

Dormammu hurried to a patch of high ground, from which vantage point he could survey the Mindless Ones' movements.

"There is still time," he said. "If I can just resurrect the barrier a little further inside the realm…"

He began summoning the necessary power. Strange, beside him, doubted he would succeed. Everything about Dormammu, from his voice to his posture, betokened debility. His magic would not be adequate to the task.

"I can reinforce you," Strange said. "I'm going to open the Eye of Agamotto and bathe you in its light. Stand still and let its power seep into you, adding to your own."

"Agamotto? But he represents everything I am not. You are not mixing like with like."

"It won't be easy for you. It may well hurt. A lot. But it's the only option."

Dormammu's growl was like hot coals settling in a grate. "Get on with it."

Strange commanded the Eye to project every last ounce of its power into Dormammu. As its glow enveloped Dormammu, he began to scream, a hoarse, wretched sound that almost made Strange pity him. Almost.

"The barrier, Dormammu," he said. "Concentrate on that."

Trembling, grimacing in agony, Dormammu directed his gaze on the encroaching Mindless Ones. The nearest of them were just a few dozen yards away and making for the mound where Strange and Dormammu stood. Their dogged implacability was menacing in itself, but made all the more so by their stony silence. They were little more than organic machines. Locusts serving a single cause: destruction.

Now they were closing in, almost within touching distance. Dormammu was quaking with effort as he absorbed the Eye of Agamotto's power and transmuted it into a form that could augment his own. Without his barrier, he and Strange would be overrun.

Strange did not rate their chances of survival highly.

At the very last moment, with the Mindless Ones practically on top of them, Dormammu let out a strangulated, guttural yell. Strange could not tell if it meant triumph or disaster.

He had his answer when the oncoming Mindless Ones recoiled.

Dormammu sank to his knees. "It is done," he said feebly. "It is done. Please, Strange. Turn that thing off."

Strange closed the Eye of Agamotto, bringing a sigh of relief from Dormammu.

The Mindless Ones advanced again and staggered back. The barrier was in place once more. Repeatedly they butted up against it. They battered it with their fists. Several of them lashed out at it with their optic blasts.

The barrier held.

○———○

BACK AT the citadel, Strange and Dormammu faced each other again in the arena.

This time, however, it was different.

"I am…" Dormammu began. He seemed to be having difficulty finding the words. "I am in your debt, Strange. If not for you, the Dark Dimension would have been annihilated."

"Is that a 'thank you', Dormammu?" said Strange.

"No. It's a 'curse you'. Curse you for forcing me to accept your aid. Curse you for putting me in that position. Curse you for doing what nobody has done since time immemorial: humbling the Dread Dormammu."

"You just said you're in my debt. I'm going to call it in right now. I want two promises from you."

"Name them."

"I want you to release Clea and assure me no harm will come to her," Strange said.

"Very well."

With a wave of a hand, Dormammu made the mass of crystal imprisoning Clea disappear. She sank to the floor, her limbs numb from being stuck in one position for so long.

"And the second promise?" Dormammu said.

"You vow never to invade Earth."

The Lord of the Dark Dimension was indignant. "You ask too much."

"You told me earlier that you're not without honor," Strange said. "Prove it. Give me your word. You will never invade Earth."

Dormammu looked around at the denizens of his realm assembled in the stadium. Thousands of pairs of eyes were fixed on him, awaiting his decision.

He ruled with an iron fist. He was a ruthless dictator. But he had a moral code, Strange could tell, and there was no way he could afford to look undignified before his people—the same people he had hoped to impress by trouncing Strange in front of them. He had to salvage something from this undesirable situation. He had to show strength of character. That was what Strange was betting on.

"So be it!" Dormammu snarled. "You have your promise. But don't think you've won here today. I shall have my vengeance upon you, one way or another. I shan't rest until you've paid for what you've done."

"Whatever makes you feel better," said Strange.

Dormammu flapped a hand. "Away with you, mortal."

CLEA OFFERED to escort Strange to the portal by which he had entered the Dark Dimension.

"I cannot thank you enough," she said as they traveled there by magical, kaleidoscopic tunnel. "Not only did you save me, you saved my people. And, moreover, you have given them hope. You have shown them that Dormammu is not unbeatable. There may yet come a day when he can no longer keep them down, when they throw off his yoke of oppression and are free."

"Let's hope so," said Strange. "In the meantime, Clea, you've not exactly endeared yourself to your uncle. I imagine you've put yourself in serious danger by betraying him."

"I can handle him. Besides, you had him promise not to harm me."

"Promises can be broken. All I'm saying is, if you want to, you could come to Earth with me."

"You're asking me to abandon my home? Everything I know and understand?"

"For your own protection."

Clea gnawed her lip. "I wish… I wish I could, Stephen Strange. But there is much that binds me to this place, and while I remain, I can at least try to exert a positive influence on Dormammu."

They reached the portal. "Last chance," Strange said. "You're sure I can't get you to change your mind?"

She looked at him, and he saw something in her silver-flecked eyes, something he suspected was in his own eyes too: hope and regret. He was sure the two of them could become friends. And perhaps, possibly, probably, more than friends. But only if they had time. Only if the circumstances were anything other than what they were.

She shook her head. She laid a hand on his cheek. It rested there just briefly.

"You must go," she said. "Now. That portal is barely holding together."

She turned round and walked off.

Strange hoped she would glance back. She didn't.

He turned too and stepped into the portal.

ON EARTH, he found the Ancient One in a state of near-collapse.

"Master, I'm back," he said.

The Ancient One blinked up at him. He was sallow-skinned and scarcely seemed able to focus his eyes.

"Stephen?" he said in a faint croak. "You're alive. You made it."

"I did. Dormammu is dealt with. You can close the portal."

"Thank Oshtur!" the Ancient One sighed.

The portal buckled and imploded, snapping out of existence. Simultaneously, the Ancient One sagged back onto the cushions beneath him, his eyelids fluttering shut.

Anxiously, Strange checked his pulse and his breathing. Both were stable and steady, if a little weak. The Ancient One had merely fainted. Given rest and time, he ought to be fine.

He went in search of Wong. The Ancient One's trusty servant would want to know his master's status. He would also, if asked nicely, rustle up a meal for Strange.

Strange was famished. Defeating an all-powerful otherworldly entity was hungry work.

o———o

THE AFOREMENTIONED all-powerful otherworldly entity was in an aggrieved, restless mood. On a rooftop terrace on the highest tower in his citadel, he paced back and forth. He muttered to himself. If he had had teeth to gnash, he would have gnashed them.

Yes, he'd promised Strange he would not invade Earth.

Yes, he would have to adhere to that promise.

But he didn't necessarily have to renounce his ambition to conquer that other realm, did he?

Dormammu had given his word, but words were malleable.

He was sure he could find a loophole in his vow.

There were always loopholes.

TWELVE

DAYS PASSED at the Ancient One's retreat. After returning from the Dark Dimension, Strange had stayed to help look after his master and ensure he made a full recovery. He and Wong took it in turns to keep vigil at the Ancient One's bedside, and thanks to a combination of Strange's Western medical knowledge and Wong's traditional Eastern remedies, the elderly Tibetan rallied. He still needed plenty of sleep—not surprising given the ordeal he had put himself through—but his vital signs were strong, remarkably so for a man of his age.

One morning, Strange came in to find him sitting up in bed. His wizened cheeks had much of their old color back.

"Master, you're looking well."

"I'm feeling well," said the Ancient One. "Maybe not 'firing on all cylinders', as you might say, but getting there. I have something for you, Stephen. Take a look in there."

He gestured with a gnarled hand at a chest in the corner of the room. It was a beautiful object, made of teakwood with polished brass fittings and intricately carved motifs of mountains, clouds and birds.

Strange undid the clasp and opened the lid. Inside the chest lay a folded cloak and an amulet. The amulet looked like a more ornate version of his own Eye of Agamotto, circular rather than square, with a petal-like pattern molded around the perimeter.

"That," said the Ancient One, "is an older Eye of Agamotto. It is, indeed, my own. It's more powerful than yours, thrice blessed personally by Agamotto himself. Take it."

"I can't," said Strange. "Don't *you* need it?"

"I haven't used it in many a year. You stand on the frontlines between good and evil, far more than I do these days. I'd rather you had it."

"But…"

"Do it. Make an old man happy."

"All right. And the cloak?"

"Watch."

The Ancient One nodded his head back, as though in greeting.

The cloak unfurled itself from the chest, rising to hover in front of Strange. It was full-length and woven from a rich red cloth, with bright yellow, filigree-pattern trim. Its collar jutted up in crescent shapes on either side of the wearer's head. It bobbed in the air, in a manner he could only think of as eager.

"The Cloak of Levitation," the Ancient One said. "A useful addition to any magician's arsenal. Again, it was once mine, but I bequeath it to you. Try it on."

Strange draped the cloak around his shoulders.

"Use the amulet to secure it at the neck."

He did as suggested, removing his old amulet first. The cloak seemed to hug itself to him, as though they belonged together.

"You are not Sorcerer Supreme yet," the Ancient One said, "but with your defeat of Dormammu you have taken a significant step towards that goal. I present you these gifts as a milestone on your journey. They mark an evolution, but also increased risk and responsibility. The path of magic is ever upward, and the higher you climb, the greater the hazards. It has always been that way. It always will be."

STRAIGHT AWAY Strange began practicing with the cloak. His first attempts were awkward and hesitant. It was an unnerving sensation, lifting off from the ground, buoyant as a balloon, and he wasn't sure he liked it. He and the cloak had a mental link, and through this he could regulate how high it flew, its speed and its direction. The cloak, although designed to be responsive to its wearer's wishes, seemed keen to show off its abilities, and he kept having to restrain its exuberance, scared it was going to propel him into a wall or shoot him into the stratosphere. It was like breaking in a wild colt.

In time, his confidence grew, and the cloak became more responsive and controllable, until eventually they were a unit, man and garment in complete sync with each other. Borne aloft by the billowing fabric, Strange soared among the Himalayan peaks, as agile in the air as any eagle. Flight became a pleasure, almost second nature.

With the Cloak of Levitation mastered, and the Ancient One's recuperation coming on nicely, Strange contemplated returning to New York. He broached the subject with Wong privately one evening.

"Duty calls," he said. "You don't need my help when it comes to tending to our master's needs any more. I'm not sure you ever did. Just call me if he takes a turn for the worse or there's any significant alteration in his condition."

"Of course," Wong said. "You needn't worry. The Ancient One may be old, but he has the constitution of an ox."

"I worry only because he doesn't seem to take care of himself. For instance, overexerting himself to keep that portal open."

"Good thing he's got me to take care of him, then," said Wong. "Go home, Doctor Strange. Everything here is under control."

NO SOONER did he arrive back in New York than Strange was called on to battle the Devious Demon, a wizard who had ambitions to conquer the world. Born Devon Darlington III, this scion of a wealthy Bostonian family had spent much of his life and a large proportion of his inherited fortune on occult pursuits. He believed that the rest of the human race should bow down at his feet and worship him. Strange soon disabused him of that notion.

Shortly afterwards he fought Tiboro, a mystic despot from ancient times who had once been venerated as a god, and who had kidnapped the cast of a hard-hitting paranormal-skeptic TV show via an idol of himself that had recently been unearthed in Peru. He regarded these captives as the first of millions of mortals he would dominate, seeing a moral vacancy at the heart of modern civilization that he could exploit to further his tyrannical ends. Strange forced Tiboro, the self-styled "spirit of decay", into surrendering, and retrieved the television presenters, whose experiences completely overturned their previous dogmatically held views.

To someone who'd not long ago put the Dread Dormammu in his place, adversaries like the Devious Demon and Tiboro were comparative walkovers, but Strange was careful not to become complacent. He knew from bitter experience where *that* could lead. Fate had a way of bringing low those who thought too highly of themselves. He maintained a state of vigilance, and more than once his mind turned to Baron Mordo. Mordo would not have taken kindly to finding his vacant body in a dumpster on the Lower East Side. If he hadn't loathed Strange already, the insult would have tipped him over the edge. Strange knew it wouldn't be long before Mordo struck at him again.

"Well," he said to himself, "the Fantastic Four seem to be at constant loggerheads with the Latverian autocrat Victor Von Doom. Spider-Man is forever fighting the Green Goblin. Everyone has a nemesis. Mine just happens to be an aggrieved European aristocrat who needs a better barber."

STRANGE MIGHT not have been so dismissive of Mordo if he could have seen him just then.

For several days Mordo had been communicating across the membrane dividing Earth and the Dark Dimension. A mystical conduit had been set up between his castle and Dormammu's citadel, and every morning Mordo received a charge of magical power through it, direct from Dormammu himself. He would kneel before the conduit, like a supplicant, and allow the power to infuse him. For an hour it would fill his body like cold, beautiful fire, lighting up his nerve endings, igniting the marrow of his bones, sending a rush of ecstasy through his brain. Every time, he would stagger away afterwards feeling dazed but exhilarated.

The transfer of power had to be done piecemeal like this. The total amount Dormammu planned on imparting to Mordo would have been too much to cope with all at once. It would have scorched him from the inside out and left him a smoldering husk. Receiving it little by little meant his body could acclimate to it and absorb it. It was like sunbathing, fine in small doses but in excess it could roast you.

Mordo was not a patient man, but he understood this was the only way he could achieve the levels of magical ability he aspired to. He chafed nonetheless. How long would it be before he was ready? How long before he could at last avenge himself upon that wretched miscreant Stephen Strange?

He put this question to Dormammu, who replied, "The human anatomy is a frail thing, Mordo. We are having to make accommodation for that. But I must say, your complaining gives me pause. Perhaps I should rescind my offer and take it all back. You hardly seem deserving of my munificence."

"No!" Mordo cried. "Oh no, Dread One. Don't do that. I was merely expressing my eagerness to get started, that's all. I want to see

Strange destroyed as much as you do. He cannot be permitted to live, not after the humiliations he's heaped on both of us."

Dormammu grimaced, unhappy at being reminded of his defeat at Strange's hands. "I have pledged not to attack Earth, and that implies not attacking Doctor Strange. But should *you* attack him, my vow remains unviolated, even if your power happens to be amplified by my own."

This sounded like sophistry to Mordo's ears, the sort of argument unscrupulous lawyers used to win cases, but that didn't trouble him in the least. "We both get what we desire. And with Strange gone, your compact with him is null and void, isn't that true?"

"Just so," said Dormammu. "The way for conquest will be cleared in every respect. There'll be nothing and no one to hold me back."

Mordo genuflected before the conduit. "Then imbue me once more with your essence, Dormammu. Gift me another tiny fraction of your great might."

It came in a thrilling, raging surge, and Mordo reveled in it. An hour later it was finished and he was one step closer to making Strange pay for his transgressions. That bit nearer to squashing the American arriviste like the shameless, irritating little insect he was.

THIRTEEN

DAWN GILDED the mountaintops overlooking the Ancient One's retreat as a trio of figures stole along the footpath that wound up towards that building.

Baron Mordo led the party of three. Accompanying him were Contessa Alessandra Fabrizzi and Edwin Cuthbertson, Duke of Hendersleigh, both accomplished mages themselves. Both, not coincidentally, were members of the landed gentry, with lineages going back centuries and wizardry in their genes. These two were a study in contrasts: the Italian woman tall and thin with an imperious Roman nose, the Englishman short and squat with a nose whose clay-gray bulbosity betrayed an abiding fondness for single malt whisky. Both of them belonged to the Counterclockwise Circle, an exclusive coterie of hereditary magic users who met up at irregular intervals to exchange tips on spellcasting and share news about the latest necromantic tome they had discovered or mystical artifact they had tracked down and acquired. Principally, the members of this secret organization deployed magic in the service of improving their business interests and their stock holdings, so as to increase their already eye-wateringly vast personal wealth.

Mordo belonged to the Counterclockwise Circle too and had cultivated various alliances within its ranks over the years. Fabrizzi and Cuthbertson were the two members whose worldviews most closely aligned with his own and the two readiest to assist him in any scheme he undertook, regardless of how immoral or illegal it might be. They relished any opportunity to exercise their magical skills beyond basic mind-manipulation and illusion-generating. What was the point in learning and honing such extraordinary talents and only ever using them dully, passively, to make others do your bidding? Much more fun to take them out into the field, as it were, and put them to a more dynamic purpose.

Approaching their destination, Mordo paused to remind his companions to follow his commands to the letter. "Do not underestimate the Ancient One," he said. "They don't call him the Sorcerer Supreme for nothing."

"Sorcerer Supreme!" Contessa Fabrizzi snorted. "Titles are meaningless unless they are inherited."

"It's like when commoners marry and hyphenate their surnames together," said Cuthbertson, nodding in agreement. "They think it confers class. It does not. Class is an innate quality. You are either born into it or you are not."

"Enough!" Mordo snapped. "Let's save the badinage for another time. Prepare your antipersonnel spells. This place teems with the Ancient One's acolytes. I've no great wish to see any of them hurt but equally I don't want them getting in the way. Stun them. Neutralize them. Employ more extreme methods only as a last resort. The Ancient One himself is mine. He must die, but it must be by my hand."

"You truly despise him, don't you, Mordo?" Fabrizzi observed.

"Not half as much as his disciple. Killing the Ancient One will wound Strange. He will come after me hot with anger, little realizing that I am now, more than ever, his superior."

The huge main door yielded to Mordo's ministrations, swinging silently open at the merest brush of a forefinger. He entered the retreat, Fabrizzi and Cuthbertson following.

Mordo swiftly got to work dismantling the magical wards the Ancient One had erected throughout the building. The task was absurdly easy, thanks to the power granted him by Dormammu. Locating the various alarms and defenses was like looking for lit neon signs in the dark. Shutting them off was akin to snipping wires with pliers.

Fabrizzi and Cuthbertson, meanwhile, moved through the premises. They disturbed a young acolyte who was out in the central courtyard, performing some early-morning tai chi exercises by the koi pond. He looked up, startled, only to be rendered unconscious at a gesture from the Contessa.

The pair continued on to the dormitories, dispensing further insensibility hexes left and right. They then entered the kitchen, where a handful of acolytes were readying breakfast. The Tibetans fell to the floor as though in a swoon.

By great good fortune, Wong evaded the two mages' notice. He happened to be down in the storage cellar when they arrived in the kitchen, and emerged only after they had gone.

The retreat was under siege, Wong realized instantly. He should hurry to the Ancient One's side, in order to protect him as best he could. But before that, he needed to call in outside help.

He crept along a corridor to the office, where could be found one of the retreat's few contemporary features: a phone. He dialed an international number and waited for the person at the other end to pick up. He prayed he would get through.

"Stephen Strange," said the voice at the other end.

Keeping his own voice low, Wong said, "It's Wong. We're in serious trouble. Come quickly. Now!"

A WORMHOLE of Weygg-Kalkuun brought Strange to Tibet in a flash. He arrived in the Ancient One's bedchamber moments after Mordo broke into the room. The Ancient One was warding Mordo off but every single defensive spell he wove, however powerful, was easily shattered by his attacker.

Strange didn't have time to recover from using the Wormhole. He scarcely had time to think. He launched himself into the fray, loosing off Bolts of Bedevilment at a furious rate. Mordo was startled, but that was soon replaced by glee.

"Strange!" he exclaimed. "What a delightful surprise. But the only thing you've accomplished by coming to your master's aid is hastening your doom."

He subjected both Strange and the Ancient One to an absolute blitzkrieg. Offensive spell followed offensive spell in rapid succession. It was all Strange could do to keep the shields coming. One after another, Mordo destroyed them. If he had been formidable before, he was now downright indomitable. Strange hadn't faced an opponent this daunting since Dormammu.

As if that wasn't bad enough, Mordo was joined by two accomplices, a tall woman and a short man, who flanked him and added their magical firepower to his. Neither newcomer was anywhere near as strong, but Strange and the Ancient One were now dealing with an assault on three fronts rather than just one. Their foes were rapidly wearing them down. Soon, inevitably, one or other of them would be paralyzed, or knocked out, or worse.

The only sensible tactic was retreat.

Strange opened his new Eye of Agamotto, unleashing a glare brighter than the sun. The three attacking mages were temporarily blinded. Strange took advantage of their disorientation to scoop the Ancient One up in his arms and fly out of the window using his Cloak of Levitation.

○———————○

MORDO WAS the first of the three to regain some vision. Through the pulsing afterimage blobs that clotted his eyesight he glimpsed Strange making his bid for freedom, carrying the Ancient One with him. He didn't pause to question how his hated enemy had gained the ability to defy gravity. He simply projected his astral form out of his body and gave chase.

With his Dormammu-augmented magic, he was more powerful than normal even in spirit state. As he darted after his fleeing foes, he hurled Blasts of Baphomet at them, the deadliest of offensive spells.

The Ancient One put up a protective sphere around himself and Strange that was able to withstand Mordo's strafing, but Mordo knew it would not hold indefinitely. Strange seemed to know it too, since he began veering from side to side, so as to present a harder target. He sped with his passenger across a glistening glacier. He dived into a gully and swerved along its winding course. He swooped beneath an overhang, startling a herd of mountain goats who were perched on the almost sheer rockface below.

No matter where he went, though, Mordo was able to stay on his tail. An astral form which could travel as fast as lightning had no trouble keeping pace with a physical body in motion. Meanwhile he kept up the magical bombardment. It was clear to him, as it must surely be to Strange, that there was only one way this pursuit would end: with Strange's and the Ancient One's deaths. He would eventually shoot them out of the sky like a fighter jet downing an airliner with a missile.

Then a cloudbank loomed ahead. Strange aimed for it, plunging into its misty, freezing depths. Mordo followed him straight in.

He realized almost immediately that he had made an error. All at once he was surrounded by dense, impenetrable whiteness. He had no idea where Strange and the Ancient One had gone. They could be mere feet away from him and he would not know it.

There was an easy solution, though.

"You're in here somewhere, Strange," Mordo said in a loud voice. "But rather than look for you, I'm simply going to expose you."

He summoned the Whirling Winds of Watoomb. A localized hurricane erupted around him, dispersing the entire cloudbank in mere seconds. Amid clear air, he scanned in all directions, expecting to see his quarry somewhere.

He saw no one. There was just blue sky, snowfields, crags, peaks—a mountainscape as untouched and unblemished as it had been for millennia. His astral form scoured the vicinity for an hour, two hours, and Strange and the Ancient One were nowhere to be found.

With a bellow of pure frustration, Mordo gave up the search and returned to the retreat.

○———————○

ONLY THEN, with his foe departed, was Strange able to drop the illusion he had cast.

He and the Ancient One were ensconced in a cave which he had chanced to spot on the way into the cloudbank. No sooner had he entered the cloudbank than he had ducked down and doubled back, passing beneath the pursuing Mordo. He'd flown himself and his master directly to the cave and thrown up a concealing glamor over the entrance. Even up close, the cave entrance appeared to be solid rock, indistinguishable from the bare slope around it.

Mordo might have left the area, but Strange didn't think for one moment that this was anything more than a temporary reprieve. The aristocrat mage wasn't going to let them get away that easily. He would be back, likely with those two associates of his.

"Master," Strange said, "I need to get you to a place of safety, but I don't have the strength to call up another Wormhole of Weygg-Kalkuun so soon."

"Neither do I," said the Ancient One. "I'm spent after that battle, and I wasn't at peak power to begin with. There is, however, a hermit who lives not far from here. He knows me. He was one of my acolytes once, and he'll gladly take me in."

"You think you'll be safe with him?"

"Safer than in this cave, that's for sure. Cozier, too."

"All right," said Strange. "I'll take you to him. But then I'm going to lead Mordo far away from here. While he's hunting me, he won't be looking for you. And while I'm dodging him, I'll figure out how I'm going to beat him. He's infinitely more powerful than before."

"Yes. I fear Dormammu has bestowed yet more of his might on Mordo. He's elevated him to near his own level."

Strange sighed. "So much for keeping promises."

"Dormammu supposes that Mordo will dispatch us both. Then he won't be bound by his vow anymore."

"I don't know whether that's insanely cunning or just really annoying."

"Either way, it's vital Mordo doesn't succeed."

"No argument here. Okay, let's head for this hermit friend of yours."

Strange picked up the Ancient One again, and the Cloak of Levitation conveyed them out of the cave.

MORDO WAS reluctant to report in to Dormammu but felt he must.

When he heard Mordo's news, the Lord of the Dark Dimension was, predictably, not best pleased.

"Eluded you?" he raged, volcano-loud. "Both of them? You mortal bungler! How?!"

"Strange tricked me," Mordo said. "I don't know how, but he did. He won't hide from me for long, I assure you. While he's with the Ancient One, his options are limited. That old fool was weak already and is weaker still after my attack. He's a burden to Strange. He'll always be his Achilles heel. Strange will never abandon him, and that's how I'll get them. Just you see."

"I've invested greatly in you. Don't allow my time and trouble to go to waste," Dormammu said.

Mordo was left head-bowed and ashen-faced after the conversation, and both Fabrizzi and Cuthbertson expressed concern.

"You seem shaken," Fabrizzi said, furrowing her brow.

"Not your usual ebullient self at all," Cuthbertson chimed in, pursing his lips solicitously.

In fact, neither the Italian woman nor the Englishman felt anything but delight at seeing Baron Mordo so clearly unsettled. The members of the Counterclockwise Circle all nursed a secret hatred for their compeers. They feigned fraternity but, underneath it, they were riddled with jealousy and resentment, paranoid about their own status and the status of others, as only the refined rich can be.

"Has either of you tried collaborating with the Dread Dormammu?" Mordo said. "Until you have, I'd suggest you keep your critiquing to yourselves." He straightened up, fixing a look of determination on his face. "Now then, time to find Doctor Strange."

"Shall we form a search party?" said Cuthbertson.

"No. I have something more efficient in mind."

THE HERMIT, name of Hamir, lived in a tiny mud-brick hut on the banks of a gurgling stream. A string of tattered prayer flags hung above the door, and a yak grazed out front, tethered to a pole. It was a crude, meager dwelling but it had the virtue of being hard to spot from the air, thanks to its turf-covered roof, and there was every chance that anyone looking for the Ancient One would pass it by, presuming that so august a personage would never stoop to lodging somewhere so humble.

Hamir himself was a gaunt man, weathered by the sun, in his thirties but looking about two decades older thanks to his harsh, ascetic lifestyle. He welcomed the Ancient One in as though he were a royal guest.

"My bed is yours to sleep in, master," he said in Lhasa Tibetan.

"My food is yours to eat. My fire is yours to warm yourself by."

"Ancient One," said Strange, "please tell your friend that he must keep you out of sight and pretend he has no one living with him."

"I speak perfect English," Hamir said to Strange, in perfect English. "I was in the Ancient One's care as a youth, and one of the things I learned under him was your language. I then went off to study at Harvard for four years with his encouragement, majoring in psychology. I wanted to understand the mysteries of the human mind, but decided that my own mind was the greatest mystery of them all. Living out here on my own, with few modern distractions, I'm able to pursue that subject in complete peace and isolation."

"I envy you that," Strange said, meaning it. "I just hope you understand that you're putting yourself in danger, letting the Ancient One stay with you. Powerful enemies want rid of him."

"They'll have to get to him over my dead body," Hamir declared, thumping fist against chest.

"Let's hope it doesn't come to that," Strange said. He turned to the Ancient One. "I don't know where I'm going or how long I'll be gone. Whatever happens, whatever it takes, I intend to settle things with Mordo once and for all."

"Take care, Stephen," the Ancient One said with a gentle nod. "May the All-seeing Agamotto watch over you."

WRAITHS SPILLED out from the Ancient One's retreat, dozens upon dozens of them, like hornets from a nest. They dispersed to all four points of the compass, with but a single collective thought: find Doctor Strange and his master.

A normal magician could not control so many wraiths at once. The usual maximum was two, three at most. But Baron Mordo was not a normal magician anymore. Commanding a whole army of unruly evil spirits was nothing to him now.

The wraiths hunted high and low. Shortly, a small band of them encountered Strange flying eastward, once again carrying the Ancient One.

For an hour or more they pursued him as he crossed the border into mainland China. Strange stayed low, hugging the contours of the ground, at an altitude of around three hundred feet, and the wraiths copied him. Now and then people below—farmers in a rice paddy, factory workers on a break, children playing in the schoolyard—would glance up to see him whisk by with that man-shaped bundle in his arms, followed by a cluster of semi-translucent, phantom-like figures. It was a startling sight, no doubt, but this was an age when super-powered beings were cropping up all over the world and commonly featured in the media. The People's Republic had some of its own, such as the nuclear physicist Dr. Chen Lu, better known as Radioactive Man, and a warlord by the name of the Mandarin who wielded a mighty personal arsenal in the form of ten psionically powered finger rings. A man flying, with what looked like ghosts in hot pursuit, was a fascinating phenomenon but nowadays not all that peculiar.

The wraiths stayed on Strange's tail but were unable to catch up to him. He traveled at a speed they could equal but not outdo. Finally it dawned on them that their pursuit was futile, and they about-turned and headed back whence they had come. They had information to report to their master, if nothing else.

THE GREAT thing about wraiths, as far as Strange was concerned, was that they were not very bright. Scary, yes, and vicious, but distinctly lacking in the brains department.

Which meant they were easily deceived. The moment he realized he had some following him, he couldn't help but smile to himself. Mordo had doubtless instructed them to look for him and the

Ancient One, possibly airborne together as they'd been when he last saw them. That was what the wraiths had expected to be presented with, and lo and behold, that was what they found and duly chased.

Unfortunately for them, and for Mordo, it was not the Ancient One in Strange's arms but a rolled-up yak-wool rug, supplied by Hamir the hermit. From a distance, and to the lusterless, lugubrious eyes of a wraith, it would have looked like a person.

After the wraiths broke off their pursuit, as Strange had known they would have to eventually, he carried on for a few miles further before at last descending to earth.

He was in a remote, hilly region. First he disposed of the rug. Then he cast a glamor over himself, so that he appeared to be dressed in civilian clothing, and went in search of a road. He hitchhiked his way to the nearest big city, which turned out to be Kunming, capital of Yunnan province. Although he couldn't speak Mandarin, he had access to Dengroth's Spell of Universal Translation, which made him effectively multilingual. He passed himself off as a freelance photojournalist for New York's *Daily Bugle* who'd come to China in search of Fin Fang Foom. To anyone who asked, he said that that infamous anthropomorphic dragon had been spotted around these parts recently, or so rumor had it—although he himself had seen neither hide nor hair of the creature, not even a gigantic footprint in the soil. He was met with knowing grins whenever he mentioned Fin Fang Foom's name. Plenty of people came looking for the dragon, it seemed, the same way they did the Loch Ness Monster in Scotland. Invariably Fin Fang Foom proved just as hard to find. Which wasn't to say it did not exist or wasn't dangerous. It was just—for a rapacious, destructive hundred-foot-tall monster—oddly shy.

From Kunming, Strange caught a train to Hong Kong. It was a long, slow journey, lasting some thirty hours, but it gave him breathing space—time to ponder, to weigh up his options. He had every reason to believe the Ancient One was safe for now in Hamir's care. His own priority was to keep going, keep leading Mordo astray, for as long as he could. That involved leaving a trail for him to follow, and Strange felt this shouldn't be too difficult. A man like Mordo, especially when backed by Dormammu's power, would have eyes everywhere.

<hr>

MORDO'S "EYES" were members of the Counterclockwise Circle. Telepathically he contacted his fellows in that secret society across the world, inviting them to keep a lookout for Doctor Strange and the Ancient One and, if feasible, take them prisoner.

The inevitable response from all of them was to ask what was in it for them. These weren't the type who did charity. There was always a quid pro quo. Fabrizzi and Cuthbertson, for instance, had only agreed to provide backup for Mordo after he'd promised them positions of authority in his Central European empire once Dormammu took over Earth. Likewise, the others now wanted to know how he would repay them in return for leads on, and the possible capture of, Strange and his master.

Mordo knew better than to offer them money. Each of them had more of that than anyone could ever need. Instead, he said their reward would be the transfer of a portion of the Dormammu-given power he currently possessed.

This was a more than satisfactory incentive, and the members of the Counterclockwise Circle unanimously agreed to do as he requested. In truth, Mordo didn't think the power was his to share with them, and Dormammu might well want it back after its use was at an end. But then what could they do if Mordo didn't hold up his side of the bargain? Sue him for breach of contract? The worst that could happen was he'd be ousted from their ranks, and he was hardly worried about *that*. When the world was under Dormammu's sway, with Baron Mordo as his most trusted lieutenant, other magicians would become outcasts and undesirables. The Lord of the Dark

Dimension was not likely to tolerate their existence, not if they might pose a threat to him or prove troublesome. He would seek to exterminate them. He would swat them like flies.

With these wheels set in motion, Mordo returned to Varf Mandra.

Ironically, the chartered helicopter that picked him up from the Ancient One's retreat passed directly over Hamir's hut on its way to Lhasa Gonggar Airport. Mordo didn't even register the presence of that rickety little shack in the landscape below. He was too busy ruminating on Strange's elusiveness. The man was as tricksy as a mongoose. But his luck had to run out sometime, surely. Soon he and the Ancient One would be in Mordo's grasp, and he would not let them slip away again. He would crush them.

FOURTEEN

IN TEEMING, sweltering Hong Kong, Strange lay low for a while. He booked into a waterfront hotel in Kowloon, part of an international chain, nothing too snazzy, and spent a couple of days sequestered in his suite, ordering room service and admiring the view of Victoria Harbour, where traditional junks and fishing vessels jostled for space alongside ferries, tour boats and billionaires' mega-yachts. So that he wouldn't need to maintain a glamor on himself the whole time, he ordered some civilian clothes from one of the city's famous 24-hour bespoke tailors. The man came to his room, measured him, then returned the next day with the shirts and lightweight suits, all excellently made.

He knew he couldn't hide away indefinitely. He had to divert Mordo away from the Ancient One. So he started going out and about, frequenting restaurants and nightspots. He didn't do anything to make a spectacle of himself. It shouldn't be obvious that he was trying to get noticed. He just showed his face here and there, waiting to see if he would be recognized and word would get back to Mordo.

It was while he was visiting the Man Mo Temple on Hollywood Road that he had his first inkling that someone was on his tail. A local woman was sidling slyly along in his wake. She was small and slender, with long black hair that hung down to her waist in a graceful plait. When he paused to admire the temple's Qing Dynasty murals, so did she. When he stopped to gaze up at the mass of incense coils that hung from the rafters, so did she. It was conceivable she was interested in him romantically and just plucking up the nerve to approach him. But he didn't think so.

He went to one of the many Taoist fortune-teller stalls around the temple and paid to have his fortune read. The fortune teller shook the bamboo tube full of *kau shim* sticks until one fell out. The number on the stick corresponded to an oracle in a book which predicted "a difficult journey ahead, with many hazards and impediments, before safe haven might be reached". Strange thanked the fortune teller and turned round to find the woman strolling away from the temple, without a backward glance.

Perhaps he'd been mistaken.

But then the same woman reappeared later that day as he was wandering through one of the city's parks, enjoying the shade from the banyan trees and watching parakeets and cockatoos squabble in their branches. She had changed her clothes, swapping the elegant silk sheath dress and chiffon blouse she'd worn at the temple for everyday T-shirt and jeans. She also had on a pair of huge designer sunglasses this time, which covered most of her face. Still, it was definitely her, and Strange was now convinced she was keeping tabs on him.

Then, in a secluded corner of the park, she attacked.

One moment, Strange was traipsing along a path, minding his own business. The next, he was face to face with a giant cobra, at least forty feet long and as thick around the middle as a man's thigh. Its tail was coiled and its head swayed from side to side, hood flaring, enormous white fangs bared.

Suddenly the snake lashed out at him. Strange threw up a shield, which the cobra penetrated as though it wasn't there. Its maw gaped inches in front of his face, amber-yellow venom dripping from the tips of those fangs.

It was an alarming sight, but Strange stayed calm. He understood that the cobra was merely an illusion. If not, it wouldn't have got past his shield.

He dispelled the shield and turned round, showing the snake his back even as it continued to rear over him menacingly.

"Nice piece of witchcraft," he said to the woman, who stood with her legs akimbo, hands splayed, orchestrating the cobra's movements. "And it'd scare the living daylights out of most folk. But you know and I know that it's all sizzle and no steak."

"Maybe so," the witch said. She dismissed the sham serpent, then changed her stance, windmilling her arms. "This, however, is not."

Bringing the heels of her hands together, she thrust them forward, palms out. A cloud of white dust came billowing towards Strange—some kind of powder.

Here, he knew, was something more serious than the snake. Clearly the witch wasn't adept in just illusion-casting but also, if he didn't miss his guess, in toxins and poisons.

Before the powder reached him he summoned the Winds of Watoomb, which hurled it straight back at its originator. The witch was caught unawares. The powder blew in her face, and she staggered back, coughing and retching.

"I hope that wasn't anything deadly," Strange said.

"Just… meant to… knock you out… for a…" The words tailed off as she crumpled limply to the ground.

"When you wake up, tell Baron Mordo that the Ancient One and I only want to be left alone."

The witch's only response was a dry gurgle. Then her mouth went slack and her eyelids closed.

Strange put her in the recovery position, just in case she accidentally swallowed her tongue while unconscious or there was some kind of fluid obstruction in her pharynx. She hadn't tried to kill him, so the least he could do was return the favor.

Mordo must now know where he was. That meant "goodbye, Hong Kong". Where to next?

THE ANSWER was Madripoor.

Strange flew to Jakarta and took a boat across the Strait of Malacca to that island principality, known for its lawlessness and its extremes of wealth and poverty. This economic inequality was at its most apparent in the main city, also called Madripoor, which was divided into Hightown, home to business tycoons and mob bosses, and Lowtown, a crime-ridden shanty slum. In the past the place had been a magnet for smugglers and pirates—still was, to some extent— and legend told of a vast dragon that slumbered beneath it.

Strange put himself about in both Hightown and Lowtown, haunting the plush casinos and sleek glass skyscrapers of the former and the smoky gambling dens and fetid, fish-stinking wharves of the latter. It wasn't long before he came into the orbit of a banking magnate called Jason Batubara, who approached him at the bar of the Imperial Hotel one evening. Batubara wore an immaculately cut seersucker sportscoat and slacks, and kept ordering Singapore Slings for them both. He reeked of magic.

Strange was unsurprised when Batubara dropped the pretense of befriending him and revealed himself as a fellow sorcerer. He knew the man must have some opening gambit planned. He just wasn't expecting it to take the form of an offer.

"Baron Mordo has put out an all-points bulletin to the Counterclockwise Circle," Batubara told him. "There's a contract on your head, and the whole of the group are gunning for you."

"You included, I suppose."

"I'm with the Counterclockwise, I admit."

"Bully for you," said Strange. "That's one club I'd never be tempted to join, even if I qualified financially and socially, which I don't. But why are you just chatting with me here and buying me drinks? Why so civilized? Why aren't you trying to take me down?"

"Because I've had a better idea. I can shelter you and the Ancient One from Mordo. Bring your master to me, and the pair of you can stay with me in my magic-proofed penthouse condo, in perfect comfort and safety, for as long as you wish."

Strange took a sip of his cocktail. "And in exchange…?"

"In exchange," said Batubara, "while you're under my roof, both of you help me improve my mystical skills. I'll even pay you. Handsomely." He had a winning smile, his teeth as gleamingly white as the pearls on his tiepin and cufflinks. "What do you say? Seems like a sweet deal to me."

"Oh, it does, Mr. Batubara. It really does. Trouble is, charming company though you are, I just don't trust you. I can see it even now: lure us in, lock us up, sell us out."

"Would I do such a thing?"

"I don't know. Would you?"

Batubara's smile faltered, but only fractionally. "So, that's a firm no."

"Very firm."

"Well, your prerogative, Strange. I shan't do battle with you personally. Certainly not here. This is one of my favorite watering holes and I'd like to be allowed back. Besides, a public brawl, even a magical one, is beneath my dignity and would draw unwelcome attention. No one here needs to know about my more esoteric inclinations. I'm just going to give you a polite, friendly word of advice. Don't venture into Lowtown again. Not if you know what's good for you."

NATURALLY, STRANGE ventured straight into Lowtown again. He wasn't going to let someone like Jason Batubara intimidate him. Bring it on, he thought.

No less naturally, Batubara's warning was really a provocation, bait in a trap he had laid.

It was late at night, and Strange drifted into an area of the waterfront that was seedy and run-down, even by Lowtown standards. Soon enough, a group of thugs coalesced around him, emerging from darkened doorways and unlit passageways. They had leering faces and muscled bodies, they carried hammers, meathooks and cleavers, and there wasn't an ounce of magic in any of them. Strange was half-persuaded this was an ordinary mugging, until one of the thugs, the largest and ugliest among them, spoke.

"Mr. Batubara says hi. He also says we're not to kill you, only have some fun with you."

"I think your idea of fun and mine may differ," said Strange. "And there are, what, eight of you? Nine? All to tackle just one of me? Talk about overkill."

"Yeah, well, we were told you're dangerous," said the same man, clearly the ringleader. "Didn't want to take any chances."

"Although, looking at you," said another of the thugs, "I don't see the problem. You ain't so tough. Just a soft-handed white guy who's never done a proper day's work in his life."

"By a proper day's work," Strange said, "you mean tooling yourself up with the contents of a butcher's drawer and ganging up on an unarmed man to beat the hell out of him?"

"Pays well," the ringleader said with a shrug. "Let's get him."

"Or," said Strange, "shall we see how this pans out if I even up the odds?"

"Huh?"

All at once there were not one but two Stranges standing in the midst of the thugs. Those two Stranges divided, like cellular fission, into two more Stranges. The four then became eight.

The thugs were aghast. One of them just dropped his weapon and ran away howling. The rest exchanged baffled looks.

"Some kinda trick," the ringleader said, sounding none too certain. "Done with, like, mirrors or holograms or such."

"Yeah," agreed one of his cohorts. "Think maybe I saw one of those Las Vegas guys on TV pull off the exact same thing."

Strange doubted that. It was unlikely any stage conjurer knew the art of Manifold Bifurcation—although he had heard of someone in San Francisco, going by the name of Moondark, who scraped a living in various low-rent theaters doing sleight-of-hand illusions for undemanding audiences and was reputed to embellish his act with genuine magic.

"The question you should be asking yourselves," he said, "is which is the original and which are the copies."

The answer would have been easy to deduce if only one of the eight Stranges had spoken. In fact, all of them had uttered the words in unison.

"More to the point," they went on, "if we all start running, which of us are you going to chase?"

Suiting word to deed, the eight Stranges scattered. They slipped past the thugs, who, still thoroughly disconcerted, were at a loss.

The ringleader managed to gather his wits enough to yell, "Don't just stand there. All of you, pick one and get after him!"

This galvanized the rest, and they split up and hared off after the Stranges, who by now had a twenty-yard lead on them and were disappearing around corners or down alleyways. Each overtook his particular Strange and swiped at him with his chosen weapon. In seven instances out of eight, the blow had no effect, passing through its target harmlessly. It was like striking thin air. In the eighth instance, the Strange in question ducked sideways and the weapon, a meathook, missed.

The man wielding the meathook was a blocky, square-headed type. He was wearing an undervest which exposed arms so densely bedecked with blurry prison tattoos that hardly any skin showed through the ink. He grinned, revealing several absent teeth. He lunged with the meathook again, and again his intended victim sidestepped.

"It's you," he said. "You're the real one. Gotta be. Them fakes wouldn't be dodging, would they?"

"Guilty as charged," said Strange. "And speaking of fakes… Are you sure that's a meathook you're carrying?"

The man frowned. "Sure I'm sure. What else would it be?"

"A scorpion, perhaps? A really, really big one?"

The man looked down at his hand and shrieked in fright. He was clutching a black scorpion, so large it was practically a lobster. Where there'd been the metal curve of the hook, there was now the scorpion's tail, arched over and poised to sting.

He dropped the thing with a shudder of horror, then stamped on it several times. His face was a mask of disgust.

When he thought the scorpion must be thoroughly dead, he peered at the patch of ground where its mangled remains ought to be. He didn't see the heap of smushed arthropod he was expecting. All he saw was a now slightly bent meathook.

He glanced up again to find that Strange was gone. While he'd been busy dealing with the scorpion that wasn't a scorpion, the guy had slipped away. The thug swore in a combination of English and Tagalog, then trudged off to rendezvous with his pals.

All the other Stranges had abruptly vanished, and the thugs were left empty-handed, their mission unfulfilled. Jason Batubara would not be pleased. He'd paid them a lot of cash to bring the white man in, and Hightown types did not like being disappointed.

Then again, there'd be no comebacks. As much as Hightowners looked down on Lowtowners, they feared them too, and no amount of money could fix that. Each side had its form of leverage over the other. That was how the balance of power, uneasy as it was, was maintained in the city. That was the Madripoor way.

STRANGE MOVED on.

After two populous cities, he tried somewhere small and remote. Alice Springs was an oasis of human habitation in the middle of the great ocean of red sand known as the Australian Outback. Tourists used it as a staging post on their way to Uluru, and there wasn't much to do in the town itself except stay indoors, out of the ferocious heat, and drink cold beer. This was how Strange passed the time, until an Aussie media baron, a Counterclockwise Circle member, tracked him down there and set a pack of hellhounds on him to flush him out of hiding.

Like the eldritch equivalent of paparazzi, the demonic canines were hard to shake off and didn't much care what happened to innocent bystanders who got in their way. To minimize potential collateral damage, Strange decoyed them out into the Simpson Desert. There, amid the coolabah trees and the baking-hot rocks, he stood his ground, but the hellhounds' savagery and sheer relentlessness began to wear him down.

Just when he could have done with some help, help arrived. It took the form of an Aboriginal Australian, who entered the fray whirling a bullroarer over his head. The device—a lozenge of wood on the end of a cord—sounded its rhythmic vibrato drone and opened up a teleportation warp which sucked the hellhounds into an empty nether-dimension.

Strange thanked his newfound ally and asked for a name, receiving a shrug in response and the laconic answer, "I make gateways, mate, so I guess you can call me Gateway." And then the man vanished into the scrub as swiftly and silently as he had appeared.

LEAVING THE Land Down Under, Strange flew northeast across the Pacific to South America and holed up in Delvadia. His thinking was that here in this fractious and impoverished equatorial country, surely, the Counterclockwise Circle's reach did not extend.

On the first full day of his stay, a revolution broke out. This, it transpired, was not an uncommon event in Delvadia. Civilians rioted in the streets of the capital and there were exchanges of gunfire between paramilitary factions. By evening, it had all been settled and a new regime was installed in government.

Then, the next day, another revolution occurred, the political pendulum swinging from whichever extreme it had been at previously to the opposite extreme. Again the streets around Strange's hotel resounded to rifle reports and the baying of an angry mob, until sunset saw calm re-established once more. During the unrest a stray bullet came through the window of his room and put a hole in the wall opposite, but he personally remained intact.

The faction who'd seized power on the first day and lost it on the second took it back on the third. By this point Strange was beginning to wonder whether something untoward was going on. The seesawing upheaval seemed ceaseless.

When a counter-counter-counter-revolution started on the fourth morning, he became convinced the problem was supernatural in origin. He went out in his astral form to look for answers and rapidly homed in on a chronomancer. The magician had generated a fluctuating 24-hour time loop and trapped Strange within it. What had appeared to be a continual to-and-fro of turmoil was actually the same day repeating itself over and over, with just enough divergences to make it feel different each time.

Dealing with the chronomancer was fairly straightforward. The man was a specialist and Strange a generalist, and generalism trumped specialism every time.

Then Strange caught the first flight out of Delvadia.

BOCA CALIENTE in the Caribbean was his next and, as it happened, final stopover.

The island had everything you could want from a tropical paradise—gorgeous weather, swaying palm trees, crystal-clear azure waters, unsullied coral reefs—and Strange's rented beachfront villa looked out over a jungle-fringed bay of such surpassing beauty you might wonder why you'd ever want to live anywhere else.

But there was, unfortunately, a downside: zuvembies. The reanimated corpses encircled the villa one night and subjected Strange to a prolonged siege. Their numbers seemed infinite, and he was in genuine danger of being overwhelmed when salvation arrived.

It came courtesy of a Haitian houngan, who appeared in a cloud of smoke to the accompaniment of throbbing, unseen drums, just as the zuvembies had Strange cornered and were about to bury him under a tide of reeking necrotic flesh. The man cut a striking figure, with a scarlet cape, a diamond-patterned V-shaped sash over his bare torso, and a finger-painted mystic symbol on his brow.

His name was Jericho Drumm and he used Vodou magic to repel the zuvembies, invoking the power of the loa to grant him strength. He also called on the spirit of his late brother Daniel, which was merged with his own, to spring forth from his body and assist him in the fight. It was a close-run thing, but together Strange and Drumm prevailed, and the zuvembies were reduced to heaps of dust and bone.

Afterwards, as they shared a restorative tot of rum together on the villa's veranda, Jericho Drumm told Strange that he had traveled over from Haiti because he had received a warning from the loa.

"It was during one of my regular prayer rituals," he said. He was exceptionally handsome, with sharp cheekbones and a steady, penetrating gaze. Like Strange, his dark hair was streaked with white, in his case a broad band of it that ran from his forehead, over his crown, all the way to the nape of his neck. "The spirits advised me that someone in Boca Caliente needed my help, urgently. So I hopped aboard the first available puddle-jumper."

"And I'm very glad you came when you did," Strange said. "In the proverbial nick of time." He frowned. "Jericho Drumm. The name rings a bell. Aren't you a psychologist? I think I read an article by you in the *American Journal of Medicine* about the misdiagnosis of schizophrenia and bipolar disorder among followers of African diasporic religions."

"I did practice as an accredited psychologist in the States for several years. But I returned home to Port-au-Prince not long ago. Circumstances there led to me becoming a Vodou houngan, which, it transpires, was my destiny all along."

"Ah-ha. Yes, I can sympathize. I started out in conventional medicine and ended up a magician too."

"You are presently on the run, so the loa say. Fleeing from a foe."

"More like leaving a false trail, in order to draw my enemy away from a vulnerable ally. Have been for nearly a month."

"It can't continue indefinitely, can it?"

"No. The point has been to draw fire and take flak, and I've been managing that pretty damn well. Those zuvembies are only the latest instance. I've no idea who sent them. Someone from the Counterclockwise Circle, that's for sure. Someone local."

"It would most likely be Wilson J. Brown. He's a popular Jamaican politician who doubles as a Vodou bokor. He's with the Counterclockwise."

"Ah yes," Strange said. "Sounds like a plausible candidate. But you're right, what I've been doing is only a holding tactic. I can't keep it up forever."

"Perhaps you should consider being less reactive and more proactive."

"Is that Jericho Drumm the psychologist talking, or Jericho Drumm the houngan?"

"A little bit of both," said Drumm, with a wry smile.

Strange laughed. "Then you'd better bill me only half your usual fee for the therapy session, Dr. Drumm."

"I'll at least guarantee you a professional discount, Doctor Strange."

"Funnily enough, I've been thinking along those lines myself. Getting proactive, that is. Enough of all this globetrotting and jetlag. It's time I figured out how I'm going to take the fight to the enemy."

"Where do you reckon the best place to begin that would be?" Drumm asked.

"Where else?" said Strange. "Home."

FIFTEEN

THE SANCTUM Sanctorum looked much as it always had. As he stepped out of the cab into a sleety night-time rain, Strange cast an eye over the building. It had been four weeks since his abrupt departure. The brownstone cladding, the arched windows, the circular skylight with its swooping, crisscrossing pattern—he'd missed the old place.

He tightened his overcoat around him as he crossed the curb to the front doorstep. His round-the-world journey had taken him to some sultry climates. The chill of New York in the fall felt unusually biting to him now.

At the door, he hesitated. Even though he'd had to leave in a hurry, he had made sure to erect the customary protective wards around the house.

They were gone.

Someone had dismantled them.

Some had broken in.

Someone was inside.

Strange retreated into a shadowy corner of the porch where the streetlights didn't reach and he couldn't be seen from the roadway. It was risky, abandoning his body out in the open, but he didn't plan on leaving it unoccupied for long.

Out leaped his astral form, sinking through the wall into the

Sanctum Sanctorum. Cautiously he explored the house, gliding ghostlike from room to room.

He found the intruder in his Chamber of Shadows, among his collection of magical artifacts.

Instantly he recognized the man as Devon Darlington III, the Devious Demon, whose attempt at world-conquering he had thwarted not too long ago. The outlandishly clothed wizard was busy picking the intangible locks Strange had placed over his library of arcane books. Standing in front of the bookshelves, he rotated his hands, much like a safecracker working the tumblers, only he was manipulating not metal dials but shapes in the air, a series of intermeshing cogs of light. One by one the cogs winked out of existence as he undid them.

Strange retreated before the Devious Demon could sense his presence. He was puzzled. During their previous encounter, he had overcome Darlington in his subterranean lair by using the Eye of Agamotto to absorb every spell the other man threw at him. He'd then put him into a trance and implanted a subconscious command. The idea was that, when the Devious Demon came round, he would remember his defeat at Strange's hands and, knowing he would never be able to win against him, renounce the mystic arts. It had seemed an elegant and humane solution, and it had appeared to work. The Devious Demon had wandered away from the battle scene, tossing aside his horned headgear in disgust and muttering about the futility of sorcery.

Now he was back and quite obviously practicing magic again.

As his astral form rejoined his body, Strange deliberated on what to do. He was weary after his travels and had been looking forward to sleeping in his own bed for the first time in a long while. He didn't relish having to engage in magical combat tonight. He wondered if there was some more practical approach he could take in order to evict the Devious Demon from his house.

Call the cops? But then the Devious Demon might attack them magically. A badge and a gun were no defense against the mystic arts.

Summon one of New York's super heroes to help? But again, for all their extraordinary abilities, none of them was immune to magic so far as he could tell. A sophisticated, high-tech suit of armor or some sticky, high-tensile webbing could easily succumb to a well-chosen spell.

Just then, a delivery truck pulled up on the opposite side of the street.

Strange smiled to himself.

Providence had given him his answer.

———○———○———

A FEW minutes later, there was a rapping at the door to the Sanctum Sanctorum.

Devon Darlington III paused in his labors. How irritating. An interruption. Well, whoever was calling, he would ignore them. He had better things to do.

The rapping came again, louder and more insistent. This time it was accompanied by a voice. "Hello? Anyone in? Package for a Dr. Strong."

Darlington clucked his tongue. A delivery driver. What rotten timing.

"Is there somebody home?" said the delivery driver through the letter slot. "Can't just leave the package on the step. I'm gonna need a signature, see."

With a sigh, Darlington broke off from picking the locks on Strange's library. He would see the idiot fellow off. Better that than have him keep hammering on the door and yelling. It shouldn't take more than a moment.

"Yes?" he said, opening the door.

The driver stood with a parcel in his hands. He wore a set of monochrome uniform overalls with the logo of the delivery company stitched onto the breast pocket. His peaked cap was pulled down over his face.

"You Dr. Strong?" he said. The cap's peak cast his features in shadow. If he was in any way surprised or bemused by Darlington's outfit, he gave no sign of it. Perhaps he met all sorts on his rounds, especially in Greenwich Village. For him, a man clad in purple and pink, with dangling, tapered sleeves, a batwing collar and a hat with hornlike projections, might not be such an unusual sight.

"Strange," Darlington said.

"What's so strange, buddy?"

"No. The name is Strange, not Strong."

The driver shrugged. "Okay. That's not what's on the label here."

"Then there has been some sort of error."

"Clearly. This is 177A Bleecker, right?"

"It is."

"And you're this Strange guy?"

"Yes," said Darlington. "Yes, I am."

"Great. That'll do. So, you gonna sign for this or what?"

"Will you go away if I do?" said Darlington.

"Of course. That's kinda how it works in this job. Hand over the package, then move on to the next address on the list."

"Give it to me, then."

The driver proffered the parcel. Darlington reached for it. The driver dropped it.

"Oh man!" he said. "Butterfingers."

"Moron," Darlington snapped.

"Sure hope whatever's in there ain't fragile. Didn't hear anything smash. Did you?"

The driver showed no inclination to pick the parcel up. It seemed this blithering incompetent just could not do anything right. Tutting testily, Darlington stooped to retrieve it.

He didn't see the right hook coming.

HE RESURFACED into consciousness sometime later. He was back in Strange's museum of mystical books and artifacts, but this time bound to a chair with the Crimson Bands of Cyttorak. His jaw ached and his head throbbed. In front of him stood Strange himself, now dressed in his magician's attire, complete with a new amulet and a cloak he hadn't had last time.

"You know, I really thought I'd neutered you," Strange said.

"Only goes to show," said Darlington gruffly. "You're not as smart as you think you are."

"Says the man who just got cold-cocked by a delivery driver."

"You."

"Of course. There was a chance you'd see through any glamor I put on myself, so I opted for a conventional disguise. I used a low-grade persuasion cantrip on the actual driver, and he let me borrow his uniform and a parcel while he stayed in his truck, in his underwear, listening to talk radio. He's dressed again now and heading off to his next port of call. No memory of anything that happened. All he knows is he's somehow fallen a few minutes behind schedule."

"How disgraceful," Darlington snarled. "Resorting to such a cheap trick to beat me."

"If it works…" said Strange with a shrug. "You might argue that a magician overcoming another magician without using magic is the greatest magic of all."

"You might, if you're the type who finds silly paradoxes amusing."

"Now then, I have questions. First, how did you break the mental block I imposed on you?"

"I had help."

"Whose?"

"Baron Karl Amadeus Mordo's," said Darlington. "Wait. I didn't want to tell you that. Why did I tell you that?"

"You know Mordo?"

"We're both members of the Counterclockwise Circle. Now hold on." Darlington flicked his head from side to side. "I didn't want to say anything about that either."

"I'll bet you didn't," said Strange. "Shame those Crimson Bands have got St. Germain's Mandate of Sooth bound in with them."

Darlington spat out a litany of oaths, accusing Strange of all sorts of illegal acts and debauched behavior. "And," he finished, "I mean every word I just said."

Strange smiled. "I know you do. Under the Mandate of Sooth, you're compelled to believe everything you say is true and say nothing you believe is untrue. Why did you come here to my house? Was it just to raid my library?"

"Mordo told me to. I owed him for releasing me from your spell. He said I could break in and steal whatever I wanted. You wouldn't be around to prevent me."

"Nice of him to tip you off like that."

"Wasn't it just?" said Darlington. "It seemed like he was doing me another favor."

"And then I came along and ruined things."

"You did."

"Where is Mordo now? Do you know?"

"At this precise moment? No idea. I've had no contact with him since he came and unraveled your spell. That was a week ago."

"And you have nothing else to tell me?"

"Nothing you would want to hear," said Darlington truculently.

Strange appeared satisfied with the answer. He turned towards the plinth in the middle of the room. "I think the Orb of Agamotto will be a bit more informative than you've been," he said, adding under his breath, "Some kind of homecoming, this. One night of peace and quiet, that's all I wanted, and now I'm looking for Mordo already."

Darlington kept his mouth shut. During the last portion of their dialog, once he knew he was in the grip of the Mandate of Sooth, he had been choosing his words very carefully. What he had told Strange was not as important as what he had left out.

Strange opened the lid of the plinth to reveal the Orb. Darlington looked on as he placed his hands over the scrying sphere. Lights began to flicker and swirl within its depths.

Strange was expecting to commune with the Orb. What he had not anticipated was that the Orb would suddenly emit a burst of sheer, unbridled energy—a massive outward pulse of power accompanied by a deep, bassy *wwwowww* sound. It hit him like an electrical feedback surge, sending him flying. He crashed against the nearest wall, hitting the back of his head with such force that he was stunned into insensibility.

Darlington, who had known what was coming, had closed his eyes and braced himself. The energy burst wasn't directed at him, but there was a chance of residual impact. In the event, he was rocked back in the chair but unhurt. Strange had taken the full brunt of it.

With their summoner rendered unconscious, the Crimson Bands of Cyttorak instantly vanished, freeing Darlington. He got up from the chair stiffly and walked over to Strange.

"You're in for it now," he said. The Mandate of Sooth had dissolved simultaneously with the Crimson Bands, but even if it hadn't, Darlington wouldn't have been lying. Strange was doomed.

AT CASTLE Mordo, a mystical alert was activated. Baron Mordo had been eagerly awaiting it, and although it came during the pre-dawn hours, while he was fast asleep in bed, he didn't mind. The moment he felt the alert, like someone giving part of his forebrain a forceful tweak, he sprang awake with a grin.

Within minutes, he was dressed and opening a Wormhole of Weygg-Kalkuun. Moments after that, he arrived in Strange's Sanctum Sanctorum, looking fresh and fit and ready to take on the world.

For him, with his Dormammu-boosted power levels, generating a wormhole required practically no expenditure of resources. It was little more effort than shoving open a heavy door.

DARLINGTON GREETED Mordo with a curt nod. "There he is," gesturing at the limp form of Strange. "It all went exactly as you predicted."

"Well done." Mordo patted Darlington on the back. "I was wise to choose you for this task."

"I'm just glad I could humble Strange like this."

Mordo eyed the lump on the other man's jaw. "For that bruise?"

"For burrowing into my mind."

Mordo nodded. "You can leave Strange to me now."

"You're sure you don't need any help?" said Darlington.

"I can manage," came the firm reply. "You may go."

Darlington was disappointed, but like everyone else in the Counterclockwise Circle he was well aware of Mordo's newfound abilities. With that upgrade in power there had come no improvement in the man's temperament, and although incurring his wrath had never been sensible, it now seemed suicidal.

And so Devon Darlington III, the Devious Demon, quietly exited Doctor Strange's Chamber of Shadows. A last look back showed him an exultant Mordo bending over his fallen foe.

In a way, Darlington was glad he wouldn't be around for what came next. Whatever reckoning Mordo was about to inflict on Strange, it would surely be hideous.

"WAKE UP."

Mordo slapped Strange's face.

"I said wake up."

Groggily, Strange opened his eyes.

"Booby trap," he murmured thickly. "Orb was... booby-trapped."

"Indeed it was," said Mordo. "Undetectably."

"Not... Devious Demon."

"Obviously not. He would never have had the skill."

"You did it."

"Me. Then I left him here to mind the place. A housesitter-slash-guard-dog. The point was not that he'd overcome you when you eventually returned, but that his presence would provoke you into consulting the Orb." Mordo made a voilà-type gesture. "And so it went, just as I foresaw."

Strange stirred his limbs, only to find that he was bound in the Crimson Bands of Cyttorak, as the Devious Demon had been. These ones felt extra-secure, like a solid iron cocoon. Even if he hadn't been nauseous from the blow to the back of his head, even if his faculties had been in full working order, he doubted he could have broken free.

"So this is it?" he said. "You finally get your wish: me dead."

"Believe me, Strange, I derive no great pleasure from eliminating you."

"Of course you do."

"No. You are little more than an irritant. I feel for you as much as I would feel for a mosquito I swat."

"That sounds like your master talking, Mordo."

"Dormammu is not my master. Not as such. What he and I have is... an alliance."

"And in return for your servitude—sorry, *alliance*—what has he promised you? A seat at the table? A little throne next to his big throne?"

"When the Earth is his, some of it shall be mine."

"Sure," Strange drawled cynically. "He'd never go back on his word."

"Trying to sow seeds of doubt?" Mordo said with a sneer. "Pathetic. I will offer you this, though, Strange. Give up the Ancient One's whereabouts, and your death will be mercifully swift. Otherwise, expect it to be long and agonizing."

Strange's expression hardened. "Yes, that isn't going to happen."

"I'll find him anyway, you know. Eventually."

"Good luck. You won't get any help there from me."

Mordo drew himself up to his full height. "Well then, that's that. Prepare to suffer as no man has ever suffered." Each of his hands became surrounded with a nimbus of pulsating black energy. "So many things I can do to you. Where to start? How about I alter your blood so that it burns like acid? No, what if I inflict you with a dozen cancers at once? Or maybe I'll make you feel as though you're drowning. Drowning forever. All well within my capabilities now. Thanks to Dormammu, any torment I can dream up for you, I can visit upon you. And rest assured, I will be keeping you alive as long as humanly possible, Strange. In the end, you'll be begging me to put you out of your misery, and I will steadfastly refuse."

"Please just get on with it," Strange said, teeth bared. "Anything's better than having to listen to you jabber on all night."

The clouds of black energy swelled, even as Mordo's face darkened with rage. He loomed over his captive, and Strange screwed his eyes shut, as if flinching in anticipation of the unendurable torture that was coming his way—although it could equally have been a sign of intense concentration.

With a cry that was almost ecstatic, Mordo unleashed the power within him. The horrors of his imagination poured out onto Strange, and Strange…

…was not there anymore.

Mordo looked down, aghast.

His hated rival had vanished. The Crimson Bands that had been holding him were reduced to thinning wisps of red vapor.

Mordo glanced around him.

No Strange.

He expanded the scope of his sensorium to encompass the entire house, then the entire block.

No Strange.

No sign of him in the immediate neighborhood.

Not a trace of him anywhere nearby.

"This…" Mordo breathed. "This cannot be. Where?"

He clutched the air.

"*Where?*"

He clamped both hands to the sides of his head and let out a roar of pure frustrated rage.

"WHERE HAVE YOU GONE, STRANGE???"

SIXTEEN

STRANGE FELL

                and fell

                                and fell

        through one dimension

then another

            then another

                      caroming between planes
                          of reality

       careering from world to world

rocketing like a comet

       from a place where cities lived, mated,
         and gave birth to smaller cities

to a place where androids dwelled
in houses made of organic matter

from a place where every person was a
vampire and every home a graveyard

to a place where dinosaurs drove vehicles
fueled by the fossilized flesh of extinct humans

from a place where everything was in reverse

to a place where everything was upside down

from a place where everything was in negative

to a place where everything was

warped as in a funhouse mirror

from a place where everything sagged
beneath crushingly heavy gravity

to a place where every ending was a beginning

and he saw sentient clouds

a civilization of anthropomorphic animals

humanoids and fungi living in symbiosis

oceans where merfolk inhabited jellyfish cities

a race of indistinguishable clones all walking in lockstep

and in one universe he was a giant

and in another universe he was tinier than a molecule

and in yet another, an electrical
impulse shooting along a neuron

and he flitted through countless lives

some of them his own

some of them other people's

living them from birth to death in an instant

and he was solid

liquid

gas

and he forgot his name

and he remembered
he was Stephen Strange

and he knew this must stop eventually

it had to stop

it would stop

and it did stop.

IT STOPPED when the propulsion provided by Mordo's spell finally ran out of momentum. Strange had used the dark magical energy as a boost to his own magic, like a burst of nitro in an engine or an adrenaline injection into the heart. It had been an incredibly dangerous course of action, not only to propel himself into the dimensional void at random but to do it with power borrowed from, ultimately, a quasi-deity. Then again, he could not even have attempted the feat without the added impetus of Dormammu's magic. In essence, he had temporarily become godlike, able to slip the grasp of the Crimson Bands of Cyttorak as though they were no more than water, able to travel between dimensions as easily as riding the subway.

Well, no, not really. Not riding the subway. It had been more like jumping out of a plane and freefalling. Without knowing whether your parachute would even work. A soft landing had not been guaranteed. He might not ever have landed at all. He might have continued plummeting between worlds indefinitely.

But he *had* landed.

He was somewhere.

The question was: where?

MORDO HAD no choice but to relay the news of Strange's disappearance to his "partner".

Dormammu did not take it well.

"Again?" he bellowed, his voice deafeningly loud, for all that it was being conveyed across a dimensional barrier via communication flames in a brazier. "How many times can you let him slip through your clutches, Mordo? How often must we have this conversation?"

"I—I had him bound and helpless, Dread One," Mordo said. "I think he used my own magic to effect his escape. Your magic, rather. Only yours would have been powerful enough for him to do what he did."

"Oh, don't try to shoulder the blame for this onto me!"

"If it's any consolation, Strange has made a grave error."

"How so?"

"As I understand it, he hurled himself through a dimensional rift without planning a particular destination. He wouldn't have had time to. It was a desperate, last-ditch escape, like jumping off a sinking ship into a maelstrom. Where he'll have wound up, not even he knows. It could be anywhere in the Multiverse. Right now, he could be a million, million dimensions removed from Earth, a million, million years away. He could be at the outermost reaches of a lost and dying universe, with no memory of how he got there and no idea how to get back."

"You cannot know that for sure."

"It's the likeliest scenario, given how much magic he channeled," Mordo argued. "Strange prides himself on his ability to outsmart others, but it seems the person he has outsmarted this time is Stephen Strange. His chances of finding his way back to Earth are infinitesimally small."

"Strange has proved resilient before now. There is no saying that state of affairs won't continue," said Dormammu.

"I agree. He's as wily as a cat, and with the proverbial nine lives too. But I'm confident his days of plaguing us are over. Wherever he may he, he is not coming back."

"If so, Mordo, then a major plank of opposition to my conquest of your world has been removed. What of the accursed Ancient One?"

Mordo ruefully shook his head. "Alas, the old man remains elusive."

"See that he is found and eliminated," Dormammu said.

"He will be. Trust me, the Ancient One will soon be ancient history."

If the Lord of the Dark Dimension found Mordo's little witticism in any way amusing, he didn't show it. "Only contact me again when he is dead."

"Very well. And in the meantime, Dormammu, I get to keep the additional power you've granted me?"

"For now," Dormammu growled. "Do not squander it."

○———○

EAVESDROPPING ON this conversation was Clea. She had long ago learned the art of listening in on Dormammu and observing his activities remotely. At first, when she was younger, she had simply been curious about what her uncle got up to. She would watch him with interest as he ranted to his underlings, and meted out random punishments and casual cruelties. He fascinated her the way a predatory animal might, and she knew what she was doing was dangerous—the consequences, if he caught her at it, might be dire—so she made as sure as she could that her scrying went undetected. She had inherited an aptitude for the mystic arts from her mother, Dormammu's twin sister Umar, who had been driven into exile by her brother after the two of them quarreled and fell out. Over the years she had honed her talents until she was as skilled a practitioner of magic as anyone in the Dark Dimension, save its ruler.

The older she got, however, the more she was appalled by her uncle's behavior, and her fascination with him turned to contempt. Dormammu had no respect for the people he reigned over. He despised them and kept them in squalor and degradation. He ruled through terror and thought only of annexation and subjugation.

She continued to spy on him from a distance solely to reinforce her belief that he was a monster. More and more she was convinced that anything she could do to curb his malignancy, she would.

The man from Earth, Stephen Strange, had shown her that Dormammu was not invincible, besting him in front of an audience of his subjects and proving that even those who were weaker than him might win against him. Strange's example had stoked the fires of insubordination that already burned in Clea's heart. Now, more than ever, she wished to defy Dormammu and yearned for a popular uprising against him.

That mood was shared by the people. Clea had contacts outside the citadel. Since Dormammu's defeat at Strange's hands, she had heard that mutinous talk was growing among the citizenry. In taverns, in alleys, in backrooms, rumors of insurrection. Perhaps it was nothing, just the usual fearful grumbling of a bitterly oppressed populace. Equally, perhaps Dormammu's throne was not quite as secure as he believed.

Strange had stoked another fire, too. Clea had felt an instant, powerful attraction to him the moment she set eyes on him, and only a fool would have failed to see that it was reciprocated. He was very handsome, but he was also brave, confident and slyly funny. Turning down his offer to come with him to Earth had been one of the hardest decisions she'd ever had to make. To leave life in the Dark Dimension behind, with all its injustices and limitations, and start a new life for herself elsewhere? And in the company of so captivating a man? Saying no had not been easy.

Now, learning that Strange was lost somewhere in the infinite multiplicities of the Multiverse—maybe still alive but, if so, how long for?—Clea felt a pang. It was regret, and it was fear, and it was compassion. It was also guilt. Perhaps if she'd gone with him to Earth, none of this would have happened. She might have been able to help him, stand by his side against Baron Mordo, use her magics to reinforce his. She might have been in a position to save him.

Wherever Strange was, Clea prayed he would be safe. Meanwhile, her hatred for Dormammu deepened, curdling into something close to abhorrence.

STRANGE LAY in lush meadow grass, winded, breathless, his head whirling. He was in a valley, with steep, forested mountains rising on both sides. It was night, and amid a mass of unfamiliar constellations a trio of moons shone, their collective brightness lending the landscape a golden sheen and casting complex, overlapping shadows. At the far end of the valley sat a vast, sprawling castle, like something out of a storybook, a fairytale fantasia of flying buttresses and toadstool-like turrets, surrounded by a glittering moat.

He'd barely had time to register these impressions when a commanding voice addressed him.

"You. Whoever you are, wherever you're from, run. Get away from here. You're in terrible danger."

Strange sat up. The owner of the voice was a slender blonde woman in high-heeled boots, leather pants and a ribbed tunic. Long lashes surrounded eyes that gleamed intently in the multiple moonlight.

"I'm... sorry," Strange said falteringly. "I'm a stranger here. I'm not even sure where 'here' is."

The woman seized him by the shirtfront and hauled him upright. "I don't know what your game is, sirrah, nor do I much care. I'm giving you this one chance. If you value your life, make yourself scarce. If Shazana finds you, she will assume you're a spy from another kingdom. Maybe you even are. You're obviously an outlander, and spy or not, simply being out here, so near the castle, could get you arrested and executed. Being seen with me, the more so."

"With you? But I don't even know you."

"Who doesn't know Thelengra, former queen of Keletodi and Shazana's half-sister?" the woman said imperiously. "Even an outlander must recognize me."

"Ah, but I'm not an outlander," said Strange. "I'm an out-of-this-worlder."

Thelengra frowned. "What is that supposed to mean?"

After his vertiginous interdimensional plunge, Strange was finding this situation more difficult to manage than he otherwise might have. "It means, Your ex-Majesty," he said, "that I've never heard of either you or your half-sister. I can tell, though, that you and she do not get along. Why else would you be trying to help me, unless you think I may be working for Shazana's enemies?"

"Not get along?" Thelengra rolled her eyes and uttered a derisive laugh. "That's putting it mildly. Shazana is the one who stole my throne. Yonder castle, Conneagle's Keep, was once mine. Shazana deposed me, using her dark magic, and permits me to live there still, but only as a menial, denied the luxuries I once took for granted. That way she can lord it over me all day long, rubbing my nose in my debasement. It brings her joy."

"I see." All of that would account for the haughtiness Thelengra displayed, and also the sadness and resentment Strange detected behind it. "And so you wander the countryside at night, looking for waifs and strays to scoop up and send away before Shazana catches them."

"If I can undermine my half-sister, in however small a way, I will," said Thelengra, "which includes depriving her of potential victims such as you, stranger. Be you spy, or poacher, or mendicant, or whatever, I would not have you become fodder for Shazana's insatiable bloodlust."

"Okay," said Strange. "Well, two things. First, the name is Strange, not 'stranger'. Second, your Shazana sounds like a real piece of work, but it so happens that I'm a magician too, and a none-too-shabby one either, if I say so myself. Given that you're the rightful queen around these parts, it strikes me that I might be the person to help you take back your throne."

Thelengra looked at him sidelong. "You?" She seemed hardly able to keep the contempt out of her voice. "In your jester's garb? You know sorcery? Enough of it to make me queen of Keletodi again? Forgive me if I am unconvinced."

Evidently, a demonstration was in order.

But just as Strange was debating which spell was the showiest and most impressive, Thelengra let out a small cry of alarm.

"Nurbren's holy spicket!" she gasped. "They've found us."

"Who's they?"

Thelengra pointed skyward. "Knights of the Gryphon Guard."

———○—————○———

STRANGE LOOKED up in the direction Thelengra was pointing, to see, silhouetted against the moons, a half-dozen winged beasts. Each carried a rider, and each rider carried a lance. The animals were big, sturdy things, composites of lion and eagle, while the knights saddled atop them wore heavy steel armor, with slitted visors and feather plumes on their helmets.

The lead knight gave a yell, gesticulating at Strange and Thelengra below. He lashed his reins, throwing his gryphon into a dive. His comrades all followed suit.

As the Gryphon Guard descended on them, Strange knew that here was an opportunity to prove his sorcerous credentials to Thelengra. He figured some hurricane-force Winds of Watoomb would blow the gryphons off-course, and he could follow this up with a few well-placed Bolts of Balthakk to stun the knights.

He configured his fingers and uttered the magic words.

Nothing happened.

No spell came.

No Winds of Watoomb.

Not even the slightest zephyr.

"What the…?"

Strange tried again. He was exhausted and disoriented from his trip through the Multiverse. Maybe he just needed to concentrate. Focus his will.

Still nothing.

But at least his Cloak of Levitation must still be functioning.

It wasn't. He urged the Cloak to hoist him aloft. It just hung limp from his shoulders, like a flag on a windless day.

The Eye of Agamotto was likewise inert.

The Gryphon Guard were closing in.

"We should move," Strange said to Thelengra.

"I thought you said you were a magician."

"I thought I was," Strange said flatly. "Come on. We can outrun them, maybe. Find somewhere to hide."

But even as he spoke, he knew it was futile. The nearest cover was the forest, and that lay a good half-mile distant. The gryphons were flying faster than even an Olympic sprinter could run. There was no chance Strange and Thelengra could beat them to the tree line.

Then Strange spied movement closer to hand. A few hundred yards away, a road ran through the meadow, leading to the castle. On that road a four-wheeler coach had just appeared. It was trundling along at a decent pace, drawn by a team of majestic, impressively antlered stags. In the light of the moons, and also of the coach's flickering headlamps, the animals' pelts gleamed like bronze. The driver spurred them on with a flick of his whip.

Grabbing Thelengra by the wrist, Strange set off at full tilt to intercept the coach. The Gryphon Guard had all the tactical advantages: speed, weapons, elevation. Strange just hoped that the element of surprise was in his and Thelengra's favor. The knights might have assumed their targets would stay still, rooted to the spot with fright. They weren't expecting a chase. Perhaps Strange and Thelengra could dodge and weave long enough to reach the coach, flag it down and take refuge on board.

He managed a few paces with Thelengra in tow. Then she halted, digging her heels in.

"Unhand me!" she boomed, wrenching her wrist from his grasp. "I may no longer be queen, but I allow no one to touch my personage uninvited."

"Unless we make it to that coach," Strange shot back, "your personage is going to get skewered by a lance."

Confusingly, Thelengra just smiled. "I think not. I am still the queen's half-sister. No vassal of Shazana's would dare harm me. You, on the other hand…"

The frontmost of the gryphons reached them, and its rider brought it in to land a few yards ahead. He wheeled his mount round, while another two gryphons descended either side of them with a heavy thud of paws. The remainder came to earth behind.

Strange and Thelengra were surrounded, with a half-dozen sleek, sharp lances pointed their way. The coach continued on its way, its driver and passengers seemingly oblivious to what was transpiring nearby.

Still dumbfounded by the mysterious absence of his magic, Strange balled his hands into fists. Outnumbered, unarmed, he would nevertheless fight these knights to the bitter end.

Meanwhile Thelengra stood nonchalantly by, as if curious to see how events would unfold.

"Hold there!" the leading knight barked at Strange. "Identify yourself."

"I am Stephen Strange, and I'm an innocent traveler who's———"

"Your speech and accent mark you out as an outlander, and therefore you are an interloper. By order of Queen Shazana, you must be brought in for interrogation."

"If you'll just hear me out…"

The knight depressed a button on his lance, and a beam of light shot out from the tip. In an instant, Strange was enclosed in a glistening semi-transparent bubble of plasma. The knight angled his lance upward slightly, and the bubble rose from the ground, taking Strange with it.

"Milady Thelengra, I regret that you must return with us, too," the knight said.

"If I must, I must, Sir Gellcaspur. But remember, it's no longer 'Milady'. Your Queen would not like to hear you address me thus.

She has stripped me of all titles and honorifics, and any who use them in connection with me will be punished."

"Of course... Thelengra," said Sir Gellcaspur stiltedly.

One of his comrades trapped Thelengra in another plasma bubble, which she passively accepted.

The gryphons beat their wings, and the Gryphon Guard took to the air again. They flew towards Conneagle's Keep, towing Strange and Thelengra along behind them like fishermen hauling their catches home.

AS THEY approached the castle, Strange searched himself for magic.

Normally its presence was readily detectable. He only had to think about it, and there it would be, a warmth inside, a deep-seated sensation of fullness and capability, always just within reach. Plenty of people in the world had access to the universal wellspring of magic, but few of them ever realized. Some tapped into it unknowingly, using it to perform rare feats of athleticism, intellect or creativity that were deemed genius. Under the Ancient One's tutelage Strange had learned how to draw on magic whenever he wished, to harness it and mold it to his will.

At present, there was nothing. Like opening a faucet and no water coming out.

Was this a permanent state of affairs? Was he cut off from magic for good?

If so, he was likely stuck here in this dimension. There was no way, short of a miracle, he was getting home. That left Earth with only one person to defend it against Dormammu, and he feared the Ancient One, no longer at the peak of his powers, was not up to the task.

The other possibility was that his loss of magic was temporary. The Dormammu power he'd hijacked from Mordo had overloaded his system, tripping some sort of inner circuit breaker and leaving him burned out for the time being. At some point he would mend and recover, and magic would be available to him again. There was just no way of telling when.

Soon he and Thelengra, in their plasma bubbles, were being lowered into a courtyard. They alighted with a jolt, while the Gryphon Guard landed around them. The knights dismounted, and the bubbles were deactivated. Squires came to collect the gryphons, placating the beasts with haunches of beef before leading them away by the reins to their stables. Meanwhile the knights, forming an escort, marched the two captives through an arched doorway and along sconce-lit corridors to an enormous throne room.

Thelengra still retained her air of regal detachment. Doubtless this was not the first time she had been arrested by the Gryphon Guard, and she knew she was immune to sanction. She was going along with the whole farce under sufferance. Strange, for his part, had no choice but to see how things played out and hope he could save his skin through diplomacy and negotiation.

The Gryphon Guard ushered them into the presence of Queen Shazana. She was taller and darker-complexioned than her half-sister, and had startling eyebrows that curved up her forehead like an insect's antennae. Whereas Thelengra was merely self-possessed, Shazana had a look of domineering arrogance about her.

"Who is this?" she drawled, jabbing a finger towards Strange. At her feet skulked a lizard-like creature, a gray-skinned thing the size of a large housecat, with what looked like a perpetual smirk affixed to its reptilian face.

"An outlander, Your Majesty," said Sir Gellcaspur. "We were on patrol and found him loitering within the castle environs. We adjudged him guilty of trespass at the very least. He was also," he added with an awkward cough, "consorting with Thelengra."

"Indeed!" Shazana shook her head, making her large star-shaped earrings jingle. "And I'll wager, Thelengra, that you were urging this man to flee before I could get my hands on him. As is your wont. Or was it more this time? Might you have been actively conspiring with him?"

"Queen Shazana," began Strange, "if I could just——"

She cut him off curtly. "No, outlander, you can't 'just' anything."

"All I want to say is that I'm no spy. I'm a peaceful visitor from afar, here by accident. I bear neither you nor the kingdom of Keletodi any ill will."

"I'll be the judge of that," said Shazana, and the gray-skinned creature at her ankles nodded as though echoing the sentiment. Strange had the feeling the animal was Shazana's familiar, a bestial toady gifted with a crude intelligence and psychically linked to her.

Shazana turned back to Thelengra. "Come along then, half-sister. Tell me the truth. Have you been caught in the act of sedition? Is this the first stirring of a treasonous plot against me?"

Thelengra offered her a wry look. "Now, whyever would I want to see you dethroned, Shazana?"

"Answering a question with a question—and an ironic question at that—implies guilt."

"Then if you want a straight reply, it's a firm no. Until a few minutes ago, I'd never clapped eyes on this man before."

"That doesn't mean you may not have consorted with him beforehand, perhaps through letters."

"You seem to have tried me already, in the court of your own opinion," said Thelengra, "and found me culpable. What's next? Will you have me beheaded? You've taken everything else from me, Shazana—my crown, affluence, the veneration the people held me in. Why not my life too?"

"Do not blame me for your downfall, Thelengra," Shazana said loftily. "I overthrew you because you were weak."

"You overthrew me because you adopted dark magics. You seized the throne because you coveted it, even though you had no right to it. You stole it from me unfairly and unjustly. If I was ever weak, it was only in allowing you to stay around after our father died. I could have had you turfed out of the castle and no one would have blamed me for it. But I chose not to. I showed tolerance and sympathy towards King Lammpetor's illegitimate daughter, and she rewarded me by stabbing me in the back."

Shazana's antennae-like eyebrows knitted together in anger. "Take care with your tongue, Thelengra! I've borne your sniping and your grievances thus far, but my patience has its limits. Show me due respect."

"And if I don't? Will that metaphorical stab in the back become a real one?"

Strange was growing impressed by Thelengra. She was goading Shazana dangerously. If her half-sister was any kind of sorceress, she could obliterate Thelengra with a snap of her fingers. Was Thelengra really so confident that she wouldn't? Was their familial bond strong enough to keep Shazana from committing sororicide?

Tension simmered between the siblings, like the air before a thunderstorm.

At that moment, a servant entered the throne room, bowing low.

"Your Majesty," he said, "the delegation from the city of Thosomayr are here. They apologize for the late hour of their arrival. They were held up at the River Maseine crossing. A flood has washed away the bridge and they were obliged to take a diversion. They wish to offer you their tribute at the earliest opportunity, and crave, moreover, board and lodging for the night."

Strange wondered if this delegation had been in the stag-drawn coach he had tried to catch. Probably, he thought.

Shazana grimaced irritably. "Very well. Fetch them. But they'd better have plenty of treasures for me to make up for their tardiness."

As the servant withdrew, she said to Thelengra, "You are confined to your quarters. Go now, and be grateful I don't toss you into the dungeons."

Thelengra turned on her heel and left, without offering Shazana, or Strange, so much as a backward glance.

"As for you," Shazana said to Strange, "you *are* destined for the dungeons. There'll come a time when I'm ready to question you and learn whether you be spy or traitor. Believe me, I will know the truth. And should it transpire that you are in cahoots with Thelengra, you will have company when you meet the headsman's ax!"

Two knights of the Gryphon Guard seized Strange by the elbows. He refrained from protesting or resisting. He doubted it would do much good. A few hours in a cell might be to his advantage anyway. If his severance from magic was only transitory, it could give him time to reconnect with it.

Shazana lodged herself on her throne, a great hunk of rough-hewn granite studded with inset gems. Even the smallest of these were as big as pool balls, while the largest were fist-sized, including an impressive ruby that had pride of place at the very top. Her familiar sprang up onto her lap, and she caressed its spiny, leathery back absently as Strange was manhandled away.

IN TIBET, an untold number of dimensions distant, the Ancient One lay in bed. He had lately come down with a fever, which Hamir was none too surprised about. The living conditions in his hermit hut were a far cry from the comforts of the Ancient One's retreat. The thin wooden-slat walls did not keep the cold out, and the cooking fire was no blazing hearth. Added to that, the food supplies were meager, barely enough to support one person, let alone two. Hamir had been giving the Ancient One the lion's share of every meal they ate, but the old man was frail and needed more sustenance than that to keep him healthy.

For several days now, he'd not stirred from Hamir's cot. His eyes were glazed and he sweated profusely and shivered. Hamir had gone to the nearest village—a ten-mile round trip on foot—and bought painkillers and antibiotics, which he doled out to the Ancient One at regular intervals and which helped alleviate his condition somewhat. Other than that, all he could do was keep him fed and hydrated as best he could and mop his brow.

Much of the time, the Ancient One slept. Occasionally he would awaken and, if he was strong enough to sit up, Hamir would spoon broth into his mouth. Now and then he would lapse into agitated, semiconscious mumbling, of which Hamir understood perhaps half. Amid the garbled monologue, certain phrases kept cropping up.

"Stephen… He needs me… Can't sense him anywhere… Lost… Where?"

One particular word recurred again and again.

"Eternity."

Several times Hamir enquired what this meant, but the answer was always vague and inconclusive.

"If only… he could know of… Eternity."

Hamir kept vigil over the old man, praying he would rally and the fever would break. He felt both resolute and helpless. The Ancient One would not die, not if he had any say in the matter. But what could he do, other than what he was already doing? He couldn't take him to hospital. He couldn't even call in a doctor. Nobody must know where the Ancient One was, especially not when he was so enfeebled and vulnerable.

And all the while, in his half-lucid phases, the Ancient One would repeat that word. That portentous yet inexplicable word.

"Eternity… Eternity… Eternity…"

SEVENTEEN

THE DUNGEONS of Conneagle's Keep were cold, dark, dank and miserable. They were, in other words, dungeons.

Strange shared his cell with a bucket, a set of manacles and several rats. The rodents did not trouble him overmuch. He'd always found rats to be intelligent and inquisitive creatures, and couldn't understand why some people had a phobia about them.

His jailer was a different story. The man was a sweaty human slug who took great delight in taunting his prisoner through the peephole in the cell door. "Nice and cozy in there, are we?" he would say. "Perhaps sir would care for some sweetmeats? An extra pillow perhaps?" Not that there was even a bed.

Strange tuned him out, along with the scurrying of the rats and the drip-drip-drip of water that seeped through a crack in the ceiling and formed a puddle on the floor. Eyes closed, he sent out mental feelers, scanning in all directions for a glimmer of magic. He knew magic was present in this dimension. Queen Shazana utilized it, after all, as did the Gryphon Guard's lances. He just had to find a way of latching on to it somehow.

At the back of his mind lurked the worrisome thought that the mystic arts were now forever denied him. It would be like losing the fine motor skills in his hands all over again. His second vocation ripped away from him, same as the first, in a single moment of catastrophe.

No. Fear and doubt were luxuries he couldn't afford. He *would* regain magic. He just needed to be persistent and patient.

Hours passed but Strange did not relent. In a change of approach, he assumed the lotus position. He chanted a mantra under his breath. He made himself inwardly calm and receptive. Instead of trying to find magic, he invited magic to find him. He offered himself to it as a willing vessel, a cup waiting to be refilled. So still and tranquil did he become that one of the rats he was cohabiting with clambered up onto his thigh, made itself comfortable and went to sleep.

Dawn light crept in through the tiny, barred window high up in the cell's outer wall. All at once, with a start, Strange opened his eyes. The rat, disturbed, leapt off him, squeaking in annoyance.

Strange grinned.

It had worked. He could feel it in his fingertips. In his heart. In his soul. That tingle. That exhilarating certitude.

He was a sorcerer once more.

STRANGE DEBATED whether he should simply return to Earth. That would be the sensible option. There was nothing keeping him here. He should prepare himself for a long and arduous journey homeward, and he should set off as soon as he felt able.

But he felt an inner tug that he knew all too well. A sense of obligation. The compulsion to do the right thing, the difficult thing, and do it properly. Once, that had meant performing the trickiest of surgeries, such as a thoracic aortic dissection repair or a coronary revascularization, in the certain knowledge that nobody could carry out the work half as well as Stephen Strange could. In this instance it meant rectifying the situation at Conneagle's Keep.

Resignedly Strange accepted that he could not depart leaving unfinished business. Shazana must be deposed. He did not know whether Thelengra would be a better monarch than her half-sister, but it was surely preferable to have her on the throne than a wielder of dark magic.

Just as he was coming to this conclusion, he had a visitor. It was not the taunting jailer, who had given up on harassing Strange once he realized his jibes were falling on deaf ears. Nor was it Shazana, or even Thelengra.

It was Shazana's familiar.

The lizard-like thing insinuated itself between the bars of the window. It must have climbed down the castle's outer wall to get here. Now it picked its way down the interior wall of the cell, darting glances at Strange all the while with its bulging, heavy-lidded eyes.

Strange acknowledged it with a nod. "Come to gloat, have we?" he said as the familiar sidled towards him. The rats had made themselves scarce the moment the reptile arrived, disappearing into a crevice in the floor.

The familiar halted. A fat pink tongue slithered out of its mouth and was retracted.

"I know you're watching me, Shazana," Strange went on. "Seeing through your pet's eyes. Hoping you'll find me here all wretched and miserable, every inch of me quaking with dread about my possible appointment with the executioner's block."

The familiar cocked its head. That smug little smirk did not leave its scaly lips.

"Trouble is, you've misconstrued what I am."

The Eye of Agamotto on his breast opened. Light shone forth, mesmerizing the familiar in an instant. It plonked its hindquarters down on the floor, and its expression went slack, its smirk vanishing.

The reptile, linked to Shazana, knew whatever she knew. Using the Eye, Strange probed its mind, seeking truth.

The infant Shazana, raised in the castle by her serving-wench mother, who dies prematurely of a wasting disease.

Shazana as a headstrong young girl, very much aware she is King

Lammpetor's illegitimate daughter, for secrets do not stay secret long at Conneagle's Keep.

A playmate and companion to Thelengra, the two of them making a mischievous pair, as thick as thieves, for all that Shazana labors all day as a scullery maid while Thelengra is a pampered princess.

The widower king, father to them both, never looking on Shazana with anything but fondness but always favoring Thelengra, the official daughter, lawful heir to the throne.

Shazana in her teen years nursing a growing envy of her half-sister, a bitterness.

A rift developing between the two siblings, a polite coldness, playmates no more.

Shazana, on the cusp of adulthood, plotting how she might one day supplant Thelengra in their father's affections and, maybe, more than that.

Developing an interest in sorcery.

Seeking out forbidden books of magic.

Practicing the dark arts at night.

Honing her skills clandestinely.

Shazana setting out one day on a quest to find a certain necromancer, reputed to be the most powerful in all the kingdom.

Locating him in his cathedral-like temple on a rocky, barren island in the middle of an inland sea.

Throwing herself on his mercy, demanding to be his disciple.

The necromancer, bewitched by her beauty and her forceful personality, agreeing to teach her everything he knows.

Shazana, an apt pupil, acquiring skills quickly, soon surpassing her teacher.

Shazana slaying the necromancer and stealing his greatest asset, the source of his power.

Returning to Conneagle's Keep with her booty to find that, during her absence, King Lammpetor has died of natural causes.

Thelengra, his natural successor, now anointed queen.

Shazana immediately setting about overthrowing her.

Wreaking magical havoc.

Destroying anyone who dares stand in her way.

Her victory complete, the injustices of her upbringing redressed.

Forcing Thelengra to live in humiliation, her status in the royal household as lowly as Shazana's once was.

Ruling Keletodi with an iron hand, backed up by the mighty magic at her disposal.

Demanding tribute from her subjects and also from all neighboring kingdoms, on pain of destruction.

Making an example of one city for refusing the tribute, wiping it out entirely, reducing it to rubble.

Queen Shazana perching contentedly on her granite throne, absolute master of all she surveys.

The Eye of Agamotto showed Strange all these scenes in rapid succession, like a montage in a film. As Shazana's history flashed before him, he realized how he could defeat her.

He also knew how he might be able to get home more quickly and easily than he'd first envisaged.

He shut off the Eye, and Shazana's familiar jerked back into life, its smirk returning. He made sure that it and its owner would have no memory of what had just happened, nor what he had said immediately beforehand. They would not even realize that they had been briefly enthralled.

The familiar appraised him for a little while longer. Strange gazed back at it evenly, betraying none of the triumph he felt inside. At last the reptile seemed to have had enough, and it crawled off, leaving the cell the way it had entered.

Strange settled down to wait. He didn't think Shazana would leave it long before summoning him back into her presence.

HE WASN'T wrong. Barely an hour elapsed before the jailer unlocked the cell door. Two knights of the Gryphon Guard dragged Strange to his feet and frog-marched him, still in chains, up to Shazana's throne room.

Shazana was busy looking over a small heap of valuables. There were gold coins, jewels, silverware, finger rings, some bone china, and sundry other gleaming trinkets.

There were also three piles of smoldering ashes on the floor nearby. A partly singed sandal protruded from one of these. Another contained visible bone fragments and a couple of teeth. An acrid smell of burning hung in the air.

Strange understood that he was looking at the tribute delivered last night by the delegation from the city of Thosomayr. He understood, too, that he was looking at what was left of the delegation members themselves.

"Let me guess," he said to Shazana. "You didn't like what they brought?"

Shazana nodded coolly. Her lizardly familiar was draped around her neck, apparently fast asleep. "They claimed it was all they could spare," she said. "I thought about it overnight, then this morning I bade the delegates see me again. I charged them with fetching more treasure. They said I'd already taken all they had and Thosomayr's coffers were empty. They were lying, and I told them as much. They clamored, they pleaded, they implored. I taught them a lesson. The next delegation from Thosomayr will be a great deal more forthcoming, I'm sure."

"And what about me? Have you decided my fate?"

"I shall tell you once my half-sister—Ah, but here she is."

Thelengra was ushered into the throne room by a knight.

"So, Shazana," she said, "what's the verdict? Have you finally tired of keeping me around? Do I have decapitation to look forward to? I must say, after enduring life as your trophy, death is starting to look very enticing."

"You have long been a thorn in my side, Thelengra," came the reply. "The thought of removing you is tempting."

"If I may butt in here…" said Strange.

Shazana rounded on him. "What, outlander?" she snapped.

"I was just admiring your throne."

"What of it?"

"Carved from stone—it can't be that comfortable to sit on, even with all those silk cushions. Did you have it made yourself?"

"Yes. So? Do you have a point?"

"Really, it's the gems embedded in it," Strange said. "They're the most interesting part. Quite a collection. Must be worth a lot. Particularly that huge ruby at the top."

Shazana narrowed her eyes. "You're looking at it in an evaluating way, outlander. Is that acquisitiveness I see on your face? You think of stealing the ruby, perhaps? Bartering for it? With the prospect of death hanging over you, that shows some nerve. Or is there something…?" Her voice trailed off. "Oh," she said after a long moment. "Oh, I see. Why didn't I notice it before?"

Strange spread out his hands. "That I, too, am a magician?"

"Magic fills you. It oozes from your every pore. By Saddannik's jagged teeth! A sorcerer, right here in my throne room."

"Fills you with alarm, doesn't it? A rival magician, so close to your seat of power."

"No," Shazana breathed.

"That's no ordinary ruby," Strange went on, gesturing at the gem. "Size aside, it's special. It's a vessel. It stores a vast quantity of magical power. The necromancer who owned it before you—the one you killed—used it as a repository. A battery to charge himself up with. You're using it for the same purpose. You've managed to hide that from everyone, even Thelengra. But I wonder what would happen if someone destroyed the ruby. I wonder how long you can remain as ruler of Keletodi without it."

Shazana's face hardened. "You wouldn't dare."

"Oh, I would, Your Majesty. I'd very much dare."

Strange summoned a spell. Bolts of Balthakk sprang, sizzling, into his hands. It felt good to wield magic once more. It felt fitting. Satisfying.

With a cry of dismay, Shazana moved to intercept his attack. Her familiar tumbled off her shoulders as she threw up a shield of pure, pitch-black necromantic power. Strange unleashed the Bolts at maximum strength. Shazana's shield shattered and she reeled backwards.

Strange lunged for the throne, already conjuring a fresh set of Bolts.

Shazana screamed in outrage. She ran after him, only to be grabbed by Thelengra, who put her half-sister in a headlock.

"Do it!" Thelengra yelled at Strange. "I'll hold her. Smash the damned thing into a million pieces!"

Shazana writhed in Thelengra's clutches. Her familiar danced around their feet in agitation.

Strange knew he had only seconds before Shazana broke free of her half-sister. That was if she didn't simply kill Thelengra on the spot with a lethal spell.

Seconds, however, were all he needed.

He flung the Bolts at the ruby.

At the same time, he opened himself up just as he had when Baron Mordo subjected him to that immense blast of Dormammuderived power.

The ruby disintegrated violently and explosively. Raw black magic gushed out in a torrent. Strange absorbed it all, every ounce of it, transfiguring it into interdimensional propulsion.

He took one last glance round and saw Shazana sagging in Thelengra's arms, riven with anguish. Thelengra herself fixed him with a look of sadness combined with profound gratitude.

Then, like a rocket driven skyward by its boosters, Strange was hurled away from Keletodi.

HE TRAVERSED innumerable dimensions. He'd done this before, but the difference was that he now knew what to expect. This time, he wasn't flotsam being borne along by a wave. He was riding that wave like a surfer. He had control. He had direction. He had agency.

Within instants—hours—days—years—lifetimes—he was zeroing in on Earth.

On America.

On New York.

On Bleecker Street.

During a tempestuous night, amid sheeting rain and sky-cracking bursts of lightning, Strange fetched up at the doorstep of his Sanctum Sanctorum.

He lay on the wet sidewalk in a sprawling heap. Steam rose from his body as the rain pounded down.

Eventually he raised his head.

He breathed in the city stink, which no amount of rain-washing could ever wholly cleanse from the air.

Home.

He had made it.

He'd really done it.

Incredibly, marvelously, he was home!

IN KELETODI, Queen Thelengra reassumed her crown. Proper diplomatic relations with all the bordering nations were swiftly restored. The tributes taken by Shazana were returned whence they had come, and restitution was made to the families of those she had slain. The kingdom became a place free of fear and persecution, as it had been before. It was as though a storm had passed and sunshine and blue skies had arrived again.

As for Shazana, she was broken. With the destruction of the ruby, not only was her power gone but her sanity. She had no more magic, and its abrupt loss unhinged her mind, leaving her a hollow, babbling wreck—as brainless as the lizard which had once been her familiar, but was now just an ordinary lizard again. She could no longer take care of even her most basic needs. For the rest of her life, she had to be tended to like a baby and spoken to like a simpleton. She wandered the halls of Conneagle's Keep, a living phantom, often reviled, sometimes pitied, largely ignored.

Thelengra thought this a fair penance for her crimes. Better than execution: being sentenced to live a life that was hardly a life at all.

In the years that followed, Queen Thelengra's thoughts turned often to her savior, the man who had righted the capsized ship of her life, the stranger called Strange. She never recalled him without a small, wistful smile. As far as she was aware, he had perished while ending Shazana's magic, consumed by the explosion that destroyed her ruby. Thelengra would never forget him or his sacrifice.

EIGHTEEN

"AARGH!" EXCLAIMED Hamir the hermit, nearly dropping the tea bowl he was holding. "You startled me."

"I apologize," said Strange, in astral form. "To be honest, I didn't think you could see or hear me when I'm like this."

"The Ancient One taught me a thing or two about the mystic arts when I was a resident at his retreat. I'm no sorcerer but I am sensitive to magic. Your astral form is as clear to me as, well, mist. But slipping in through the roof the way you just did… You'd have turned my hair white, if I had any." Hamir patted his clean-shaven scalp. "Not that I'm unhappy you called, Doctor. The Ancient One is not faring well."

You didn't need to be a trained physician to tell that the elderly Tibetan was in poor shape. His breathing was wheezy and labored. His skin was deathly pale. His cheeks were sunken. The likeliest diagnosis was pneumonia, which was bad enough if you were young and otherwise healthy, but was apt to be fatal in someone as old and frail as the Ancient One.

"How long has he been like this?" Strange asked.

"Ten, eleven days," said Hamir. "I've been giving him acetaminophen and over-the-counter antibiotics, and it's stabilized him, I think. But his fever won't break." He looked hopeful. "From the fact that you're putting in an appearance, I'm assuming Baron

Mordo is no longer a threat, and that means I can get the Ancient One to a hospital, where he needs to be."

Strange shook his head. "I've been away from Earth. Mordo doesn't know I'm back yet, but there's every chance he'll find out soon enough. It's risky me coming here even in astral form, but I had to look in on my master."

Just then, the Ancient One stirred in his sickbed. He began muttering.

"Stephen… I sense you… Your presence… Stephen, you must listen to me…"

"Oh yes," said Hamir, "he's been doing that. A lot. Your name keeps coming up. I think he's delirious."

"There is a way… Dormammu… Defeat Dormammu… You must seek…"

The Ancient One's voice trailed off.

"Seek what, Master?" said Strange.

"Eternity…"

It was the faintest of whispers, more exhalation than speech.

It came again.

"Eternity…"

Then the Ancient One lapsed back into insensibility.

"Yes, that's been a constant refrain throughout," said Hamir. "He keeps repeating the word again and again. 'Eternity.' Any idea what he might mean by it?"

"Not a clue," said Strange. "But it's clearly important."

"I think so too. That's if it's not just the name of some nightclub he goes to."

"Hamir, I'm going to have to come back here in person. This is going to expose you to potential danger. Mordo's spies could be anywhere, and if you're with me when they discover me, you could be in the line of fire."

The hermit shrugged gamely. "Ah well. What's the point of a life of isolation and contemplation if you're not getting attacked by evil magicians every once in a while? I'll put the kettle on for you."

A BOWL of fresh, steaming tea was waiting for Strange when he arrived at Hamir's hut in his physical form, via a Wormhole of Weygg-Kalkuun. In the Tibetan custom, yak butter had been added to the tea rather than milk, along with plenty of salt. Strange had disliked the drink when he first tried it at the Ancient One's retreat—it tasted more like soup than a beverage—but in time he had become quite partial to it. He emptied the bowl gratefully, then turned his attention to the febrile old man.

Even without a thermometer, it was obvious to him that the Ancient One was running a high temperature. His skin burned to the touch. Strange made a cold compress and placed it on his forehead. He took his pulse and found it predictably rapid and erratic. He put his ear to his ribcage and heard the crackling sounds that indicated fluid in the lungs' air sacs. He scowled. The signs were ominous. The Ancient One's immune system was doing its utmost to fight the infection, but the infection was winning.

All at once, the old man's papery eyelids flew open. He let out a hoarse gasp and grabbed Strange's wrist. His grip was surprisingly strong.

"Stephen! Eternity! Eternity holds the key!"

"Tell me, Master," Strange said. "Tell me what 'Eternity' means."

Bloodshot eyes stared at him, but Strange wasn't sure if the Ancient One was even seeing him.

"Eternity, Master," he urged. "It seems I need to seek something known as Eternity. You have to explain what it is and why."

But nothing more was forthcoming from the Ancient One. He subsided once more into uneasy unconsciousness.

Strange sat back, thinking.

"What's the plan, Doctor?" Hamir enquired. "How do you think you can get an answer out of him?"

"The plan," said Strange after a moment, "is to dig around inside his mind and see what I can unearth. I'm going to have to go into a trance, Hamir, and while I'm doing that, I'm counting on you to keep me safe. If Mordo or any of his cronies turn up, you're going to have to hold them off long enough for me to pull out of the trance and come to your aid. You think you can manage that?"

By way of reply, Hamir produced a penknife from his pocket. "Well, I've got this. But it's not really adequate."

"Hardly."

He fetched out a wooden trunk and rooted around inside it. "I've also got this."

Out came a bolt-action hunting rifle.

"I guess I shouldn't ask why you have that," Strange said, "but I'm going to anyway."

"It's for scaring away snow leopards and yetis."

"Yetis?"

"You'd be surprised."

"Not sure I would, actually."

"It's also handy for shooting magicians who might wish to do me and my friends harm."

Strange, in spite of everything, smiled. "Just keep that thing pointed away from me."

"Don't worry, I'll only aim it at the bad guys," Hamir said.

STRANGE PROPPED the Ancient One up against his pillows, then sat down cross-legged at the foot of the bed.

"You've done this before, right?" said Hamir.

"Never."

"But it'll work?"

"Theoretically, yes. Theoretically, it could also fry my brain and leave me a drooling vegetable."

"Seriously?"

"Not really. At least, I don't think so. But the Ancient One will have plenty of mental blocks in place to prevent just this sort of intrusion. I've no idea how easy those'll be to get around. Not easy, is my guess."

The Eye of Agamotto opened and Strange projected its light onto the old man's wrinkled brow, using it to establish a link between his mind and his master's. He sent his consciousness along this glowing bridge, probing tentatively forwards.

He encountered an obstacle straight away. His thoughts became clouded. It was as though he was lost in a fog, searching this way and that in order to regain his sense of direction.

"Master," he said mentally, "it's me. Stephen. Allow me in. I need to speak with you. I need your wisdom."

Gradually the fog lifted. Strange's mind ventured further forwards.

Suddenly, swift as a steel trap, a mesh descended from above. Strange was flailing around like a fish in a net.

"Master. Let me through."

He continued with this imprecation, until at last the mesh melted away.

There was a brick wall, reaching all the way up to the sky and, right and left, to the horizon.

There was a sentry, standing at a guard post, armed with sword and shield.

There was a fire-breathing dragon, big as a house, with lambent eyes and a tail that lashed back and forth in anger.

There was a river in full spate, rushing by at Strange's feet, its current too fast and its waters too deep for him to ford across.

These were psychic constructs, images designed to deter and confound. Strange overcame them one after another by patiently, painstakingly, entreating their creator to dismantle them.

"Trust me, Ancient One. It's your disciple. You know who I am. You know I mean you no harm. Open yourself up to me."

At last, through persistence and concentration, Strange was past all the obstacles.

He was alone in a plain, monastic room with the Ancient One. There were no windows, no decorations, no door. This was the innermost recess of the Ancient One's mind, the very heart of him. His pure, unadorned self.

"Ah, Stephen." The old Tibetan was standing upright and his eyes were clear. He looked healthy and vigorous. "I was hoping you'd come. How am I doing, out there? My body, I mean. Be honest. I know I'm unwell."

"Not great," Strange replied. "I believe, with the appropriate treatment, you can pull through. But Hamir's no doctor and his hut's no hospital, which is where you really ought to be. At the very least, you should be at your retreat with Wong looking after you."

The Ancient One waved a dismissive hand. "If I die, so be it. Death holds no terror for me. It's just the next step in the journey."

"I'd prefer it if you stayed alive."

"Me too, but we don't always have a say in the matter, do we? Now, you probably want to know about this message I've been trying to get across to you. That's what's important right now."

"Yes. What is 'Eternity?' A place? A person? A concept?"

The Ancient One nodded.

"Which one?"

"All three," said the old man. "And more."

"Oh-kay," Strange said. "Can you be any more specific than that?"

"Eternity cannot accurately be explained, Stephen, only experienced."

"And how do I accomplish that?"

"The Eye of Agamotto. The Eye is the portal and the path. Give your amulet free rein. Surrender yourself to it, and Eternity will be yours."

•—•

STRANGE STOOD on a ledge on a windswept crag overlooking Hamir's hut. The sun was starting to set, its dying light turning the snowy peaks rose-pink.

He was about to undertake a journey into the unknown. Even the Ancient One was unsure where he would be going, how safe it would be, and whether he might return.

"I wouldn't be proposing this to you, Stephen," he had said during their psychic dialogue, "if I did not think it utterly necessary. Dormammu will make his move on Earth sooner or later, probably sooner, with Mordo as his catspaw. It's inevitable, and it must be stopped. You are our best hope, and that is why you must take such an awesome risk. All my many years of occult learning and study have taught me that, in times of dire need, Eternity's aid may be recruited. In none of the books is it made clear what this entails. It is a mystery which even the greatest magical scholars cannot explain. They only know it to be a truth."

"Or, to put it another way, I'm doing what I'm about to do on faith alone."

"That's it. It's a leap of faith. You can be forgiven for not wanting to take it."

"Sounds like there isn't much of a choice."

"That, I'm afraid, is what leaps of faith are all about. May Agamotto guide you, Stephen, and may Oshtur protect you."

Strange gazed out over the Himalayan sunset vista before him, a scene as breath-stealingly spectacular and beautiful as any Earth had to offer. Here was a world worth saving. Here was a prize worth hazarding everything for.

He set the Eye of Agamotto in front of him, wedging it between two rocks so that it stood upright. The Ancient One had told him the incantations he required. He spoke them, and the amulet began to grow. It expanded until it was the size of a doorway. Then it opened.

Through it, he saw star-filled blackness.

Strange took a breath, clenched his fists, and stepped in.

TIME SLOWED.

Strrrrrrretched like taffy.

Strange strrrrrrretched with it.

TIME ACCELERATED.

Accelerated faster.

Acclrtd fstr.

Acdfr.

TIME LOST meaning.

Time lost.

Lost meaning.

Meantime.

Losting.

Time.

Mean.

Lost.

THEN...

nothing

blankness

silence

a void

and now

a

tiny

dot

that

became

a

figure

shaped like

a

man

at

first

a silhouette

black

on white

but

growing

in size

at

speed

as

though

getting nearer

and

nearer

its

features

becoming clearer

and

better defined

until

it stood,

titan-tall and

looming,

and spoke:

I

AM

ETERNITY

DOCTOR STRANGE: DIMENSION WAR

STRANGE REELED, body and soul. The voice was like a thousand gongs striking at once, a thousand church bells chiming, a thousand calls to prayer resounding across rooftops. It sang loud and clear through his mind, crowding out all other thought. It seemed to come as much from within himself as from the figure before him.

That figure resembled a man, but it was not. It was the outline of a man, but it was composed of universes. Stars scintillated inside it. Galaxies spun. Interstellar clouds of dust and plasma drifted. White dwarfs dwindled. Black holes pulsed.

A suggestion of a face hung amid the cosmic vastness. There appeared to be a cloak, a collar, perhaps some kind of headgear.

But it looked like a man only because it was making itself intelligible to Strange. It spoke like a man for the same reason.

This huge, imperious thing, with its somber expression and shadowy gaze, was an abstraction given form. It was the essence of everything, modified so that the senses of a mere mortal could interpret it.

It wasn't a god, because "god" was too small a word for it. It was an entity embodying unfathomable endlessness.

Or, as it had declared…

Eternity.

I KNOW YOU, STEPHEN VINCENT STRANGE, it said. SPEAK NOT. I KNOW THE REASON FOR YOUR QUEST. I KNOW WHY YOU HAVE COME TO ME. YOU STAND FOR THE HUMAN RACE AT A CRUCIAL HOUR. YOU ARE HERE TO BEG MY HELP. TRULY YOU WOULD NOT HAVE SOUGHT ME IF YOUR NEED WAS NOT GREAT. YET WHY SHOULD I CARE WHAT BECOMES OF YOUR SPECIES OR WHO RULES YOUR WORLD?

Strange wanted to respond, but Eternity had commanded him to silence. There didn't seem much point answering, in any case. He figured anything he had to say, Eternity already knew.

WHAT MATTERS THE FATE OF A SINGLE PLANET TO ONE

WHO IS ALL THINGS AT ALL TIMES? Eternity went on. YOUR WORLD'S CONCERNS ARE AS MOTES OF DUST TO ME. IF A BILLION OF YOUR KIND WERE TO PERISH, I WOULD SCARCELY NOTICE.

Eternity raised a hand, holding it above Strange's head. Where human beings had fingerprint whorls, Eternity had star clusters.

BUT, FOR ALL THAT, YOU HAVE COME AS A SUPPLICANT, STEPHEN VINCENT STRANGE. YOU HAVE BRAVED MUCH THROUGHOUT THE COURSE OF YOUR LIFE. LIKE ALL HUMANS, YOU WERE BORN IN INNOCENCE. FOR A TIME, IN ADULTHOOD, YOU STRAYED FROM THE WAY OF TRUTH AND WISDOM, AND YOU WERE PENALIZED, BUT IN THE END YOU RETURNED TO IT. YOU LEARNED FROM YOUR SUFFERINGS AND YOUR HEART HAS EVER REMAINED GOOD.

Although a compliment like this was nice to hear, Strange was more preoccupied with the notion that if Eternity was all things at all times, as it had just claimed, then it already knew the outcome of this encounter.

ALL IS PREORDAINED, Eternity said, as though intuiting his thoughts. THE RESULT CANNOT BE CHANGED, NOR CAN IT BE PRE-EMPTED. THE SEQUENCE OF EVENTS CANNOT BE DEVIATED FROM, LEST CHAOS ENSUE. ORDER MUST BE OBSERVED.

Eternity's hand continued to hover over Strange, like that of a parent reaching out to their offspring. It could be taken as a loving gesture, or one of reproof. Which of the two it was remained to be seen.

YOU ARE PART OF ETERNITY, Eternity said after a pause, seeming to come to a decision. YOU HAVE SHOWN YOURSELF TO BE A STAUNCH DEFENDER OF EVERYTHING THAT MATTERS. YOUR WILLINGNESS TO PUT YOURSELF IN SERVICE OF OTHERS AND SET THEIR NEEDS BEFORE

YOUR OWN IS COMMENDABLE. ON BALANCE, I FIND YOU WORTHY. THUS, SHALL I GRANT YOU THE BOON YOU DESIRE.

Eternity withdrew its hand.

WHEN YOU REQUIRE IT, it said, IT WILL BE YOURS. YOU WILL KNOW THE HOUR. YOU WILL KNOW THE PLACE. IF YOU ARE AS WISE AS I SENSE YOU TO BE, I NEED SAY NO MORE THAN THAT. AND IF YOU ARE INSUFFICIENTLY WISE, THEN YOU DO NOT DESERVE WHAT I CAN OFFER.

With that, Eternity took a step back. All at once, it enlarged, swamping Strange, engulfing him, swallowing him into its infinitude.

There was a moment of falling.

A brief but seemingly everlasting plummet.

Then Strange was back on the ledge.

The Eye of Agamotto was back to its usual size and position on his chest.

Night had descended.

○━━━━━━━○

STRANGE SAT for a while, discouraged and oddly dissatisfied. Had he really just communed with the living personification of the totality of existence? Such an extraordinary experience, with such enormous spiritual ramifications, and yet he was left underwhelmed. Eternity had promised him something, but what that something was remained nebulous. *If you are as wise as I sense you to be, I need say no more than that. And if you are insufficiently wise, then you do not deserve what I can offer.* Talk about cryptic. Not to mention conditional.

Perhaps this was how all supreme cosmic beings behaved. They just did not care about making their intentions crystal clear, and maybe even enjoyed causing confusion and obfuscation. Either that was the case, or they were so far above mortals, so removed from the mundane, they had trouble making themselves understood.

Strange might encounter similar difficulties trying to interact on a meaningful basis with a flea.

Regardless, he had gone in search of reassurances and come away empty-handed, or so it seemed. Where the Dread Dormammu was concerned, it looked as though he was going to have to rely on himself after all.

The Cloak of Levitation flew him back down to Hamir's hut...

...where everything lay in disarray and the Ancient One was missing.

NINETEEN

THE HUT walls were pocked with bullet holes: a dozen or so of them, by Strange's count. A similar number of shell casings littered the floor, and the tang of cordite hung in the air. Hamir's few sticks of furniture were overturned; much of it was splintered and broken. The cooking fire was out, reduced to just a few glowing embers. There'd been a violent altercation here, and Strange judged it to have occurred not long before he returned from his audience with Eternity.

Hamir himself sat huddled in a corner, clutching his hunting rifle to his chest. He appeared physically uninjured but was in a catatonic state, staring into space.

Strange knelt beside him and gently but urgently spoke his name.

Little by little, the light returned to the hermit's eyes. He gave a sudden start and leveled the rifle at Strange. Strange shoved it aside just as he pulled the trigger. The firing pin clicked uselessly. The weapon was empty.

"Hamir, it's me. Doctor Strange. What happened here? Who attacked you?"

"They... They came out of nowhere," Hamir stammered. "Magicians. Five, maybe six of them. I opened fire but they just deflected the bullets. As in, bent the shots through the air so they missed. Then one of them encased me in these—these sort of red straps. Intangible, but I couldn't break out of them. The more I tried to, the tighter they coiled. All I could do was watch as they grabbed the Ancient One out of the cot. Lugged him outside. That's the last I saw of him. Then they came back and started smashing up the place because, apparently, I had to be taught a lesson—and I lived in such a hovel anyway, what difference did it make? The only thing I remember after that is one of them waving a hand at me, the same guy who put those red straps on me. This was the man in charge, giving the orders. Short, kind of round, bad hair, bad goatee."

"Mordo," said Strange.

"Guessed it might be. After he did that... Well, everything's a blank, till just now, when you showed up."

A pained expression came over Hamir's face.

"They kidnapped him," he wailed, "and I couldn't stop them. I let the Ancient One down. I let you down."

"Nonsense," said Strange. "Half a dozen magicians against you, Mordo among them—you didn't stand a chance, gun or not. If anyone's to blame for this, Hamir, it's me. I left you alone and undefended. I thought I had time. I didn't think Mordo would be able to pinpoint my location so quickly. Just count yourself lucky he didn't want you dead."

Hamir got to his feet, with Strange's assistance. "What now? Please tell me you found this Eternity and you've been given whatever you need to beat Mordo and Dormammu and get the Ancient One back."

"I..."

But before Strange could begin encapsulating his astonishing but also somewhat frustrating escapade with Eternity, a voice called to him from outside the hut.

A voice that was all too horribly familiar.

"Strange," said Baron Mordo. "I know you're in there. Come on out."

Hamir unclipped the spent magazine from his rifle and started hunting around for a fresh one. Strange put a hand on his shoulder, staying him.

"No. You've done plenty, Hamir. No point putting yourself in harm's way anymore. You'll only get yourself killed. This is up to me now, and me alone."

The hermit looked obstinate, but in the end saw sense and relented.

"Whatever happens, Doctor Strange," he said, "please know that it's been an honor and a privilege to meet you."

"Same here, Hamir."

Strange shook the hermit's hand, then stepped outside.

Mordo stood gloatingly near Hamir's yak. The beast snorted and tugged at its tether in agitation, still upset by the recent gunfire.

"Where is he?" Strange demanded. "Where is the Ancient One? What have you done with him?"

"He is where you and I are about to go," Mordo replied. "You have pranced and capered long enough, Strange, and Dormammu and I are heartily sick of your shenanigans. It's well past time we brought this whole business to its denouement. Come with me now."

"And if I don't want to?"

"Oh really, Strange! If you wish to see your precious Ancient One again, you'll do as I say."

Strange had had a feeling this would be Mordo's answer. At least he now knew the Ancient One was still alive. That was something.

"All right then," he said. "Where are we going?"

"Where else?" said Mordo.

THE DARK Dimension.

To be precise, the main chamber in Dormammu's citadel.

Gathered here were thirty-odd mages from Earth. Strange

recognized several of their number from his earlier run-ins with them. There were the tall woman and the bulbous-nosed man who had supported Mordo in his assault on the Ancient One's retreat. There was Devon Darlington III, the Devious Demon. There was the witch Strange had battled in Hong Kong. There was Jason Batubara from Madripoor.

Others he knew by face and reputation, or could identify by drawing inferences from their appearance. They included stately Bavarian wizardess Annalise Varnhagen, Margravine of Winzeldorfstadt, with blue-black hair so elegantly coiffed and stacked it looked like the funeral equivalent of a wedding cake; a fierce-eyed Russian called Mr. Rasputin who claimed descendance from the notorious Mad Monk of that name; and Wilson J. Brown, the politician and Vodou bokor who had sicced those zuvembies on Strange in Boca Caliente.

All were members of the Counterclockwise Circle, and Strange could only assume the rest were as well. The entirety of that group was in attendance, doubtless keen to see him defeated once and for all.

In addition, there were the flamboyantly clad warlocks he had fought on his last visit here when making his way through the city to the citadel. The Counterclockwise mages were dressed smartly and, in the Devious Demon's case, elaborately, but looked dowdy and drab in comparison with these particular denizens of the Dark Dimension—penguins next to peacocks.

Most importantly, as far as Strange was concerned, the Ancient One was there. The old Tibetan had been given a heap of blankets to lie on, and looked sicker and frailer than ever. Strange would have gone over to him, but Mordo restrained him with a hand.

"Let him alone," said Mordo. "His welfare is not your concern right now. Your own should be."

Strange shot him a look of pure venom, at which the European aristocrat merely sneered.

Dormammu was not present in the chamber, but Strange thought he would surely be arriving soon. Also absent—Strange didn't know whether to be relieved or dismayed—was Clea. He would have liked to see her again, but not under these circumstances. Unless he was very wrong, he'd been brought here to meet his death. He was glad Clea wouldn't be on hand to witness that.

"When's the big chief coming?" Strange asked Mordo. "I presume he's on his way."

"Why so impatient?" Mordo replied. "Are you in a hurry to die?"

There was no good answer to that.

○——○

CLEA WAS in another part of the citadel, the tower which served as her quarters. She shared the living space with her father, Prince Orini.

Orini was many things. He was a doting parent. He was the son of King Olnar, who had ruled the Dark Dimension before Dormammu rose to power. He was an obedient supporter of Dormammu.

He was also ineffectual, weak in a myriad of ways. When Olnar died, Orini had been too young to assume the throne, and Dormammu and his twin sister Umar, fugitives from the Faltine Dimension, had been installed as regents in his stead. When he attained manhood, Umar had seduced him. Clea was the product of their union, but Umar, disgusted by her own displays of humanity, left Orini to bring up the child alone.

Never once, upon becoming an adult, did Orini contest the throne, as he perhaps ought to have. Even after the Faltine twins had their rift and Umar was exiled from the Dark Dimension, he remained meek and supine, a loyal retainer to Dormammu. If he felt any animosity towards his usurper, he kept it to himself.

Much though Clea loved her father, she loathed his passivity, and she wasn't averse to telling him so.

Which she was doing now, while elsewhere in the citadel Baron Mordo and his fellow magicians from Earth were waiting for Dormammu to appear and put paid to Stephen Strange and his master once and for all. It was common knowledge that Mordo had arrived with his brace of human prizes a short while earlier, laying them before Dormammu's feet like a dog retrieving rabbits for its owner.

"Father," she said, "you know as well as I do that Dormammu is going to slay the two of them. Then he is going to take over their world, and plunder and pillage it remorselessly. And here you sit, twiddling your thumbs, while all this happens under your roof. This is your citadel, Father. Your realm. You are the rightful ruler of the Dark Dimension. You should be over there right now challenging my uncle for the crown. You should have done it ages ago."

Orini sighed. "What hope would I have of success against one as mighty as he? My father was a great mage, of a lineage going all the way back to G'uran the Great and Oka'an of the Azure Throne, and even he was helpless before Dormammu."

"That's because Dormammu and my mother deceived him," Clea said. "They tricked him into releasing the Mindless Ones, who killed him and his wife, my grandmother. They then drove the Mindless Ones back and erected the barrier that keeps them out. The people, in misplaced gratitude, appointed them as regents. You've told me this countless times, and always more in sorrow than in anger. Dormammu and my mother as good as murdered Olnar themselves! If I were you, I'd have done anything and everything I could to get revenge. At the very least, you could depose Dormammu. Don't forget, you too are of your father's lineage. You could stand up to him."

"And die in the process?"

"If need be. Better that than live as his perpetual houseguest."

"Clea, my child," said Orini, "your passion does you credit, but you are unversed in the realities of life. Don't think I didn't dream of ousting Dormammu. But while you were younger, I didn't dare.

Were I to have died, you would have been left without a parent. Who would have raised you then? Dormammu himself? Certainly not Umar. She entirely disavowed you. And now... Well, now it is too late. Dormammu is well entrenched, and whatever magic I had has long since fallen into decay through disuse."

"But I am not without magic, Father," Clea said hotly. "And I am no longer prepared to stand idly by while Dormammu wreaks havoc across the dimensions. Nor while he threatens the life of the man from Earth, Stephen Strange, who has defied his plans for conquest at every step."

"And what would you do, my daughter?" Orini asked. "What do you think you can possibly achieve?"

"I am Umar's offspring. I have much of her magical prowess."

"And much of her strident, fiery temperament too," her father observed, with some ruefulness.

"I also have the ear of the people," Clea went on, "and I know they are girding themselves, waiting for an opportunity to overthrow Dormammu. I can give them that."

"How?"

"That's my business. Just be prepared, Father. If ever the time was ripe for revolution in the Dark Dimension, that time is now."

"YOU LOVE an audience, don't you, Mordo?" said Strange. He was getting tired of waiting for Dormammu. He had time to kill, and since he was prohibited from ministering to the Ancient One, needling Mordo seemed as good a way of occupying himself as any. "You could have done this without all your Counterclockwise pals present, but no, you had to drag them along for your moment of triumph. You're just a great big showoff. What's in it for them, I wonder. I can't believe they've gone to the trouble of traveling to the Dark Dimension just to see me die."

"You'd be surprised, Strange," Mordo retorted. "My colleagues have cause to resent you, especially those whose efforts to capture you, you foiled."

"Yes, them I can understand, but the rest? What's that about?"

"They…" Mordo faltered. "They are supportive."

It sounded like hogwash to Strange. "Supportive? They're a cadre of the most self-centered bunch of humans as ever lived. They don't do anything out of the goodness of their hearts. There's always an angle." He turned to address the assembled Earthly mages. "Is that a fair assessment? I mean, let's be frank. You people are the type who'd kill their own mothers to get ahead in life. In fact, I believe a couple of you have done exactly that."

In response, there were growls and curses, but also one or two nods of shameless acknowledgement.

"What did Mordo promise you?" Strange continued. "Power? An exalted position after Dormammu takes over Earth? Immunity from Dormammu's wrath? Something like that, I'm sure."

From the expressions on several of the magicians' faces, he saw that he wasn't wide of the mark.

"Thought so," he said, warming to his theme. "There has to be something in it for yourselves. Makes me think, though. Aren't you, all of you, masters of the world? You have everything you could possibly want: wealth, status, influence. And now look what's happened. Karl Amadeus Mordo has come along and formed a pact with Dormammu. He's offering the Lord of the Dark Dimension our planet on a plate. Do you genuinely think your services are going to be required once Dormammu takes over? What use are you going to be? To Mordo? To Dormammu?"

"Strange," warned Mordo, "you'd do well to still your tongue."

"I'm not saying anything that hasn't already occurred to them. Maybe they haven't given it as much thought as they should. Maybe they're in denial. But they must know there's unlikely to be room for them on Earth under Dormammu. You, Mordo, have carved out a nice little niche for yourself in his designs, and that's very sensible of you. I think he'll treat you well. But the rest of them? He won't want them around. *You* won't want them around. Rivals. Potential competitors. I foresee a purge."

"Strange…"

He grinned at Mordo. "What are you going to do? Kill me? I doubt Dormammu would appreciate it. That honor is supposed to be his."

He turned back to the Counterclockwise Circle.

"Mr. Batubara," he said, focusing on the Madripoorian banking magnate. "You're a clever man. You've got a head on your shoulders. Where's the benefit for you in living in a world ruled by Dormammu? I don't suppose your business will thrive. More likely there'll be financial chaos, runs on currencies, economic contagion, a stock market collapse that'll make the Wall Street Crash look like a blip, followed by a second Great Depression that nobody will ever crawl out of. What'll you personally have left at the end of it? A garage full of Lamborghinis, and you won't be able to afford the gas to run them."

Jason Batubara looked uneasy. "I imagine we can come to some sort of accommodation with Dormammu."

"You keep believing that. And you, Devon Darlington III. All your connections. All that family money. It'll be meaningless under Dormammu's jackboot. You'll have to hole up in your Boston mansion while angry mobs howl outside, like Marie Antoinette during the French Revolution. Same goes for you, Frau Varnhagen. For all of you. You haven't thought this through. Mordo's been stringing all of you along."

"This is nonsense," Mordo said. "The words of a desperate man. Strange is just trying to sow discord in our ranks. He is doomed and he knows it, and so he lashes out. It is all he has. You may rest assured, my friends, that Dormammu will look kindly on you when he is our overlord. I shall advocate for all of you. There won't be any of the problems Strange predicts. He is scaremongering."

The bulbous-nosed man—Edwin Cuthbertson, Duke of Hendersleigh—piped up. "You said, Mordo, that we could share in the magical power Dormammu has given you. That was the condition for our assistance in catching Strange."

There were grumbles of assent from other Counterclockwise members.

"Is that still the case?" Cuthbertson continued. "I mean, speaking for myself, I'm beginning to wonder whether we haven't put our money on the wrong horse."

"A lying horse," chimed in the tall woman, Contessa Alessandra Fabrizzi.

"No," said Mordo. "No, no, not at all. Believe me, there will be a distribution of power. We will all be better off in Dormammu's Earth."

"You know what you sound like?" said Strange. "A politician. All bluster, no action."

The other Counterclockwise mages were now restless, murmuring to one another and glaring sullenly and suspiciously at Mordo. Whatever faith they had had in him, they were losing fast.

Strange was pleased. It hadn't taken much to turn them against their colleague. Their trust would have been tenuous to begin with, liable to break under the slightest strain. What Strange had managed to do might well result in Mordo's jealous, resentful peers abandoning him. They might even gang up on him and ensure that his tenure as Dormammu's flunky did not last long. Strange himself would probably not live to see that day, but it was gratifying nonetheless to think it might happen.

He turned to Dormammu's warlocks. "Same goes for you people. I know you're here because you've been commanded to attend. You surely can't bear much love for your lord and master."

"Dormammu looks after us," said one of them.

"For as long as you're useful to him."

"He has our respect," said another of the warlocks.

"But do you have his? How was your little vacation in the Pitiless Pit of Neverness, by the way? Not a whole heap of fun, I'll bet."

The warlocks shuffled their feet. In their eyes there was a haunted look. They did not like to be reminded of the punishment they'd suffered.

"That great, eh?" he said. "Maybe you can tell these visiting magicians about it sometime. They'll be keen to hear how Dormammu treats his workforce."

Before he could go on, a tremendous fanfare of trumpets sounded, although there were no trumpets to be seen.

This was followed by the appearance of a ramp made of overlapping discs of light, manifesting out of nowhere.

At the top of the ramp, amid a sun-bright glow, a figure stood silhouetted.

Everyone turned to stare.

The figure came swaggering down the ramp, and it was Dormammu, clad in finery, his flaming head more brightly ablaze than ever.

He halted at the foot of the ramp, looking around.

"I expect some show of appreciation when I make an entrance," he said.

Immediately Mordo started applauding. The other Earthly mages and the Dark Dimension warlocks joined in, if a little reluctantly. Strange, of course, did not.

His eye was caught by a second figure who appeared on the ramp, loping down it in Dormammu's wake.

His mouth tightened in grim surprise.

The Lord of the Dark Dimension, it seemed, had a guest. A visitor from the Dream Dimension.

Nightmare.

A KALEIDOSCOPIC tunnel transported Clea to the farthest reaches of the realm, the broken lands bordering on the Mindless Ones' home.

A handful of the thickset, charcoal-gray creatures were stumping around in the fogbound region on their side of Dormammu's barrier. Clea felt a small chill at the sight of them. She felt a greater chill at the thought of what she intended to do.

Release them.

One of the things keeping the people of the Dark Dimension from trying to overthrow Dormammu was his ability to restrain the Mindless Ones. As long as his barrier held, so did his subjects' fealty to him, just about. It was a kind of unspoken blackmail.

The last time the Mindless Ones broke through, Dormammu had managed to repel them only with Stephen Strange's aid. Since then, the people had not forgotten how frightened they had been. Dormammu's guarantee of safety had begun to look fragile.

If the Mindless Ones broke through again, it might be enough to precipitate an all-out rebellion. Dormammu could drive the creatures back as before and reseal the barrier, but nobody would have reason to trust his assurances anymore. The population would rise up. The unspoken dissent would become vocal. A groundswell would become an earthquake.

So Clea hoped. She was even willing to be the figurehead for the rebellion. She would rally the people and lead the charge, pitting her magic against her uncle's. She might die as a consequence, but death in the name of a righteous cause was preferable to living beneath the heel of a tyrant.

Of course, her scheme was fraught with uncertainties and potential pitfalls. For one thing, what if Dormammu wasn't able to fend off the Mindless Ones this time? What if they overwhelmed him and proceeded to rampage throughout the length and breadth of the Dark Dimension, killing indiscriminately, laying waste everywhere they went, like some apocalyptic plague?

Then again, if she did nothing, the misery here would continue. There would also be misery for places such as Earth as Dormammu spread the tentacles of his empire further. Freeing the Mindless Ones was Clea's least bad option, a radical solution to a radical problem.

There was also the chance that this solution might also be the solution to Strange's current predicament. The last time he faced Dormammu, he'd been saved when the barrier thinned and Mindless Ones came through.

Perhaps the same thing might happen this time: Dormammu would have to suspend their fight in order to deal with an incursion by those creatures into the Dark Dimension. At the very least, Clea might gain Strange a reprieve. She might even save him.

She steeled herself for the task ahead. There was much riding on it.

Umar the Unrelenting. That was the nickname given her mother. A mark of her inner mettle, her ruthlessness.

Now it was time to see if Clea was truly her mother's daughter.

THE PALLID dream-lord greeted Strange with a sardonic wave.

"I imagine you're asking yourself why I am here," Nightmare said.

"You imagine wrong," said Strange. "The only thing I'm asking myself is how many lackeys can one despot need. There's Mordo there. There are his warlocks over there. Now you."

Nightmare bristled. "Lackey? I am no lackey. Dormammu invited me to the Dark Dimension as a courtesy, one leader to another. He knows of my contempt for you. He told me he was going to finish you once and for all, and asked if I would like to be in on the kill. I could hardly say no to that."

"Interesting."

"What do you mean, interesting?"

"Didn't you have plans to conquer Earth?"

"What of it?"

"And Dormammu made you give them up."

"How do you know that?"

"He told me himself. Right, Dormammu?"

The Lord of the Dark Dimension had been following the conversation with detached amusement. Now, in answer to Strange's query, he simply nodded.

Nightmare bobbed his head, as though in embarrassment. "Perhaps he did dissuade me from the idea. But if so, I ask again, what of it?"

"Well, you're claiming you and he are equals," Strange said. "'One leader to another.' But Dormammu slapped you down, and now he's dragged you all the way over to his dimension just so you can watch him polish me off. Me, the man who's ruined your fun on more than one occasion. I wouldn't call that a courtesy. I'd say it was kind of a snub. 'Look how much better I am than you.'"

"Good grief, Strange!" Mordo declared. "Do you *ever* stop talking?"

"You would deny me my last words?"

"You're stalling, Strange. What is it, are you giving yourself time to think? Time to figure out a way out of this situation?"

"You see right through me, Mordo."

"But don't you realize? There *is* no way out," Mordo said. "You and the Ancient One are about to die. This is what it has come down to. All the times you and he have interfered, all the times you've got in our way... That's over now. I have brought you to Dormammu, and his will be the honor—indeed the pleasure—of dispatching you. Slaying the Ancient One, in his enfeebled condition, will prove no problem. As for you, something special awaits. You are—"

"No, Mordo," said Dormammu, interrupting. "I, not you, will enlighten Strange as to the manner of his demise."

"Of course, Lord Dormammu."

"Strange," Dormammu said, "you and I are to engage in combat."

"Another duel?"

"Indeed."

"Okay," said Strange. "Just for the record, our previous duel didn't work out so well for you. As I recall, it ended with you vowing to me you'd leave the mortal realm alone."

"That vow holds, so long as you live."

"And today's duel is going to be the same type as last time?"

"No."

"I thought not."

"No, this time I felt something more classical would be appropriate. Hence you and I are going to fight using the dueling weapons that have been favored among my race, the Faltine, for untold centuries."

"I see."

"The terms of the duel, as is traditional, stipulate that neither participant employs magic, other than to power the weapons themselves. No spells, no incantations, no shields."

"So that explains it. This way, you won't have to draw on as much magic as last time. You don't want to endanger the integrity of the barrier that keeps out the Mindless Ones again, do you?"

"That is neither here nor there," said Dormammu.

"But I have a point?"

Dormammu brushed it aside with a flick of his hand. "Your amulet and cloak, both being magical items, must be discarded. Each of us must rely solely on his martial artistry and his willpower."

"And suppose one of us isn't too hot on martial artistry?" Strange said.

"Then you will perish. Do you agree to abide by these rules, Strange?"

"Do I have a choice?"

"You do not."

"And if you kill me—"

"*When* I kill you."

"Sure. When that happens, Earth is yours for the taking."

"You *are* stalling, Strange."

"I'm just making sure of the stakes."

"With you no longer around," Dormammu said, "my vow is null and void. Not only that, there is nobody to stand in my way. The Ancient One?" He cast a glance at the elderly Tibetan, shuddering and sweating on the blankets. "Killing him will be an act of mercy."

"Earth has other defenders apart from him and me," Strange pointed out.

"You mean its so-called super heroes? Yes, I have observed them and their antics. Do you honestly believe a few mortals, enhanced by just science and mutation, can withstand the full mystical might of one such as me?"

"I think they'll give it a darned good try. Captain America, for instance. He never backs down, never surrenders, no matter the odds. The same can be said for the rest of the Avengers. Then there's Spider-Man, Daredevil, the Fantastic Four... They'll resist you with everything they've got."

"Let them. They shall regret it. But that's enough prevarication. Nightmare, you have the weapons I gave you for safekeeping?"

Nightmare stepped forward, producing a pair of golden bracelets in each hand.

"Fetching and carrying," Strange said wryly. "That's definitely not something a lackey would do."

Nightmare shot him a look that could have soured milk.

Dormammu took one of the bracelet pairs and placed them around his wrists. "Strange. The other ones are yours. Take them. Put them on."

Strange did as bidden. "Now what?"

"Now... this." Dormammu held out his arms. A frown of concentration came over his fiery face.

Abruptly, twin curved blades of magical energy extended from each bracelet, their tips almost meeting and forming a circle. The blades—several inches long, serrated on the sides, wickedly pointed at the end—shimmered and crackled.

"These," the Lord of the Dark Dimension said, "are the Pincers of Power. Sharper than razors. Immune to blunting. And in the right hands, quite deadly."

TWENTY

STRANGE REMOVED his Cloak of Levitation and the Eye of Agamotto. Baron Mordo took them from him, setting them aside. Strange had become so used to wearing them that he felt a little naked in their absence.

He gave the bracelets on his wrists the once-over. They were made from lightweight metal, infused with a receptiveness to magic. They needed to be activated somehow. From what Dormammu had said, the wielder's own will powered them.

A thought occurred to him. He had an ace in the hole. He wasn't sure it would win the day. He wasn't sure it was even worth playing. It was also potentially dangerous. But he had it nonetheless. Was this the time to try it?

No. Not yet. Some instinct told him he should keep it in his back pocket for now.

He focused on the bracelets. He channeled magic from its fountainhead within him, through himself, into them.

After a couple of false starts, twin blades of light sprang out from each.

He had only a few seconds to adjust, to familiarize himself with the Pincers of Power.

Dormammu attacked.

The Lord of the Dark Dimension jabbed his Pincers of Power at

Strange, a double-handed blow.

Strange brought his own Pincers up to block. More by luck than judgment, he parried Dormammu's strike. Both sets of Pincers sparked and sizzled as they collided.

Dormammu came on the offensive again straight away. He swung. Strange ducked, coming up with a blow of his own, aimed at his opponent's belly.

Dormammu batted Strange's Pincers aside.

The two combatants stepped back, eyeing each other.

"Not bad," Dormammu said.

"For an amateur, you mean?"

"For one destined to lose."

Dormammu lunged. Strange body-swerved and struck out at him sideways. Dormammu deflected, then whirled round and slashed at Strange from behind. Strange sidestepped, but not quickly enough. One of Dormammu's Pincers scored his flank. There was coldness, followed by searing agony. Strange reeled, hissing in pain.

Dormammu pressed his advantage, raising both Pincers and bringing them down at Strange. Strange, despite the injury in his side, got his Pincers up just in time. Dormammu bore down on him. Strange pushed upward as hard as he could, legs braced. He felt blood seeping down through his shirt, soaking into the sash at his waist. He didn't think the cut was very deep, but it hurt like Hades.

Dormammu continued to push down. All at once, his Pincers closed, snapping shut on Strange's. The combatants were locked together now.

"Submit, mage of Earth," Dormammu said. His flaming face was so close to Strange's that Strange could feel the heat radiating off it. "Why prolong the inevitable?"

"Why does anyone fight, Dormammu? I'll tell you. Because it's always better than surrendering."

At that moment, he slackened his resistance. Dormammu, taken by surprise, fell towards him. Strange used his opponent's momentum against him, flipping Dormammu round so that he tumbled.

Their Pincers were still locked together, and Strange barely managed to remain standing. Dormammu, on the floor, kicked out at his legs. Strange was off-balance and fell too.

Dormammu released Strange's Pincers from his, so that he could get back onto his feet. Strange also scrambled upright.

They paused again, hunched over, facing each other. Around them, the magicians of the Counterclockwise Circle were looking on with unalloyed glee. For the moment their disgruntlement towards Baron Mordo was forgotten. Doctor Strange's suffering and eventual death was all that interested them.

Much the same could be said for Dormammu's warlocks. Their feelings towards their master might be ambivalent, but they owed him loyalty still. If he beat Strange, it would prove their allegiance to him was justified.

Mordo himself was observing the fight with great satisfaction. He would have liked to end Strange's life by his own hand, but watching Dormammu do it was the next best thing.

As for Nightmare, his white lips were pursed, his scarlet eyes narrowed. He was looking intently at Dormammu, searching for a chink in unbreakable armor, a flaw in the perfect warrior.

"You are not unskilled in hand-to-hand combat," Dormammu said to Strange.

"The Ancient One taught me some tai chi as part of my magical training," Strange replied. "I wouldn't say I was a master of the martial arts, but I can hold my own."

"But you are bleeding."

"Just a scratch."

"Let's see how many more such scratches I can put on you before I deliver the killing blow."

Dormammu hurled himself at Strange.

THERE!

Clea sensed a thinning in Dormammu's barrier.

It was all but imperceptible, the slightest diminution of strength.

But it was a weak point she could exploit.

Summoning her magic, she delved into the barrier. She extended her arms, hands back to back, palms facing outwards. Concentrating, she slowly drew her hands apart sideways. The action was a symbolic physical manifestation of the magic she was wreaking. As her hands separated, it was as though they were wrenching open an aperture in the barrier.

Her face showed intense mental exertion. Her teeth ground together. Her forehead was as furrowed as a plowed field.

She could do this. She was Umar the Unrelenting's daughter. She was the hope of the people of the Dark Dimension. She would prevail. She had to.

The aperture widened. She couldn't see it but she could feel it. An invisible hole in the invisible barrier.

She tore further. She was ripping the fabric of the barrier apart. She was creating a wound.

The effort was nigh unbearable. She had no idea how much longer she could keep this up. She was straining the sinews of her mind, using every magical muscle she had. She'd never pushed herself so hard before. She'd never had to.

Gradually, incrementally, the aperture grew until it was the size of a doorway.

Clea could bear it no more. She had nothing left to give.

She collapsed, sinking to her knees. She was exhausted. She could barely think. Barely move.

But she had done it! There was a gap in the barrier now. Not big, but large enough to afford the Mindless Ones access to the Dark Dimension.

But would they realize? Would they use it?

The answer wasn't long in coming. A Mindless One shambled

towards the aperture, seeming to sense that the barrier had been breached. It groped around, found the gap, and stumbled through.

On the other side, it halted. If a thing so expressionless, so devoid of character and soul, could be said to show delight, it was delighted. The slit which served as its eye glowed with dumb, avaricious brightness.

Another Mindless One saw that its fellow had somehow pierced the formerly impenetrable barrier. It walked up to a different section of the barrier, only to bounce back. It looked confused. Was the barrier solid again? It didn't take long, however, for this Mindless One to locate the aperture and follow the first Mindless One through.

More of the creatures were emerging out of the fog and approaching the barrier now. It was as if some silent message had gone out, a signal alerting every Mindless One in the vicinity. *There is a gap. The Dark Dimension can be ours.*

Clea struggled to her feet. The frontmost Mindless Ones were already plodding towards her. They would tear her to pieces if they caught her. They would stamp the bits of her body into the ground.

She was too tired, her magic too depleted, to do anything but run. She bolted towards her tunnel and hurled herself within.

The nearest of the Mindless Ones fired an energy beam at her from its eye-slit.

But Clea had closed the tunnel just in time. The optic blast hit nothing but thin air.

The Mindless Ones were undeterred. The whole of the Dark Dimension lay before them. They lumbered onward, while yet more of them funneled through the gap in the barrier.

STRANGE CROUCHED, bent almost double. His sides heaved. Sweat dripped from his face and plastered his hair to his scalp.

He was cut in a dozen places. His shirt hung in ribbons. His torso was soaked in his own blood. The floor of the chamber was spattered with it.

Dormammu prowled around him triumphantly. He too was injured, but not as severely as Strange. In the places where the blades of Strange's Pincers of Power had slashed his body, a lambent, magma-like ichor oozed out. A Faltine's blood.

"You are nearly spent, Strange," the Lord of the Dark Dimension crowed. "Your strength is failing. Your willpower likewise. See? Your Pincers grow faint. Soon they will give out altogether, and you will be defenseless."

This was true. Strange was drawing on his last reserves of magic, and it wasn't enough to keep the Pincers at full potency. They flickered and guttered like expiring candles.

"You've been a formidable opponent," Dormammu went on. "No duel I have fought with the Pincers of Power has lasted this long. But that will only make my final victory all the sweeter."

"I don't know… about you…" Strange panted, "but I'm just… getting started."

"Bravado to the end. I like that about you, mage of Earth. You never give up. Even when it is hopeless."

Strange steeled himself. Dormammu was winding himself up for his next attack.

It came.

Strange's Pincers met Dormammu's. They held them at bay. But only just.

He couldn't go on much longer. Another minute, perhaps, then he'd be running on empty.

He remembered his ace in the hole. Yet for some reason, again it didn't feel like this was the moment to play it. There was still a chance he could turn things around without resorting to drastic, untried measures.

Suddenly Dormammu stiffened, looking distracted.

"No," he murmured. "The barrier… It's…"

Strange took advantage of the momentary lapse. He disengaged one of his Pincers from Dormammu's and thrust it at his opponent's leg. The edge caught Dormammu on the side of the thigh. As some of that glowing, ichorous blood welled out, Dormammu staggered backwards with a cry of distress.

Strange, with the failing strength in his body, dived at him, shoulder-barging him like a linebacker and knocking him over.

Dormammu fell to the floor, rolling onto his back.

Strange placed a foot on each of Dormammu's forearms, pinning them so that Dormammu couldn't bring either of his Pincers to bear.

He poised one of his own Pincers at Dormammu's neck.

"Yield," he said.

Dormammu glared up at him.

"I said yield. I'll give you this one chance. Otherwise I slit your throat."

"No," said the Lord of the Dark Dimension. "No, you won't. You don't kill, Strange."

"I can make an exception this once."

"Go ahead, then. Let's see if you can."

Strange was in a quandary. Dormammu was correct. He did not kill.

Or did he? The fate of the Earth was at stake. What was Dormammu's life, set against the future of the entire human race?

He decided to give Dormammu one last chance. There was a way out of this dilemma which would mean he himself wouldn't have to commit murder and Dormammu could retain his dignity.

"Reaffirm your vow never to conquer the mortal realm," he said, "and we'll call it quits. And this time no exceptions, no niceties, no takebacks, no 'it doesn't count if Doctor Strange is dead'. A complete, blanket vow with permanent effect."

He would never find out if Dormammu would have agreed to it.

Because, just then, he was zapped from behind by a Bolt of Balthakk.

He was sent flying.

He slid across the floor, fetching up near the Ancient One.

He lay stunned. His Pincers of Power sputtered out.

The Ancient One was in no fit state to defend him. Strange was utterly at Dormammu's mercy.

○———————○

DORMAMMU, HOWEVER, was not so concerned about Doctor Strange just then. He was too busy upbraiding Baron Mordo.

"What," he boomed, "did you just do? Did you just strike Strange?"

"I did," Mordo replied forthrightly.

"What for?" Dormammu loomed over him.

Mordo looked a little less sure of himself. "He was about to kill you. He had his Pincers at your neck. I… I saved you."

"*You* thought you were saving *me*?"

The European aristocrat began visibly quailing. "I was only trying to help."

"Help? You interfered in a Faltine duel. That's a transgression in itself. But you also assumed, just because Strange had me at a temporary disadvantage, that I was going to lose. You bungler! You utter, blithering imbecile! How dare you?"

"Lord Dormammu, please," said Mordo. "Forgive me. I made a misstep. I overreached."

The assembled members of the Counterclockwise Circle were finding Mordo's discomfort very entertaining. They loved seeing people squirm, especially someone known to them, someone so arrogant. Someone, moreover, who'd made bad faith promises to them. It couldn't be happening to a more deserving victim.

"You, Mordo, have been merely a tool of mine," Dormammu said. "A hireling. But then you had the impudence to go over my head, to act of your own accord and not at my command."

"I—I meant no harm. Sincerely, My Lord, I did what I thought was right."

"You blundered greatly. And do you know what I do to blunderers?"

Mordo had all of a sudden lost his voice. He was too afraid to reply.

"For one thing, I do not tolerate them holding on to power borrowed from me."

Dormammu deactivated his Pincers of Power and held both hands aloft over Mordo.

It wasn't possible to see the actual magical power being transferred from Mordo back to its original possessor. That happened invisibly.

It was possible, however, to see the effect on Mordo.

He jerked and spasmed like a marionette in the hands of a mad puppet master. His limbs flailed. An eerie, strangulated wail escaped his throat. It was as though some essential part was being pulled out of him. As though some of his vigor was being forcibly siphoned upwards into Dormammu's hands.

Then he crumpled.

"The other thing I do to blunderers," said Dormammu, "is dispose of them. In your case, death would be too great a mercy. I shall banish you and give you time to repent. An indefinite amount of time to suffer exquisite, unending torments."

Mordo recovered the ability to speak. "Mighty Dormammu," he croaked, "Dread Dormammu, please. I beg you. Don't. Don't do this."

"I'm thinking the Dimension of Demons is the place," Dormammu said.

"No," Mordo whimpered.

"Yes."

Dormammu conjured a portal. Through it could be glimpsed a landscape of jagged, blood-red rocks, interspersed with bubbling lava pools and steaming sulfurous pits. Hellish beings loitered around in various states of repose. Some had forked tails. Some had piglike snouts. Some had goat legs. Some resembled reptiles. Some were akin to insects, some to sea creatures, some to birds. Some simply defied description.

One of the demons carried a barbed-wire whip. Another was sharpening a long, curved knife with a stone. Yet another was heating up a branding iron over one of the lava pools.

As soon as the portal opened, a frisson of excitement went through the demons' ranks. They danced, squabbled, and jockeyed for position, like zoo animals at feeding time.

Mordo was a puddle of abject, groaning horror. He was too incapacitated to escape, too terrified to resist. Dormammu lifted him up as though he weighed no more than a child and flung him bodily into the portal.

Mordo screamed as he hurtled headlong into the Dimension of Demons. Its denizens closed in on him.

The portal snapped shut, cutting off his pitiful cries. All that remained to mark his passing was a lingering whiff of brimstone.

TWENTY-ONE

STRANGE HURT all over, both from the wounds inflicted by Dormammu's Pincers of Power and from the body blow delivered by Mordo's Bolt of Balthakk. Through a haze of pain he watched Dormammu consign Mordo to the Dimension of Demons. It was a terrible fate but he couldn't honestly say he was sad. Mordo had brought it on himself.

Now Dormammu stalked over to Strange. "That's one irritant from Earth dealt with," he said. "Time for another."

He reactivated his Pincers of Power.

"Slit my throat, Strange? Was that what you threatened me with? Seems only fair I should return the favor."

Strange forced himself up onto all fours. He raised a hand to summon a shield. Nothing came. The pain blurred his thoughts, making concentration next to impossible.

Dormammu brought one set of Pincers to Strange's neck. "This gives me little pleasure," he said. "No. I tell a lie. It gives me quite a lot."

"Stop!"

CLEA BURST into the chamber. In a flash, she took in the startling tableau before her. Dormammu, with his Pincers of Power at

Stephen Strange's throat. Strange himself, bloodied and bedraggled. Dormammu's warlocks, gathered round, along with men and women dressed in Earth clothing, magicians all. And a figure clad in dark green, with white skin and red eyes, whom she did not recognize but who, like the Earth mages, clearly hailed from outside the Dark Dimension.

Clea's cry of "Stop!" was ragged and heartfelt.

Dormammu paused. "Ah, niece. A very dramatic entrance. And just in time to see Doctor Strange receive his long-overdue comeuppance."

"No. Leave him alone, Dormammu."

The Lord of the Dark Dimension canted his head quizzically. "You've developed a fondness for this man. I can see it in your eyes. You cannot bear the thought of him dead. Would you plead for his life now? Is that the reason for your intervention?"

"I know that I would be wasting my breath," Clea said. "You would hear me out, then slay him just to spite me."

"You know me well."

"No, I come to inform you that the barrier between the Dark Dimension and the world of the Mindless Ones has been breached. Even as we speak, Mindless Ones are invading."

"I am aware," Dormammu said.

"You must do something about it. If not, people will die. Your people. Would you abandon them in their hour of need?"

"I shall attend to the Mindless Ones after I have dispensed with Strange."

"It might be too late. You should go right now, before too many of them come through even for you to handle."

Dormammu straightened up. Clea was relieved that his Pincers of Power were no longer at Strange's throat.

"Tell me, Clea," he said, "this breach in the barrier which has so mysteriously and conveniently occurred… You wouldn't have had something to do with it, by any chance?"

"Why would you suspect me?"

"I am not ignorant of your seditious inclinations, niece. Little happens in this dimension that escapes my notice. You feel that by letting Mindless Ones loose, it will somehow turn my subjects against me, perhaps even provoke an uprising. You underestimate how bovine the populace is. Oh, they mutter rebelliously, some of them, and talk big talk about overthrowing me. But by and large they are timid, docile things who would rather just get on with their miserable lives. You are a deeply misguided young woman, Clea. You have my sister's intensity of spirit in you, but also her waywardness and her contrariness. What did not serve her well likewise disserves you."

Clea shook her head. "So you're simply going to let Mindless Ones conduct a rampage?"

"For a time. Then I shall round them up and beat them back, and after that, restore the barrier. And do you know what the people will do? They will praise me. They will be eternally grateful. They will say, 'Dormammu has delivered us from terror. All hail Dormammu!' Yes, there will have been deaths. A massacre, even. But those deaths will merely remind my subjects that their existences are contingent on me. Without my power protecting them, they have nothing."

"You have miscalculated their hatred for you."

"No. You have miscalculated their dependency on me. Now, if you don't mind, there is business to be conducted here." Dormammu bent down towards Strange again. "Well, mage? Anything to say before I end your life? Any great insights to impart with your last dying breath?"

"Eternally grateful," said Strange.

Dormammu half-laughed. "And what is that supposed to mean?"

"Eternally grateful," Strange repeated.

"Yes, I heard you clearly the first time."

Strange chuckled.

Dormammu frowned. "You seem unusually cheerful for someone about to die."

"Not really," Strange said. "It's just that you've confirmed it."

"Confirmed what?"

"That it's ace-in-the-hole time. Finally."

"Have you gone insane?" said Dormammu. "Make sense, mortal!"

"You see, Dormammu, powerful though you are, there's always someone greater."

"No. I am Dormammu. I am all-conquering. Everyone bows before me."

"Of course. You've got every reason to believe that. But the trouble with autocrats like you is that you can't see the bigger picture. You never appreciate just how small and insignificant you actually are."

"This?" Dormammu sneered. "This is how you wish to depart life? With a diatribe against me?" He looked round at Nightmare, his warlocks, and the members of the Counterclockwise Circle. "It only goes to show. Petty mockery is the last refuge of the loser. When all else fails, insult."

"But Dormammu," said Strange, "you know of Eternity, surely."

"Eternity?"

"The embodiment of all that is, all that was and all that ever will be."

"I am cognizant of the existence of such a being. I have given it no great heed. Eternity dwells on a plane so far removed from this one as to be irrelevant."

"That's where you're wrong," Strange said. "Everything you do is part of Eternity. You're enfolded into it. We all are. Every step you take, every decision you come to, every course of action you follow, is beholden to Eternity. You are not all-powerful, Dormammu, and never will be, while you remain Eternity's subordinate."

"I am subordinate to nothing and nobody!" declared the Lord of the Dark Dimension.

"Keep telling yourself that, but you must know, in your heart of hearts, that you are a pawn of Eternity. You will never escape that fact. Conquer as many worlds as you wish. Impose your yoke on countless people. Become absolute ruler of the Multiverse, if you can. But at the end of it all, there'll always be something greater than you. You'll never have everything as long as Eternity *is* everything."

Dormammu straightened up. "This is nonsense," he said, but his tone was unconvinced.

"Stephen Strange is right, Uncle," Clea piped up. "Your ambitions are meaningless. However much you reign over, Eternity will always reign over you."

"No." The word came out slowly, musingly. "No, not if I vanquish Eternity. Not if *I* reign over *it*."

Nightmare joined in the debate. "That is impossible," he said. "Vanquish Eternity? It would be madness even to try."

Briefly, behind Dormammu's back, Strange and Nightmare exchanged glances. The dream-lord gave Strange the tiniest of nods. He knew Strange was goading Dormammu. He was in on the ruse. For the moment, his goals and Strange's aligned. Both of them wanted the same thing.

"Lord Dormammu," Nightmare continued, "I urge you strongly against this policy. It will not end well for you."

Dormammu turned and fixed him with a derisive glare. "When I want your counsel, Nightmare, I shall never ask for it."

"I'm simply suggesting——"

"Hush!" Dormammu wagged an admonishing finger. "Cease your chatter. On balance, Strange, I am minded to think you are right. You show wisdom in your desperation. After I am done with you, and have corralled the Mindless Ones, the next item on my agenda will be Eternity itself. If I can trap it, even destroy it, then I shall be free. There will be nothing I cannot overcome, no limit to what I can achieve!"

"Why wait?" Strange said.

"What do you mean?"

"Why put it off? Why not confront Eternity now? I can summon it here, if you'd like."

"Don't be absurd. Eternity is not at your beck and call."

"You might be surprised."

"I would be astounded."

Strange got to his feet, effortlessly. Standing hurt. Breathing hurt. He had lost so much blood, he felt faint. He could barely hold himself upright. Added to that, he was unsure whether this gamble of his would pay off. There was no guarantee it would and no reason it should. Eternity had said it would grant him a boon, but would it even remember doing so, let alone honor its offer? Supernal entities had greater things on their minds than fulfilling promises made to beings who, to them, were infinitesimal, inconsequential specks. It could be pardoned for having forgotten its pledge to Strange within instants of giving it.

And yet Strange felt the moment, at last, was right. All at once, things seemed preordained. *You will know the hour,* Eternity had said. *You will know the place.* If this wasn't exactly what Eternity had been referring to, he didn't know what was.

"Hear me, Eternity," he said. "I call on you. Your boon is due. Grace us with your presence."

For several long moments, nothing happened. Strange caught Clea's eye. She was looking at him with compassion and perhaps a touch of pity. Maybe she thought he had gone insane. Maybe he had.

Dormammu undoubtedly thought so. "Ridiculous," he snorted. "I thought you desperate. Now I see you are hopelessly deluded."

"Give it time," Strange said, with more confidence than he felt. "Eternity can't be rushed."

He glanced down at the Ancient One. The old man's rheumy eyes were half open—and was that the ghost of a smile on his lips? As if he was congratulating his disciple on a ploy well orchestrated?

Then…

THE CHAMBER had been just a chamber.

Suddenly it was filled with *everything*.

A vastness manifested.

It took the form of a man.

A gargantuan man comprised of stars, universes, cosmic debris, meteors, nebulae, untold numbers of planets.

A man who gazed down with somber knowingness on the negligible creatures arrayed around the room.

The Counterclockwise Circle mages, in various states of cringing incomprehension. Dormammu's warlocks likewise.

Clea, her silvery eyes wide with astonishment.

Nightmare, no less dumbstruck than her.

The semi-comatose Ancient One.

Doctor Strange, whose evident physical traumas were somewhat mitigated by the gratification he felt at Eternity's arrival.

And Dormammu, Lord of the Dark Dimension, who was striving to keep his expression inscrutable but whose jaw nonetheless gaped.

Eternity surveyed them all like a scientist studying bacteria under a microscope, detached, mildly curious.

I HAVE COME, Eternity said. YOU HAVE SUMMONED ME IN ACCORDANCE WITH OUR AGREEMENT, STEPHEN VINCENT STRANGE. WHAT WOULD YOU HAVE ME DO?

"It's not me, as a matter of fact," Strange replied. "It's him." He motioned at Dormammu. "May I introduce Dormammu, Lord of the Dark Dimension. I think he's got a bone to pick with you."

I KNOW OF DORMAMMU. HIS DEEDS HAVE CAUSED MANY A DISTURBANCE WITHIN THE FABRIC OF EXISTENCE. HIS MOTIVES REEK OF IMPURITY. WOULD YOU, DORMAMMU, CHALLENGE ME?

Dormammu had no choice but to confirm it. His pride would allow nothing else. "I do indeed. I cannot permit you to be master of all, not when that is a role I covet for myself."

Something like a smile flickered across Eternity's indistinct features. YOU ARE BOLD. YOU ARE ALSO UNWISE. DO YOU NOT UNDERSTAND THAT ETERNITY IS ALL-

ENCOMPASSING? UNFATHOMABLE? UNCONTESTABLE? DUST CANNOT CHALLENGE A WHIRLWIND. A MINNOW CANNOT CHALLENGE THE OCEAN.

To Dormammu's credit, he didn't flinch. "I am mighty," he said. "I am unafraid."

RECANT YOUR DECISION. YOU WILL ONLY REGRET IT. "Never!"

Dormammu gathered his magic around him. Titanic forces swirled within the chamber. His flaming head burned more brightly and fiercely than Strange had ever seen it burn. His body seemed to expand from within, swelling as he drew on every last erg of power that was his to command.

It was at that moment that Strange wondered if he'd made a misjudgment. Might Dormammu actually stand a chance against Eternity? Might he unleash a holocaust right here and now which could destroy that entity and therefore all that existed? Was it possible? He wouldn't put it past Dormammu, drunk with arrogance and indignation, to do just that. Oblivious to the consequences, he could very well end the Multiverse. The cataclysm would consume him along with everything else, but Strange doubted he was concerned about that. For Dormammu, daring superseded caring.

The Ancient One spoke softly. "Fear not, Stephen. Dormammu will not prevail."

Strange wished he could be so sure.

Dormammu hurled himself at Eternity, letting loose a discharge of pure, unbridled magical power. It was enough to level mountains, to halt a tsunami in its tracks, to raze a city to the ground.

And Eternity…

Didn't even blink.

Dormammu sent forth a second blast, and a third. It was as though the chamber suddenly housed a tempest, all blinding flashes of light and deafening bursts of thunderclap-loud sound. The warlocks and the Counterclockwise mages cowered and reeled. Even

Nightmare appeared taken aback.

Eternity calmly absorbed everything Dormammu threw at it.

This only incited the Lord of the Dark Dimension to try harder. Howling energies crackled and roared. The whole citadel shook. Parts of the chamber ceiling broke free and crashed to the floor. In the floor itself, zigzagging fissures opened up.

As Dormammu assailed Eternity, so Eternity got larger. It wasn't clear to Strange if Dormammu even realized this. Eternity was reaching for him, growing around him, incorporating him into itself. Dormammu fought on, loosing off magic with reckless abandon. He was so lost in the frenzied fury of his assault, he failed to appreciate that Eternity now surrounded him.

All at once, he seemed to grasp the immensity of it. The immensity of Eternity itself, and the immensity of the mistake he had made.

He was inside the cosmos.

He was as nothing.

Relative to the universes of which Eternity was comprised, Dormammu was utterly without importance.

He was tiny.

Literally.

Before the eyes of all those watching, Dormammu was shrinking. Diminishing within Eternity's unending, star-speckled limitlessness, a dot among galaxies, a particle, an atom. Vanishingly small.

Then gone.

Eternity stood, unchanged. Swallowing up Dormammu had made no difference to it. Neither had Dormammu's assault. Eternity was just as it was, as it had always been, as it would always be.

Eternity.

"Thank you," Strange said, but Eternity gave no indication it had even heard him. Its colossal form turned round, as though heading for an exit. Then it wasn't there anymore. All that remained behind was an impression of magnitude beyond comprehension and, in the hearts of those present capable of feeling it, a sense of humbleness.

TWENTY-TWO

STRANGE LEANED against a pillar for support, head bent. Clea hurried to his side.

"Your injuries," she said. "How bad are they?"

"How bad do they look?"

She cast an eye over his torn body. Her expression was her answer.

"That bad, huh?" he said. "Well, it's nothing a few days' rest and maybe some of Wong's healing ointments won't cure."

"Who is this Wong?"

"Great guy. You'd like him if you met him. Everyone does. But listen. Mindless Ones are on the loose, yes?"

Clea nodded. "I made a hole in the barrier and freed them."

"And your timing was excellent. It distracted Dormammu at just the right moment. I'd have had him, if Mordo hadn't got involved. But we need to put them back where they belong. Without Dormammu. Somehow."

"It's worse than that," Clea said. "With Dormammu gone, the barrier is no more. Every single Mindless One can enter this realm."

Strange shunted himself off the pillar. "Then we have to fight them off and resurrect the barrier."

"How? Look at you. You can hardly stand. As for me, I don't know if I can summon the magic needed yet. I burned myself out opening the barrier. It'll be a while before my power is replenished."

"All is not lost," Strange said.

He moved over to the warlocks and Counterclockwise Circle mages. They were still in consternation after the tumultuous events they'd just witnessed.

"Ladies, gentlemen," he said. "I don't expect any of you act in a way that's not in your own interest. Nevertheless, I'm offering you the chance to do exactly that. This realm, the Dark Dimension, is under threat of extinction. There are Mindless Ones out there, terrible creatures that exist only to destroy, and they are moving in. They have this city in their sights: when they reach it, they'll kill everyone who lives here. Now, you from the Counterclockwise Circle can head back to Earth if you like. I imagine most of you will. You'll flee because saving your own skins is always the most important thing to you. I, however, am going to combat the Mindless Ones, and some of you might want to stay and assist me in that. And you, Dormammu's warlocks—well, this is your home. You've surely got to want to protect it and whatever loved ones here you might have."

He couldn't tell if he was getting through to them or not. Any faces in front of him that weren't stubborn were nonplussed.

"You saw what happened to Baron Mordo," he persisted. "A man who put himself before everything else, a man who chased power for power's sake. Look how well it worked out for him. That ought to be an object lesson to you. You also saw Eternity. I don't know about you, but for me, having met that entity, everything's been put in perspective. We're small, all of us. We're tiny and unimportant. Brief, minuscule sparks of light in the yawning enormity of the cosmos. And that may make you think, 'Well, what's the point of anything, then? Why bother at all? Good, evil, what does it matter? Just go ahead and act as you please.'"

He paused.

"If I've learned anything since I became the Ancient One's disciple and started studying magic, it's that that's the point. The small things count. Not only people. What we, as people, do. How we behave. It all contributes. It may seem insignificant, but it mounts up. It's exponential, in fact. The more of us who do good, the more likely it is that others will do good too. Here, now, you have a chance to change yourselves. You can step up and be part of something better. Join with me and take on the Mindless Ones and save the Dark Dimension. It won't be easy. It will be dangerous. Not an appetizing proposition at all, to be honest. But if some of you help— even just a few—it could make all the difference."

He waited. The members of the Counterclockwise Circle looked at one another. The warlocks did the same. Several of them went into huddles and discussed.

He noticed that Clea was holding his hand. He'd been so busy making his speech, he hadn't been aware of her fingers slipping in between his and clasping them. He liked how it felt. He clasped back.

The Counterclockwise magicians finished their conferring, and the bulbous-nosed Englishman, Cuthbertson, stepped forward. It seemed he had been elected spokesperson.

"Mordo rallied us against you, Strange," he said. "He made us believe you were our enemy. Now that we've seen you in action, though, we're moved to reconsider. The consensus of opinion among us has shifted. And there's... there's just so much more to existence than we realized. That being, that Eternity—until we were confronted with it, we really had no idea how things work. I certainly didn't. It's all connected, isn't it? We're minute, each of us, yet we're all part of a greater whole."

"Does this mean what I think it means?"

"Not all of us are in, but most of us are. We'll help."

"Thank you," said Strange. "And you?" he said to the warlocks.

One of them spoke up. "This is our home. We'll defend it."

"That goes for all of you?"

There was assent among the warlocks, expressed in nods, cheers and the odd clenched fist.

"Good," said Strange. "Clea, would you explain to the people from Earth what the Mindless Ones are? Give them some idea what they'll be facing. I'm going to go and have a chat with that fellow over there."

He disentangled his hand from hers, with some regret. Then he approached Nightmare, who'd been observing the foregoing conversation with mild curiosity.

"You won't persuade *me*, Strange," Nightmare said.

"Then why are you still here? Why did you come to my aid with Dormammu?"

"I wanted to see the back of him, and I saw a way of helping to achieve that. I know his type. I know what levers to pull."

"Because you and he are alike."

"Precisely. Just because I did what I did, however, it won't mean I'll volunteer for your little army."

"We could do with the power of a dream-lord."

Nightmare conjured a portal to the Dream Dimension. "Goodbye, Strange. Assuming you survive today, we will clash again, I'm sure, in future. The waking world will be mine one day."

"Not on my watch, Nightmare," Strange retorted. "Launch as many attacks on Earth as you like. I'll always stop you."

"In your dreams, Strange," said Nightmare, striding into his portal. "In your dreams."

MINDLESS ONES were nearing the city. The bludgeoning monsters crushed everything they came across. Trees, houses, livestock, people. It seemed nothing could stop them.

A line of defense awaited them at the city outskirts. Dormammu's warlocks and a couple of dozen magicians from Earth, all led by Doctor Strange.

Strange hovered aloft with his Cloak of Levitation. This gave him a good vantage point as the Mindless Ones roved towards the members of the Counterclockwise Circle.

"Hold steady," he told his uneasy troops. "Hold steady. Not yet. You have the power to do this. Keep your nerve."

Before leaving the citadel, he'd seen to it that the Ancient One was comfortable. "I won't be long, Master," he'd said. "Then we'll whisk you back home and get you the medical attention you need."

The old man had given a weak nod. "You have acquitted yourself nobly, Stephen. I could not be prouder of you than I am now. When you return from the fray, there is something I must tell you."

That "when" had been important to Strange. Not "if." The Ancient One was confident he would win this battle.

Then Clea had approached him. "My magic is still not up to full strength, but I have enough to ease your injuries. Let me do that."

She'd run her hands over him, and everywhere they'd touched the pain had abated and a delicious numb warmth taken its place. The lacerations had gently closed, the bruises and abrasions faded away.

"Please keep an eye on the Ancient One for me," he had said.

"Come back, Stephen Strange."

"Oh, I will, believe me."

As the Mindless Ones drew closer still to the city, people began filing out from the main gate. They had brought weapons with them, both actual and makeshift. Some had swords and knives, while others brandished fire irons, chair legs, hammers, anything that could be pressed into service as an armament.

This was their city. They would help stop the Mindless Ones from overrunning it, or they would die trying.

Strange took a moment to admire their bravery.

Then he let out a cry.

"Attack!"

AN HOUR later, the battlefield was strewn with bodies.

By far the majority belonged to Mindless Ones. A handful of the warlocks and the Counterclockwise Circle mages had perished. Scores of citizens, too.

But the Mindless Ones were on the retreat. They were scurrying back whence they came, in their leaden-footed, cumbersome way. They had come up against stiffer opposition than they could have anticipated. They had seen their numbers devastated through a combination of magical spells and sheer physical violence. Brute instinct prompted them to turn and leave. Even brainless engines of destruction knew when they were outclassed and when continuing with an assault was futile.

Strange, satisfied that the creatures had been successfully repulsed, congratulated the city's defenders. The Counterclockwise magicians found themselves being applauded by the citizens, as did the warlocks. It was clearly an unusual experience for these men and women to have folk come up and slap them on the back and invite them for a celebratory drink. Strange could tell it made them uncomfortable, but they didn't dislike it.

The Cloak of Levitation carried him back to the citadel, where he rejoined the Ancient One and Clea.

"You look dead on your feet, Stephen Strange," she said.

"I am. And please, it's just Stephen. 'Stephen Strange' is too much."

"Very well, Stephen."

"So…" he began awkwardly. "I can't stay. I have to take the Ancient One back to Earth right away."

"I understand."

"My offer stands. You could come with me, Clea. Now that Dormammu's no longer around, you don't have to be here anymore to counteract him."

"That's just it." Her lip trembled. Her silver-flecked eyes were sad. "Now that he's gone, there's more reason for me to remain, not less. For one thing, you have driven the Mindless Ones back, but they are only at bay, not contained. The barrier against them will have to be re-established. I can do that. I can put up and sustain a new barrier. I may be the only person in the Dark Dimension who is able to."

"I... see."

"But also, the people need a ruler, someone to guide them now that Dormammu's reign is over. My father will assume that role, but he will need an adviser. He isn't the most dynamic or decisive of men."

"I get it. You have duties."

"And you have yours, Stephen. Our separate duties must keep us in our separate worlds. For now."

"Yes." Strange liked the sound of those words: *For now*. Nothing was permanent. Things could change. "Well then, Clea. This is goodbye, I suppose."

He went to the Ancient One's side. He wasn't sure he had the strength for any more spells. A portal to Earth might be beyond him. Even just raising his hands to start the conjuring was an almost insurmountable feat.

Clea, seeing he was having difficulties, came over. "Allow me. My magic is sufficiently recovered."

Together, pooling their mystical resources, they opened the portal. Through it, the interior of the Ancient One's retreat could be seen. A window showed Himalayan snows flurrying outdoors, but inside a hearth fire burned and the place looked warm and inviting.

Strange picked the old man up in his arms. He was not heavy. Thin anyway, he had been reduced by his fever to mere skin and bones.

Clea leaned in and kissed Strange.

"For now," she repeated.

Strange stepped out of the Dark Dimension, not seeing the tears in Clea's silvery eyes.

His vision was blurry from the tears in his own.

EPILOGUE

XANDU THE Unspeakable had both halves of the Wand of Watoomb, and this made him exceptionally dangerous. With it, he possessed the single greatest source of magical power available, or so the necromantic lore claimed at least. He could access other dimensions. He could destroy objects and people with just a thought. He could alter reality. He could command the elements. Once he had been just a minor magician and his greatest talent had been the ability to hypnotize others into doing his bidding and grant above-average strength and endurance to those who fell under his spell. Thanks to the Wand, however, nothing was beyond Xandu now, and the world was his for the taking.

Luckily, two men stood against him.

One was Doctor Strange. The other was the web-slinging wonder known as Spider-Man.

IT ALL started one night when Xandu enthralled a couple of petty thugs, gifting one with an immunity to pain and fear and the other with fists that could shatter timber. He'd found the pair, Clancy and Rocco, coming out of a Hell's Kitchen dive bar called Josie's, fresh from a brawl. They were thick-eared, big-muscled, and clearly fond of a scrap. Perfect for what he had in mind.

At Xandu's behest, the two thugs barged their way into the Sanctum Sanctorum, catching the homeowner off-guard. Strange was knocked unconscious and the intruders stole the half of the Wand of Watoomb from his Chamber of Shadows. Rocco, with his magic-hardened fists, simply smashed open the cabinet containing the artifact.

By great good fortune—or perhaps through the auspices of the Great Vishanti, who were said to exert a subtle influence on the workings of fate—the super hero Spider-Man happened to be swinging along Bleecker Street on his nightly patrol of the city just as Clancy and Rocco emerged from Strange's house. His fabled Spider-Sense told him these two were up to no good, and even if it hadn't, they looked suspicious anyway. They moved like sleepwalkers and one of them had a small sack slung around his neck with something heavy inside.

He accosted them, and they responded by attacking him. A fight ensued, during which Spider-Man kept up a constant stream of quips, because that was his way. Spider-Man couldn't battle bad guys without wisecracking.

"Are you guys kidding? Taking a poke at me is like instant annihilation! But I guess you wanna be able to brag to your grandchildren that you were once knocked out by Spidey. So here's your chance!"

His wit was wasted on the mesmerized thugs. Wordlessly, they slugged away at him. Clancy shrugged off his strongest blows, while Rocco dished out a severe beating.

Like Strange, Spider-Man was caught off-guard. He hadn't expected two ordinary-looking joes to be quite as tough a proposition as these were, and his lack of caution cost him. Between them Clancy and Rocco clobbered him into submission, then continued on their way, leaving him behind in a dazed, befuddled heap.

Spider-Man still had a weapon in his arsenal, though. He

managed to toss one of his Spider-Tracers at the departing thugs. The tiny, spider-shaped electronic device found its mark, adhering itself to Rocco's pants leg. Now, once he recovered, Spider-Man would be able to track the man down wherever he went, homing in on the Spider-Tracer's signal with his Spider-Sense.

Clancy and Rocco made their somnambulistic way to Xandu's townhouse on the Upper West Side. He placed them both in a trance-like state of suspended animation, then examined the booty they had brought. The Wand of Watoomb consisted of a pair of carved, icosahedral heads, each surpassingly ugly. The portion of the artifact Xandu already owned came with a foot-long shaft attached. Strange had had the other head. Xandu fastened the head to the shaft, and lo and behold, the Wand was complete again.

Power pulsated through the Wand. Xandu held it aloft gloatingly. Magic permeated from it, through his hand, into his very soul. He felt infused with permission to do whatever he pleased. With sheer *possibility*.

○───────○

SO ENGROSSED was Xandu in marveling over his acquisition, he failed to notice Spider-Man sneaking into his house through a skylight.

Spider-Man, for his part, recognized a super villain when he saw one. Xandu had a cape, a monocle and a white moustache that curled a long way outside his cheeks. He was also monologuing to himself about destroying his enemies, which was Bad Guy Behavior 101. He was even talking about himself in the third person, and giving himself a self-aggrandizing suffix, "Xandu the Unspeakable." In short, he couldn't have come across as more super-villain-y if he'd tried.

"Xandu the Unspeakable, huh?" Spider-Man said, clinging upside-down to the ceiling above Xandu.

The magician whirled round and looked up.

"More like Xandu the Unremarkable," the wall-crawler went on. "If I've met one bargain-basement nogoodnik like you, I've met a dozen."

"Fool!" Xandu cried. "There's nobody like me!"

He fired magical force beams at Spider-Man with the Wand, but the web-slinger evaded every blast with uncanny agility and grace. It was as though he could predict where Xandu was aiming and where the shot would land, enabling him to leap out of the way. Which, of course, he could, courtesy of his Spider-Sense.

However, magical foes were not something Spider-Man was accustomed to. Give him a man with mentally controlled steel tentacles attached to his torso, a man who threw pumpkin-shaped bombs and rode a rocket-powered glider, even a man who could turn his body to sand, and he was fine. He knew where he stood. But magic? That was a trickier proposition.

And so, when Xandu opened up a portal to another dimension beneath Spider-Man's feet, he couldn't prevent himself slipping into it.

But thanks to his swift reflexes, he didn't leave without a prize. He shot a strand of webbing at the Wand of Watoomb, figuring correctly that this was the source of his opponent's power. He snatched the Wand right out of Xandu's hand and took it with him. Xandu leapt after it but it missed. Spider-Man, to his great anger, had outwitted him.

Spider-Man found himself in a place of senses-shattering bizarreness. It was a topsy-turvy crossroads between dimensions, where strange realm collided with strange realm. There were windows to other worlds, doorways to planes of reality that boggled the mind, tunnels linking parallel universes. He could scarcely make sense of anything he saw.

"I… I don't have any idea where I am," he murmured to himself, "but one thing's for sure. It's gonna take more than a bus ride to get me back to Forest Hills."

MEANWHILE, DOCTOR Strange was gradually coming to. He had a bruise the size of a hen's egg on the back of his head, and his brain was a jumble of thoughts and impressions.

As he collected his wits, his mind went back to his last conversation with the Ancient One. This had taken place a few days after they returned from the Dark Dimension. Under Wong's care at his retreat, the Ancient One was recovering well. His fever was gone and his strength was trickling back. When Strange was confident his master was on the mend, he came to bid him goodbye.

"Stephen," the old man said, "I said it at the time, and I'll say it again. You acquitted yourself nobly in your conflict with Mordo and Dormammu. You saved Earth *and* the Dark Dimension. You have shown yourself to be a true master of the mystic arts."

"I was taught well," Strange said.

"Don't be modest. Knowledge is one thing. Using it wisely is another. The time has come for you to step into your next role in life."

"What do you mean by that, Master?"

"Simply this. I am old. Very old. I have worn the mantle of Sorcerer Supreme for an inordinate length of time, and my powers are waning. Someone else must take it now."

"Me?"

The old Tibetan smiled. "Who else? You have proved more than worthy of the title. You are our world's greatest magical defender. Take on the responsibility. I could not be handing it on to a better recipient."

Strange bowed his head. "I don't know what to say."

"Just say you agree to it."

"I do. I am honored."

"The honor is mine," said the Ancient One. "I have been blessed with a skilled disciple and an exemplary successor. It is a comfort knowing that, whatever should happen to me, Earth is in safe hands."

And so it was not just Doctor Strange but Doctor Strange, Sorcerer Supreme, who left the Ancient One's retreat and resumed his life in New York.

But, while he might now be Sorcerer Supreme, Strange was currently having difficulty reconciling his newfound status with the fact that he'd been blindsided and cold-cocked by a couple of street thugs. Maybe the Ancient One had been premature in handing the title on. Maybe he didn't deserve it after all.

It didn't take him long to figure out that his half of the Wand of Watoomb had been stolen. It was the only item missing from his Chamber of Shadows, and the theft was so specific, he could only assume that someone else had the other half of the Wand and wished to reunite the two parts.

That was very worrying.

Strange opened the Eye of Agamotto and used its light to reveal the trail left by the two crooks. His Cloak of Levitation flew him uptown through the dark, with trepidation growing in his heart. The Wand, in the wrong hands, could be the deadliest of artifacts. Apocalyptically dangerous.

He arrived at Xandu's townhouse and demanded that the other sorcerer return the Wand to him. Xandu refused, although he didn't explain to Strange why. He didn't want him to know he didn't have the Wand anymore. Instead, he engaged in magical combat with Strange.

This was as short-lived as it was futile. Xandu, with nothing to fall back on but some basic magical abilities, was hardly a match for Strange. Strange swiftly gained the upper hand in the contest.

That was when Spider-Man burst back onto the scene.

IN THE interim, Spider-Man had been battling with Clancy and Rocco at the interdimensional crossroads. Xandu had sent the two thugs after him to retrieve the Wand. Spider-Man had traded blows with them before realizing that his best chance of getting out from this place of madness was to feign defeat and allow them to take him captive. The thugs had been transported there to bring the Wand back. Why not just hitch a ride home with them?

As the trio hurtled through a portal into Xandu's townhouse, Xandu seized his opportunity. He snatched the Wand of Watoomb out of Spider-Man's grasp.

Now he had it again—all the power a man could wish for, and more!

He went on the attack straight away, beleaguering Doctor Strange with volley after volley of intense magical blasts. Strange was on the back foot, barely managing to protect himself.

Spider-Man, meanwhile, was at loggerheads with Clancy and Rocco once more. The two of them just wouldn't give up. He had registered the presence of another man nearby, wearing a high-collared cloak and bell-sleeved shirt. He hadn't a clue who this person was but presumed, because he was fighting Xandu, that they were on the same side—both of them good guys. Mostly, he was preoccupied with not getting the snot kicked out of him by the two musclebound goons. That, and berating himself for letting Xandu grab that wand thingy back.

Spider-Man wound up battling Clancy and Rocco in the townhouse's cellar, and this was where he found the solution to his situation. The property's fuse box was down here. He grabbed ahold of one of the mains cables that fed into it. He yanked the cable free and jabbed the spark-spitting bare end at Clancy and then at Rocco.

Where an ordinary human would have been electrocuted, perhaps fatally, Clancy and Rocco were merely stunned. Spider-Man had been hoping for this outcome. Banking on it. The two brawlers stood dazed and blinking, as though waking up after a long nap.

"Hey, what gives?" said Clancy. "What's goin' on here?"

"Search me," said Rocco. "How'd we get here? And why am I so tired?"

"You don't remember anything?" Spider-Man said. "Us fighting? Traveling to some crazy out-of-this-world weirdo zone? Me zinging you with some snappy one-liners? None of it? Sheesh! I wasted some of my best material on you two bozos. Now, you just hang out here for a while. I'm going to go see what the deal is with this Xandu creep."

So saying, Spider-Man trussed up Clancy and Rocco with webbing and darted back upstairs.

Clancy frowned in puzzlement at Rocco. "Gee, I thought Spidey only webbed up burglars and muggers and guys like Doctor Octopus."

"Yeah," said Rocco with a mournful look. "We didn't do nothin'!"

UPSTAIRS, THE two magicians were still locked in combat.

And one of them was not faring well.

Spider-Man may not have known much about magic, but he knew when somebody was on the losing end of a fight. He'd been in that position himself more often than he cared to think. Xandu had the other magician on the ropes. The man was struggling to defend himself against the onslaught of blasts coming from that wand. To Spider-Man, the battle was a strobing dazzle of light and color: bolts of energy crisscrossing the room, bright shields appearing out of nowhere and shattering, and lots of fancy finger configurations, some of which reminded him of the hand gesture he adopted to trigger his wrist-mounted web-shooters.

Spider-Man liked to take a logical approach to things, which was hardly surprising, given that he was a science student in his civilian identity. During his own battles, very often the resolution came not through raw strength and fisticuffs but through applied thinking. There were ways of cracking a problem that didn't require just hitting it until it fell over.

He certainly couldn't compete with the magical hoo-hah that was going on all around him. That was way out of his wheelhouse. But there *was* something he could do. A simple little shortcut.

While Xandu was busy hammering at his opponent, he was neglecting the basics of any fight: situational awareness. He didn't even seem to realize Spider-Man was there.

So he didn't notice the rope of web that jetted out from Spider-Man's wrist and tangled around his legs. He only knew about it when Spider-Man gave the web line a hefty tug and he crashed to the floor.

The Wand of Watoomb spilled from his hand. Xandu scrambled to pick it up. Spider-Man shot more webs at him, fixing him to the floor.

And just like that, it was over.

○━━━━━○

DOCTOR STRANGE and Spider-Man sat side-by-side on the roof of Xandu's townhouse. Dawn was breaking over Manhattan. The verdant expanse of Central Park stretched away at their feet, its treetops gilded by the light of the rising sun.

"Doctor Strange," said Spider-Man. "That's your actual name?"

"I'm assuming yours isn't Spider-Man."

"Nah, but what else does a guy with spider powers call himself?"

"Fair point. It seems providential that someone who deals in strangeness, as I do, should have the surname I have. I believe it's known as nominative determinism."

"Right. Our destinies are written in our monikers. But, just so's you know, in real life I'm not Johnny Arachnid."

Strange smiled. "You are full of jokes, Spider-Man. I've heard that about you."

"It's become kind of a trademark thing," Spider-Man said. "Nowadays bad guys get disappointed if I don't make gags while I'm punching them in the face. And speaking of bad guys… Those two goons I webbed up in the basement don't seem to have any recollection of what they did."

"They were under Xandu's spell."

"So it's okay for them to walk free once the webbing dissolves?"

"I'm sure they've done plenty in their lives for which they merit jail time," said Strange, "but today they are innocents."

"What about ol' Xandy himself? I watched you put sort of mystical trance whammy on him just now. How long's that going to hold?"

"It wasn't just any trance. I wiped his mind."

The big white lenses on Spider-Man's mask widened, suggesting the eyes beneath were widening too. "You did what? As in, brainwash him? Erase his memories? Because I'm not sure I'm comfortable with that, tampering with people's minds."

"All I've done is leave him without any recall of his magical knowhow, and without any of the evil ambition he had. Xandu, shorn of his baser traits, could be a productive member of society."

Spider-Man mused on it. "I'm gonna defer to you on this one, Doc, basically because you must know better how to deal with bad wizards than I do. And how about that doohickey there?" He pointed to the Wand of Watoomb, which Strange had tucked into his waist sash. "You're going to stash it somewhere safe, right?"

Strange shook his head. "I'm going to destroy it. It's safer that way, for everyone."

"Glad to hear it." Spider-Man stood and approached the parapet at the edge of the roof. He stepped over, balancing horizontally on the side of the building, clinging on with the soles of his feet and the fingertips of one hand. The sidewalk lay a couple of hundred feet below him, but it might as well have been a drop of a few inches onto a feather mattress for all the concern he showed. "Well, anyways, I gotta run. Webs to sling, walls to crawl, you know how it is. Also sleep to catch up on. It's been an education, meeting you and dipping a toe in your world, Doc. Can't say I'm in a hurry to do it again, though."

"I'm pleased to have made your acquaintance, Spider-Man, and grateful for the help you provided," Strange said. "May the Vishanti watch over you and the Omnipotent Oshtur guide you on your way."

"Sure. Okay. And, uh, may your amulet never tickle."

Webbing shot forth from Spider-Man's wrist, and he launched himself off the rooftop into the morning air.

Strange watched him swing off down the street in a pendulum motion, firing strands of web to attach to buildings left and right. Beneath that gaudy red-and-blue costume, he intuited, lay a young man—a very young man, perhaps even a teenager—who was riddled with insecurities and had known tragedy. He fought the forces of evil because he saw wrongness all around and wished to right it. While presenting a laughing face to the world, he was serious in his mission.

This was a super hero, then. This was what it was like to be one. Spider-Man said he had dipped a toe in Strange's world, but Strange had likewise dipped a toe in Spider-Man's. He suspected it wouldn't be the last time.

He was Sorcerer Supreme now. No longer could he be just that magician in Greenwich Village you went to when you had a supernatural problem. Those days were past. Much had changed. Baron Mordo was elsewhere, doubtless suffering the torments of the damned. Dormammu had been engulfed within Eternity, perhaps never to be seen again. Even the Counterclockwise Circle had been largely disbanded. Those of them who'd survived the battle against the Mindless Ones had returned to Earth very different people than before. They hadn't exactly become saints, but they were reconsidering their self-centered lives and taking steps towards bettering them.

However, there were other similar threats out there, other eldritch dangers that imperiled Earth, and that Strange was best equipped, out of everyone on the planet, to deal with.

Strange understood that a new chapter of his career had begun. From now on he would have to be more of a public figure, like Spider-

Man and the other super heroes. Doctor Strange, Sorcerer Supreme, would have to become a name universally recognized and trusted. It was a natural evolution, the way forward. No more loitering at the occult fringes of things. It was time to embrace the world of capes, cowls and codenames.

His thoughts strayed to Clea, and he felt a pang of melancholy.

No, he told himself. This wasn't a time for regrets. It was a time for looking ahead, not back.

At a mental command, his Cloak of Levitation billowed open and swept him skywards. Doctor Strange flew over the awakening city, into the clear blue light of a brand new day.

CREDITS

COMMISSIONED ON A DARE
BY "FANTASTIC" FENTON COULTHURST

EDITED WITH EXTREME CARE
BY "DAZZLING" DAQUAN CADOGAN

SCRUTINIZED WITH A SKILL THAT'S RARE
BY "SPECTACULAR" SARAH SINGER

COPY-EDITED IN A MANNER BEYOND COMPARE
BY "CULTIVATED" KEVIN EDDY

DESIGNED WITH UNTOLD FLAIR
BY "WIZARDLY" WILLIAM ROBINSON

COVER DRAWN WITH ATMOSPHERE
BY "INCOMPARABLE" INHYUK LEE

ALL OVERSEEN WITH A VERY HARD STARE
BY "GREGARIOUS" GEORGE SANDISON

Doctor Strange: Dimension War is based on the original comics by Stan "The Man" Lee, "Sturdy" Steve Ditko and "Rascally" Roy Thomas, as featured in *Strange Tales* #110–111 and #114–146, and *Amazing Spider-Man Annual* #2.

ABOUT THE AUTHOR

James Lovegrove is the *New York Times* bestselling author of *The Age of Odin*. He has been short-listed for many awards including the Arthur C. Clarke Award, the John W. Campbell Memorial Award, and the Scribe Award. He won the Seiun Award for Best Foreign Language Short Story in 2011, and the Dragon Award in 2020 for *Firefly: The Ghost Machine*. He has written many acclaimed Sherlock Holmes novels, including *Sherlock Holmes and the Christmas Demon*. As well as writing books, he reviews fiction for the *Financial Times*. He lives in Eastbourne in the UK. @jameslovegrove7

For more fantastic fiction, author events, exclusive
excerpts, competitions, limited editions and more

VISIT OUR WEBSITE
titanbooks.com

LIKE US ON FACEBOOK
facebook.com/titanbooks

FOLLOW US ON TWITTER
@TitanBooks

EMAIL US
readerfeedback@titanemail.com